Soraya's dirt-smudged face had never looked more beautiful.

Marc wanted to kiss her so much he fought to keep his hands on the reins.

"Come with me to Venice," he blurted. It was unnecessary to ask the question, but he wanted to say it aloud, hear the words of invitation hang in the air. There were a thousand other things he might also say.... Come with me to my bed. Come with me to Scotland, to my life.

But he could not. His first duty was to the king, not his heart. She held his gaze and with a jolt of warmth he realized they needed no words to know what the other was thinking. Their eyes said everything.

* * *

Crusader's Lady
Harlequin® Historical #842—March 2007

Praise for Lynna Banning

Loner's Lady
"...poignant tale of a woman's coming of age..."
—*Romantic Times BOOKreviews*

The Ranger and the Redhead
"...fast-paced, adventure-filled story..."
—*Romantic Times BOOKreviews*

The Wedding Cake War
"You'll love Banning's subtle magic with romance."
—*Romantic Times BOOKreviews*

The Angel of Devil's Camp
"This sweet charmer of an Americana romance has just
the right amount of humor, poignancy and a cast of
quirky characters."
—*Romantic Times BOOKreviews*

The Scout
"Though a romance through and through,
The Scout is also a story with powerful undertones
of sacrifice and longing."
—*Romantic Times BOOKreviews*

CRUSADER'S LADY
Lynna Banning

HARLEQUIN®

TORONTO • NEW YORK • LONDON
AMSTERDAM • PARIS • SYDNEY • HAMBURG
STOCKHOLM • ATHENS • TOKYO • MILAN • MADRID
PRAGUE • WARSAW • BUDAPEST • AUCKLAND

ISBN-13: 978-0-373-29442-8
ISBN-10:   0-373-29442-5

CRUSADER'S LADY

This edition published by arrangement with Harlequin Books S.A.

® and TM are trademarks of the publisher. Trademarks indicated with ® are registered in the United States Patent and Trademark Office, the Canadian Trade Marks Office and in other countries.

www.eHarlequin.com

Printed in U.S.A.

In memory of my husband,
Clarence Browning Woolston,
and my father, Lawrence E. Yarnes

With grateful thanks to Tricia Adams,
Suzanne Barrett, Marlene Connell,
Kathleen Dougherty, Kat Macfarlane,
Jane Maranghi, Brenda Preston, Susan Renison,
Gwen Shupe, and David Woolston.

Chapter One

Jerusalem, 1192

Marc drew the wool cloak about his shoulders and leaned toward his campfire with a weary groan. He no longer cared if it was night or day, if the desert was sun-scorched or wind-whipped, his belly full or empty. Each day brought him closer to not caring whether he lived at all.

The sun dropped toward the dry hills of Syria like a great gold coin, burning its way across the purpling sky. Usually he welcomed the smoke-coloured shadows that gathered around his camp each evening, but not tonight. He drew in a lungful of dung-scented air. Fifty steps to the west, the king's banner of scarlet and gold fluttered weakly in the dying wind. Were it not for Richard, this hated crusade would be over.

A boot scraped against the ground near him. Marc cocked his ear and reached an aching arm for the sword lying at his side.

'No need, my friend,' a hearty voice called. 'It is but Roger de Clare.' The muscular young man, a forest-green surcoat covering his chain mail shirt, squatted beside Marc's fire.

'What news, de Clare?' Marc muttered.

'None. The king is worse. The servants are lazy. The scavenger birds are hungry. All this you know.'

Marc nodded without smiling. 'Saladin himself sends a healing medicine for the king. At least that is what our spies report.'

Roger tipped his head toward the edge of Marc's camp. 'They also report Saladin's men lurk in the shadows beyond our firelight and listen to words best left unspoken.'

The whole camp knew Richard lay in his tent, sweating with fever, attended by knights and servants. Saladin, as well, knew where Richard and his warriors lay. Every move the Frankish army made, the Saracen leader seemed to know in advance.

Roger cleared his throat. 'The king sent word he would speak with you.'

Marc groaned. 'Again. No man in all Christendom ignores so much good advice. I will go later. I have not yet eaten.'

Roger glanced into the crude metal pot hanging over Marc's fire. 'Small loss, it would appear.'

Marc nodded. Roger de Clare never minced his words, as did other Norman knights. That was one reason Marc tolerated him. Other Normans, with their greedy gaze on Sicily, Cyprus, even Scotland, could go to the devil.

'Will the king die, do you think?' Roger asked.

'I doubt it. Lion Heart is well named.'

Again Marc leaned toward his fire. The bowl of boiled grain looked unappetising, but it was all he had.

'Join me, Roger.' He gestured toward the bowl of food. 'I grow weary of eating alone.'

Roger glanced at the warming wheat mixture. 'I think not, my friend. Your cooking pot would not feed a hungry rabbit, let alone a friend. And…' The young man hesitated. 'Richard waits.'

'Let him wait,' Marc grumbled. 'I am weary of killing.'

'Spies are near,' de Clare said in a low voice. 'Take care to say nothing of interest to the Saracen.'

Marc nodded. His friend rose and propped his hands on his sword belt. 'You are too much alone, man. You eat alone, sleep alone. You would fight alone if the king would let you. But, my ill-tempered friend, I will not let you do that.'

'Save your advice for the men you command.'

Roger scuffed noisily out of the firelight, and Marc closed his eyes. God in heaven, he did not deserve such a friend. Not after Acre. Richard had ordered the massacre, but on that awful, bloody day a part of Marc began to die. The heads of two thousand hostages, women and children, as well as defenders, rolled in the blood-soaked sand outside the city. Richard had betrayed them, and then slaughtered them all.

A rustle whispered into his consciousness. Not a footfall, something else. Without thought, he felt for his sword.

The sound came again, closer. Behind him. 'Who goes there?'

The silence stretched, so profound it seemed to scream. One of Richard's heavy-booted minions? A servant?

An assassin?

Marc lifted the simmering pot off the fire, rose and grasped the hilt of his sword. He had just started to buckle the leather belt around his hips when a movement beyond the flames caught his attention. He stiffened, straining his eyes into the thick night.

Sensing a motion at his back, he spun, sword raised, just as a dark-swathed figure hurtled toward him. Instinctively Marc took a single step forward, and his blade caught the intruder in the throat. A cry, then the man pitched onto the ground at Marc's feet and lay still.

Blood poured from the man's wound, soaking the turban

and the silk tunic, oozing over the dark fingers clutching at the torn throat. A Saracen. Probably a spy, this close to the Frankish camp.

A gurgling sound, then nothing. Marc bent closer. Almighty God, what had he done! The man was unarmed.

He turned away in self-loathing, covered his face with his hand. For a moment he thought he would vomit. A warrior's slaughter in battle was his duty as a Christian knight, but striking an unarmed man, even a Saracen, was against the law of God. A whisper of sound brought his head up, every nerve on edge. Something—instinct or training, or perhaps the voice of God—made him twist back toward the dead Arab. A small form flitted out of the shadows and threw itself over the body, sobbing like a girl. So, the man had a loyal servant.

Again Marc turned away. The words of regret that sprang to his lips died the instant he opened his mouth. He need not apologise to a Saracen, much less to a Saracen's servant.

He turned away, toward the fire, and suddenly a warm weight dropped onto his back. One thin arm crooked about his neck and the blade of a dagger pressed into his throat.

'*Qaatil!*' shouted a thin voice, choked with hatred. Before Marc could throw him off, the knife nicked his skin; a dribble of warm liquid ran down the neck of his tunic.

'*Taraka.*' He spoke in Arabic, but the boy did not let go. Instead he clung to Marc's back, the hand gripping the dagger flailing to find a vulnerable spot. He grabbed the servant's upper arm and twisted, hard.

With a yelp, the slight figure tumbled off and sprawled on the ground. The dagger skittered out of his fingers. A skinny hand grabbed for it, but Marc stomped his boot onto the blade, pinning it to the hard ground.

'Go.' He gestured toward the shadowy edge of his camp.

'I will not harm you.' Without thinking, he spoke the words in the Frankish tongue.

'I will kill you.' The low voice replied with a tremor. 'I will take revenge if it is the last thing I do on this earth. God knows I speak truly.'

A servant boy who spoke Norman French? 'Who are you?' Marc demanded.

The boy darted a glance at the dagger caught under Marc's foot, flicked his gaze to the body of the dead Saracen and dropped into a crouch, his forearm still imprisoned in Marc's grip. Tears streaked the lad's dirty face.

Marc bent and scooped up the knife. The hilt was silver, beautifully incised, with a single jewel embedded into the metal. A ruby, big as a sparrow's egg.

'Where did you get this?'

The hunched figure twitched but said nothing.

'Answer me!' He slid his fingers down to the boy's wrist and squeezed. 'Where did you get this blade?'

The trembling servant glanced down at the dead Arab. 'It belongs to me.'

'And I am the prince of Samarkand. Speak the truth!'

'I am no thief.'

'So you say, boy. Where did you get this blade?'

'It is mine, now.' He glanced again at the body.

So, the Arab had been armed. A spy? It mattered not, since death now sat on the man's chest.

But the boy mattered. The boy might be only half-grown, but the wiry young Arab had tried to attack him, kill him, even. Marc reached down, caught the neck of the youth's dust-smeared tunic and yanked him upright.

'Who are you?' He expected the boy to cringe, but he straightened and looked boldly into Marc's face.

'I am…Soray.'

'And who is that man on the ground?'

'That is my lord. His name is Khalil al-Din.'

Marc tightened his grip on the tunic. 'A servant? You are his servant?'

'I am his servant.'

Marc released him. It made no sense. Was a Saracen servant so devoted to his master that he would commit murder on his behalf?

'You are lying.'

The boy tensed. 'No, lord. I do not lie.'

Marc shook his head. He knew a lie when he heard one. Still, he could not linger; the king awaited him.

'Leave this camp, boy. I will see to the body of your master.' He tramped out of the circle of firelight, the dagger still clenched in his fist, to the tent where Richard waited.

Soraya crossed her arms over her waist and watched the tall knight stride off into the dark. He had a cold, hard look about him, a darkness in his face that frightened her. Not one word of regret, not even a prayer for the man he had struck down with his thoughtless blow.

Shaking with sobs, she knelt at Khalil's side and bowed her head. 'Uncle, I swear to you I will avenge your death. And I will also complete your mission—I will make sure that Saladin's written message is delivered to King Richard. But for both these tasks I must get your dagger back. God willing, I will do it this very night.' She reached out and pressed her fingers over his eyelids. Choking back a cry of anguish, she straightened Khalil's limbs and kissed both his cold cheeks.

I cannot bear for the Frankish barbarian to touch you.

I cannot allow him to lay you in the ground without the proper words.

She stood up, her hands clenched at her sides. Tearing her gaze from her uncle's body, she surveyed the camp. The barbarian had no tent, only a meager fire and one cooking pot. She peered inside the vessel. Surely a man so large must eat more than that little bit of noxious-looking paste!

An iron helmet and a chain mail shirt were partially stuffed into a filthy hemp bag. Beside it lay a rolled-up blanket, secured with a leather belt blackened with age. Ugh. These Franks were worse than pigs.

She lifted her head, listening. The knight would return soon. When he did, she would be ready. She must snatch the dagger away from him and strike before he could react. She would not give up until the miserable Frank lay lifeless beside her uncle.

And as to her other quest, the message she needed to deliver? All in good time. She would see to that once she had retrieved her dagger and dealt with the man who had killed her beloved uncle. It would be difficult to demand her weapon back from the Frank without saying why she needed it—but she was to tell no one of the message except the king. She added more dung to the fire, carefully positioned the blanket before it and lifted it away in a prearranged signal.

Marc made his way past a dozen campfires, noting how the knights he met backed away from him, neither looking him in the face nor speaking. Richard's men had always been uneasy in his company; now they seemed to fear him, as well. Did his fury show that much?

When he came to Richard's large, crimson tent, he stuffed the dagger into his belt and reached for the silk flap.

'Ah,' an oily voice murmured at his back. 'Marc de Valery. At last. I wager you will regret making the king wait.'

Marc said nothing. He shoved past the surly knight, entered Richard's tent and went down on one knee beside the cot.

'Get up,' the king rasped. The ruddy face, crowned with frizzy red-gold hair, was sweaty and flushed. Below the bushy moustache, the dry, chapped lips opened. 'Come closer.' It seemed to take all Richard's strength to utter those few words.

Marc edged forward on his knees. The still air inside the tent smelled of sour bedding. 'My lord?'

'Listen to me, de Valery,' the king wheezed. 'My strength fails me.'

'Aye, lord?'

Richard's eyelids closed. 'Tell no one what I say. Swear it.'

Marc stared at the ailing monarch. 'I swear.'

'Lean down.'

Marc bent his head, turning his ear close to Richard's open lips. The king murmured a single sentence. 'I must return to England.' He raised one unsteady hand to rest on Marc's shoulder. The heat from the man's fingers seared through his linen tunic like a hot iron.

'My brother John has made alliance with the French king. Philip wants Normandy—John wants my crown. I must go home. I need you to accompany me on the journey.'

'If I do what you ask, my lord, you will die.'

'I will not die, de Valery. You will see to that.'

Marc sucked in air. He could not refuse. No one refused Richard of England unless he ceased to value his own life.

'Very well, sire. I will do what you ask.'

'Good,' Richard uttered on a sigh. *'Très bien.'*

'One question only,' Marc murmured. 'Why me?'

The king gave a hoarse laugh. 'Because,' Richard said, 'I trust you, even if you are half-Scot. You are a good man, de Valery.'

Marc dropped his head to acknowledge the backhanded compliment. He would not bother to confess he was not the good knight Richard thought him. Not even close.

He made to rise, but Richard's limp hand stayed him. 'One more thing.'

Marc waited for the king's breathing to steady.

'Stay away from Leopold of Austria. He is blinded by his anger.'

'Yes, my lord. I have known this. You should not have desecrated his banner as you did.'

'You should have told me before now.'

Marc said nothing. No Scot would dare accuse a German baron of perfidy. Richard knew that.

It was past moonrise when Marc finished his preparations on the king's behalf and returned to his small camp. The fire had burned down to embers. The cooking pot was stone-cold. He wasn't hungry anyway, thinking of tomorrow and all the things that could go awry. Richard was shrewd, even calculating. But at times he acted on impulse rather than with the cool rationality of his father, Henry Plantagenet. It was worse with a fevered brain.

He glanced toward the spot where the dead Saracen should have been and recoiled. The body was gone! He bent over the spot and found it swept clean.

A shiver went up his spine. No blood stained the ground. No hoofmarks, or footprints. Did a Saracen ascend to Paradise so easily?

Or had the Arab boy dragged his master away?

He crossed himself in short, jerky motions. Perhaps the corpse had been spirited away by *djinns*. He fingered the jeweled dagger he'd stuffed under his belt. He had told no one of the slaying, not even Richard of England. The act made him sick to think on. But now he must look to the future and prepare to leave the camp tomorrow morning and journey back to England with Richard.

The hair at his neck prickled. Marc half turned, straining to listen. Outside the circle of firelight he could hear someone breathing.

He drew his blade and plunged toward the sound.

Chapter Two

Marc closed his fingers around a smooth, silk-covered arm and yanked the Saracen boy out of the shadows. 'What are you doing here? I told you to go.'

'Do not touch me!' a high, angry voice yelled. 'Release me at once!'

'Answer me!' Marc gritted through clenched teeth.

The small turbaned head came up. 'I kept watch over my uncle.'

'And where is your uncle now?' He gave the boy a single hard shake. 'Perhaps he rose up and walked to Paradise?'

A slap stung his cheek. 'Do not insult him. No one walks to Paradise.'

God, the little brat had struck him!

'Where is he, then?'

'I signaled my kinsmen, using your firelight. They came in secret for the body, took him away on a horse.'

'Why did you not go with them?'

The youth dropped his head, flicked a glance at the jeweled dagger in Marc's hand, then stared at his leather sandals. Marc tightened his grip on the slim arm. 'Why?'

The boy set his mouth in a tight line and did not respond. Then, quick as a cat, he wrenched his arm free and his small hand made a grab for the dagger. The blade sliced into the boy's thumb, and he cried out.

Marc collared him, dragged him over to the fire and pushed him down beside it. 'Here.' He tossed down a bit of linen he kept under his tunic. The boy wrapped it around his hand but said nothing.

Marc nodded. 'I see.' He squatted a few feet away and hid the knife behind his belt. 'You stayed behind to attack me.'

No answer. The boy stared into the glowing embers.

'You have courage, I will say that.' Still no response.

'Look at me!' Marc ordered. With his fist he tipped the scarf-swathed chin up. Eyes the colour of the sea, pale green and hard as jade, met his.

Something kicked inside Marc's chest. 'You have strange eyes, boy. Arabs are dark.'

'I am Circassian, not Arab. But I was brought up among Arabs. I know their ways.'

Marc studied the boy for a long moment. 'Unwind your headpiece.'

The layers of silk slowly fell away until Marc could see the boy's visage. True, he was not Arab. His skin was the colour of cream, the features fine, almost delicate, the nose long and straight. A mass of unruly black curls sprang to life when released from under the turban.

Again a jolt under his ribs snapped his nerves taut. The youth was handsome, almost feminine in his movements. He watched the thin shoulders hunch against the cold wind. The lad had tried to stab him, but he had neither the skill nor the strength to accomplish the deed. Disarmed, he was no longer a threat.

'Are you hungry?' he snapped.

'Yes, lord….'

Marc reached for the cooking pot, scooped up three fingers of the congealed mess, then handed over the bowl. 'It is cold, but it fills the belly.'

The boy did likewise and made to hand it back, but Marc pushed it away. The youth gazed at him, his strange green eyes assessing, then quickly devoured the rest.

Marc watched him. What should he do with the boy, who was now busy scouring the inside of the empty pot with a handful of sand? Send him back to his people, he supposed.

God, what was he thinking? The fate of the young Arab did not matter; Marc and the king would be gone before morning.

He rose, tramped over to his hemp supply bag and yanked out a ragged blanket. Bundling it into a ball, he tossed it to the boy, who stared at Marc with wary emerald eyes.

'Nights in the desert are cold, Circassian.'

The smooth, pale forehead creased into a puzzled frown. 'Yes, lord. I know. *Shukren,* lord. *Mercez.*'

There was something strange about this lad. For one thing, he spoke both Arabic and Norman French. And for another, eyes that color were rare, even for a Circassian. Eyes that mysterious made him feel…restless. Aware of something he could not name.

For the rest of the night he would sleep with his sword at his side and make sure the dagger was secured under his body. He did not trust the boy.

She would never understand these Franks. This one in particular, with those eyes blue as lapis lazuli and his gold-streaked hair. There was a darkness about him that made Soraya shudder. He had killed Khalil, yet he gave her his blanket.

She wrapped the coarse wool about her shoulders and dropped her head onto her raised knees. But she did not shut her eyes. Instead, she tipped her head just enough to watch him settle himself by the dwindling fire. He had strong features, but his eyes were shadowed, his mouth a harsh line.

No matter. She had but one purpose now—to avenge her uncle's murder and then carry out their assigned mission for Saladin. By dawn this knight would be a dead man.

She shut her eyes.

A spark exploded and she jerked her head up and peeked at the knight on the other side of the guttering flames. Sleeping. Or so he appeared. Firelight heightened the strong jaw, the cruel mouth.

She flicked a pebble at his head, striking his chin, but his closed eyelids did not quiver. Her dagger was pinned beneath his long body. She prayed he would shift in his sleep so she could snatch the weapon and plunge the blade into his throat.

She watched the knight's chest rise and fall with his steady breathing. She must do it. She had pledged her word to God. She tossed another, larger stone.

Marc flicked one eyelid open, then instantly snapped it shut. The boy still sat by the fire, his slim body hunched over his knees. Asleep, probably. Or watching him. Waiting.

The large ruby embedded in the Saracen dagger hilt chewed into the flesh of his back, but rather than roll over and ease the annoyance, he would endure. A blade secured under him was a blade that could not be used against him.

God have mercy, he had killed the Saracen in unthinking haste, and the ease with which he'd done it stunned and ashamed him. He felt sorry for the slave boy opposite him. Unending warfare ate away a man's soul, poisoned his spirit.

It had to stop. He couldn't stomach another killing, not even of a servant.

He shifted uneasily, stretching out his legs. God, the longer the struggle for Jerusalem, the less human he became. Week after week Saladin's warriors encircled the Frankish camp arrayed outside the city gates. Before them naught faced Richard's army but stone walls. If the Franks moved their camp north or south, the Saracens again surrounded them once night had fallen. It had been thus for months. The battle for Jerusalem was a stand-off.

The butchery on both sides was beginning to make no sense. Richard did not covet Jerusalem for himself. The king was attacking a city he knew he could not hold. Was this interminable siege of the high stone walls just for show? Was Richard merely playing out the slaughter to best Philip of France and the German baron, Leopold of Austria?

He studied the slight figure of the Arab boy, asleep where he sat before the dying fire. There was a time when he himself had been as foolhardy and brave as that lad. And as innocent of the ugly side of life.

At dawn, he rolled over, reassured himself the dagger was still secure at his back and came to his feet. The boy sat tipped to one side, snoring lightly. Let him sleep. He and the king would be gone before the camp awakened.

He let his warhorse nibble a handful of the grain he had hoarded, pulled on his mail shirt and blue overtunic and flung the heavy leather saddle upon the animal's broad back. When he had buckled on his sword belt and turned to mount, he found the boy grinning at him from atop the horse.

'Get down,' Marc ordered.

'I will not, lord. How am I to attend you if I do not ride with you?'

'I do not need a servant.'

'Not true, lord. You need me. I assure you, I am no ordinary servant.'

A harsh laugh chuffed past Marc's lips. That was obvious enough. 'Get down,' he repeated. 'Now.'

The youth tilted his frame to one side, slid sideways and dropped gracefully to the ground. How, Marc wondered, had he managed to mount the huge animal in the first place?

'Where do we ride?'

'I ride south. You can go to the devil.'

The boy hissed in a breath. 'Surely you would not wish it so!'

Marc clenched his jaw. 'You are an outspoken brat. Ill-mannered and stubborn.'

'Aye, lord. I am stubborn, I admit it freely.'

'Go!' Marc roared the word hoping to frighten the boy. Instead, the lad sent him a look designed to charm devils.

'Where shall I go, lord?'

'You can go to the latrine,' Marc said with a jerk of his chin. 'That way. Go.'

The boy scampered off in the direction Marc pointed. When he was sure the lad had not doubled back, he secured his sword belt, tucked his canvas utility bag behind the high-backed cantle and mounted his warhorse.

With an odd niggle of apprehension, he stepped the animal forward, toward the prearranged meeting place with the king.

Chapter Three

Soraya did not go to the latrine. She crept behind a hillock where she was hidden from view. Then she picked her way back among the sleeping camps and already bustling servants toward the knight's camp.

Yawning Frankish squires sharpened swords or scrubbed chain mail shirts with handfuls of wet sand, paying her scant attention. But her soft *massa al-khayr* to the Arab servants brought a quick smile and a polite *ahlan*.

It always surprised her that Arab slaves were common among the Franks, taken as spoils of war and traded back and forth by the victors like sacks of grain. But then she herself had been acquired by Khalil in much the same manner. She had been captured as a child by Arab raiders and taken from her mountain homeland across the sea to a sheik's harem. At least they had educated her well, but she was happy to leave when Khalil bought her at the slave auction when she was but ten summers.

The Frankish camp was a filthy place. Flies buzzed every-where, and she wrinkled her nose in distaste at the smell of unwashed bodies and horse dung. At one camp she managed to snatch a fragrant ripe pomegranate from a fruit basket, then gradually worked her way toward the largest of the tents. Made of crimson silk instead of rough canvas, it was easy to pick out among the myriad of smaller ones; a scarlet-and-gold pennant fluttered from the top. If only she could deliver her message now, but it would have to wait. She had to recover Khalil's dagger. She looked around for her quarry, then halted suddenly. The Frankish knight was approaching from the opposite direction, a scowl on his sun-darkened face. He led his huge horse by a worn leather bridle, and Soraya frowned. Already she had learned that he allowed none other than himself to mount the great black beast. She would not soon forget his look of pure fury when she'd scrambled into the saddle ahead of him.

She watched him with curiosity. He was tall and well muscled. The man was pleasing in some way; perhaps it was his voice, rich as honeyed syrup. Or his eyes.

Pah! It mattered not. He would be a dead man by nightfall.

He strode toward the large tent, his gait slightly uneven, perhaps from an old wound. His warrior's body must be battle-scarred, and that heavy chain mail shirt and leggings would weigh as much as she did.

Franks were foolish indeed. Arab warriors wore mail, as well, but it was lighter and their horses were smaller and faster. Besides, the Arabs purposely rode mares because when the mating scent was upon them, they wreaked confusion among the heavy Frankish stallions. A great many warhorses had been slaughtered in battle and still the invading Christian armies failed to realise their error.

The knight veered left, away from the great tent of red and gold, and she ducked out of sight behind a smaller, tattered canvas structure to watch him. She would snatch the dagger and then find the king. That was almost as important as avenging Khalil's death.

The knight skirted several cook fires and made his way to a cluster of boulders two dozen paces from the camp's perimeter. Soraya circled around and darted forward to the opposite side of the tumbled rocks, crouched low and cautiously peered through an opening.

The first thing she saw was the hindquarters of another horse, a lesser animal than the knight's beast but well accoutered. The leather saddle was plain but polished to a soft gleam. The wool under blanket was adorned with embroidery and decorative leatherwork detailed the harness. The stirrups were smooth pieces of curved black iron.

On the animal's back sat a cowled religious man. A monk. Was then 'her' Frank—she snorted at the designation—a Templar knight? A Hospitaller? Such knights wore white surcoats with a four-sided red cross sewn on the front, but no such cross emblazoned the knight's blue surcoat.

He was not a religious, then. Good. It would be harder to slit the throat of a servant of God...

The monk raised his hand in greeting, and the Frank inclined his sun-streaked dark head in response. So, he respected the holy man. The two men exchanged a few words in low tones, only one of which she heard clearly. *Jaffa.* Then the knight turned away to mount his horse.

She understood at once. They were leaving the camp, riding south to the port town of Jaffa. If she would kill the Frankish knight and retrieve the dagger, she must go with him! She must move now! She would think about how she would come back to the camp and deliver the message to the king later.

She bolted from her hiding place, skittered the few paces to where the Frank stood and threw herself on the hard ground at his feet. 'Lord, forgive your miserable servant, but I could not find what you commanded me to bring you.'

The tall knight glowered at her without speaking. Soraya dared not look up until she heard his voice.

'And what was it I commanded you to bring?' His voice was cold and hard as metal.

'Why, a horse, lord! You sent me to find another mount. Do you not remember?' She risked a peek at his knees, then raised her gaze to the wide leather sword belt encircling his waist. Finally, with a murmured prayer, she looked into his harshly planed face.

His expression stopped her heartbeat. Exasperation showed in the set mouth and the frown creasing his sun-darkened forehead, but a hint of grudging admiration flashed in the clear blue eyes. A blue like the azure-enameled mosaic stones on the floor of the mosque. A blue, she suddenly thought, like the sunlit sea of her native land.

'I recall no such task,' he said shortly.

Soraya sighed dramatically, flicked a glance at the holy man, then swaggered a step closer to the tall knight. 'Lord, do you never grow tired of this game? Each morning you command and I obey, and then you forget what you commanded and I appear but a foolish boy.'

'And an imaginative one,' he shot back.

'Oh, yes, lord,' she agreed, warming to her charade. 'I can imagine many fine things. But this time...' She dropped her head in sham embarrassment. 'This time I have failed. I could not find the horse you sent me for.'

The hooded monk stepped his mount toward them. 'You have a servant now, de Valery?' he asked in a raspy voice. 'Why did you not tell me?'

Her knight snorted. 'I have no servant.'

'Do not bluster at me,' the monk said with a weak laugh. 'The wind from your mouth will blow this "holy man" off his mount.'

'Your ma— Father, this boy is not my servant. He has naught to do with me.'

Soraya grasped one of her knight's gloved hands and sank to her knees before him. Where he traveled, so must she. She would stick to this man like a prickly desert burr. Like a flea under his tunic…like a sticky almond paste smeared over his loathsome skin. She would see him dead if it was the last act of her life.

"Tis a sin to lie, lord. You taught me so yourself. I am your servant, and I serve you well and faithfully.' She touched her forehead to the hand imprisoned in both of hers. 'Do not deny me, master. Where should I go but with you?'

She let herself slip down to press her brow on his leather boot. Yes. She especially liked that last part.

The monk made an impatient sound, half cough, half oath, and Soraya leaped to her feet. The holy man waved a floppy sleeve at the Frank. 'Your boy is too young and puny to walk, de Valery. Since you have not another horse, take him up with you and let us be off.'

Her knight grumbled, but the holy man cut him off. 'I did not bring my own servant lest he tittle-tattle what he knows. It is good to have one, nevertheless. Yours will do.'

The tall knight scowled at the monk, then turned his unsmiling face down at her. Seizing the moment, Soraya sprang onto the horse's withers, grasped the coarse mane and clawed herself up until she once again occupied the padded leather saddle.

The Frank swore a truly blasphemous oath about the toenails of God, dragged her off and swung himself into the saddle. Then, with a look of distaste, he reached down, grasped her elbow so tightly her arm went numb and swung her up behind him. The expression in his eyes sent a scorpion crawling up her backbone.

She wrapped her arms about his solid form and felt the lumpy hilt of the dagger—*her* dagger—he carried in his belt poke against her wrist. Her spirits soared. The weapon she needed was right there, within her grasp!

But if she reached for it now, he would pin her arm and break the bone before she could strike. She would wait until he moved or twisted in the saddle and the knife presented itself to her seeking hand.

She hid a smile. She had outmaneuvered the surly Frank with the unwitting help of the Christian holy man. Khalil would have been proud of her.

The great warhorse beneath her snuffled loudly and began to move forward, and Soraya tightened her arms around the knight's waist. The metal rings of the mail shirt he wore under his knee-length tunic prodded her chin.

God preserve her! Never before had she been so close to any man. Her senses careened crazily, making her aware of every sound and smell, the jingle of harnesses, the low murmur of men waking up, giving orders, breaking their fast, the yeasty scent of baking bread, even the sour taste of the stolen pomegranate seeds on her tongue.

And then with a jolt the horse picked up its pace and she forgot everything but staying seated.

For hours they rode south, toward Jaffa, under the burning desert sun, finally stopping at a small village late in the hot afternoon to refill their water skins at the well. Marc sent the servant boy through the town gate with the empty vessels; he and the king would rest in the protection of a shady olive grove while the lad fetched water.

Exhausted, the ailing king dropped off his horse, stretched

out beside his mount and closed his eyes. Marc frowned. Richard had developed a hacking cough, and the inferior horse he had bargained from a dying Templar was slowing their progress. They dared not dally lest someone guess that the monk's robe, with its ragged moth holes, covered the Lion Heart of England.

He cursed under his breath. No one save Richard's mother, great Eleanor, had ever been able to reason with the king. To settle his unease, he began to sift handfuls of fine grey dust through his fingers. Had he not sworn to obey the king, Richard would never have ventured outside his tent.

But the king followed his own impulses, regardless of his barons' arguments. Night after night Marc listened at the noisy council in Richard's tent and kept quiet. Only when the king asked him a direct question did he venture an opinion, and while Richard listened at length, in the end it always went Richard's way.

The Lion Heart could do no wrong. Thus far Richard had rolled his seasoned, heavily armed warriors over the Saracen forces with bloody success; in the eyes of his followers, the man was more god than king.

Until now. Marc eyed the motionless form stretched in the shade beside his horse. This was a fool's plan. A king's fevered whim.

A sharp cry brought his head up. The servant boy darted through the village gate and raced toward them at such speed he looked to be skimming above the ground. Another cry, this time a gutteral shout, and then Marc saw the reason why the boy ran.

Two—no, three—merchants tumbled through the gate, arms waving. 'Thief!' the first man shouted. 'Stop him!'

The panting boy dashed up to where Marc rested in the olive grove and stopped short. In the next instant he dropped to his knees, jerked up the hem of Richard's voluminous monk's garb and wriggled underneath. The robe twitched once and was still.

Scarcely three breaths later, the first merchant puffed to a stop before him. 'Did you see that boy?' he said in Arabic.

'Boy?' Marc replied in a lazy voice. 'The skinny one who trampled through our resting place without a by-your-leave?'

'That's the one. He stole a loaf of bread and—'

'And a round of cheese,' the second man added as he limped to a stop. The third merchant, tall and sallow with one drooping eyelid, gasped for air but said nothing.

Marc idly sifted another handful of dust through his fingers. 'The boy is gone,' he said in the same nonchalant tone. 'Into the olive grove. No doubt at this moment he is scampering on down the hill.'

The merchant swore an inventive oath. Marc understood its earthy implications, but he did not smile.

Two of the men then dashed into the grove. 'We shall catch him at the crossroads!' one yelled.

But the third man, the tall, silent merchant, eyed Marc's black warhorse, then gazed at Richard's prone body. Slowly he walked toward the ragged, motionless figure on the ground and prodded at the monk with the toe of one boot.

Chapter Four

King Richard sat up partway, propped himself on one elbow and signed an exaggerated cross over his chest. 'Yes, my son?' he said to the merchant in a pious voice. 'Do you wish to confess?'

The man's eyes blinked. *'Allahu alukhaim.'*

'There is no god but Allah,' Marc translated. The merchant backed away, then turned to follow the other two into the olive grove. When the turbaned men were out of sight, Marc spoke, directing his words to the moth-eaten habit on the ground.

'They are gone, boy. You can come out.'

The wool robe shuddered and the disheveled lad emerged, a delighted smile on his face. 'I thank you, lord.' From inside his dust-smudged tunic he pulled a flattened loaf of bread, a dirty-looking hunk of cheese and a handful of dried herbs, which he dumped into a small leather sack at his waist.

'Aha.' Marc scowled at the youth. 'You are a thief after all.'

'Oh, no, lord.' A disarming grin lit the boy's face. 'Say instead that I am a very skilled borrower.'

Richard chuckled. 'I say the lad has wit and an enterprising spirit. Considering our situation, de Valery, you may be thankful for such qualities.' The king straightened, then stood and clapped the boy's shoulder. 'You may ride with me, lad.'

The boy blanched.

Marc laughed until his eyes watered. With quick, sure motions the lad stashed the bread and cheese in Marc's supply bag, grabbed a handful of Jupiter's thick mane and wrestled himself up into the saddle.

'Where do we travel now, lord?'

With a sigh, Marc again hauled the youth down off his horse, mounted in his place and lifted the small-boned frame up behind him. 'There.' He motioned ahead. 'To the sea.'

'Ah!' The youth jerked in a hissed breath.

Richard climbed onto his sway-backed horse. 'Pray God there is a ship waiting.'

A ship! Soraya caught her breath in a squeaked-out gasp. A ship that wallowed on the water while filthy men crawled over it like scavenger ants? Her blood turned cold. She prayed to God a ship was *not* waiting!

She was not afraid of a great many things, but being tossed about on the water was not one of them. She only vaguely recalled such a voyage, but the memory of the experience still haunted her. Her stomach roiled at the thought of standing once more on a ship's deck.

And, she realised in growing horror, she was getting farther and farther away from Jerusalem and the English king.

She must devise some way to lay her hands on a weapon and end this miserable Frank's life at once. Twisting her head slightly, she eyed the scabbard hanging from the knight's belt. Could she slip the sword out? Yes, that might work. Perhaps when he next dismounted. She would ask for a swallow of water. Then, when his attention was diverted to his horse, or the saddle, or the water skins...

Yes! When he reached for the water…

The monk's rough voice spoke behind them. 'Look ahead, de Valery.'

'I see it.' The destrier stepped up its pace.

Soraya stretched her neck as high as she could to peer over the rise, yet could see nothing but sand and more sand. But when they reached the top of the hill, a cooling breeze brushed her face and all at once there lay the sea ahead of them, smooth as a porcelain plate and so blue the dancing light made it look bejeweled. It was so bright she couldn't look at it for very long.

And in the harbor—*God preserve me!*—boats bobbed on the water. Hundreds of them! Fishing vessels. Canopied barges. Arab dhows. Ships with rows of oars and sails and men crawling up and down the masts.

Her mouth went dry. She ducked her head, restudied the position of the knight's scabbard. It hung at his belt just so, and if he turned to his left, away from her…

The horse moved forward a few yards and halted. 'Climb down, boy.'

Soraya slid off the destrier's back so fast she lost her balance and stumbled onto her knees. She clenched her teeth at the holy man's raspy laugh, and just as she started to scramble to her feet, the Frankish knight grabbed the front of her tunic and heaved her to a standing position. She stood so close to him she could see the beads of sweat on his upper lip.

His glance strayed to the water skins. Now was her chance. She inched her hand toward the protruding hilt of his sword. Focused on the skins, the knight turned away to his left just as her fingers closed over the cold steel.

Lord be praised. She did not have to drag the heavy weapon from its leather covering; the knight's own motion away from her tipped the scabbard and separated it from the sword she gripped. Then he pivoted toward her, opening his mouth to speak.

Foolish man.

She wrapped both hands around the hilt and heaved the tip of the blade into the air. Lord, but it was heavy, like a great iron sewing needle balanced over her head.

Now. She would crash the weapon down and split his head right between those two puzzled blue eyes. She aimed for his nose and drew in a breath of resolve.

With a surge of strength, she extended the blade over her head as far back as she could and willed the cutting edge down for the killing blow.

Chapter Five

The first thing Soraya became aware of was the sound of laughter. Men's laughter. Deep voices whooping out guffaws of hilarity.

She opened her eyes. What was she doing flat on the ground?

The knight's sword lay at an odd angle, just out of her reach. Had she brained him and then fainted? Surely not. She never fainted. The women in the harem had taught her a trick to prevent such a breach of manners. Had that been so long ago she had forgotten?

She spat out a mouthful of grit. 'What happened?' Her tongue felt thick as a caliph's chair cushion.

'Far less than you expected,' the holy man said with a chuckle. '*Certes*, I have not enjoyed such a joke since I left England.'

Joke! Speechless, she glared up at the two sets of blue eyes peering down at her. Two sets. So she had not killed her knight. The last thing she remembered was lifting the sword over her head, raising it higher…higher…

She recalled that it took every ounce of strength she possessed. And then what?

Her knight bent forward and hauled her upright by one

arm. 'What do you think happened?' he growled. 'The weight of my sword unbalanced you. You toppled over backward.'

He scowled at her while the holy man alternately coughed and chuckled. The look of black fury on the knight's face sent a cold chill up her spine.

'I can explain,' she said quickly. 'Truly, I—'

'Don't even try, boy. Your intent was plain enough.'

'Oh, but—'

'Silence!'

Soraya shrank away from him. His voice was like thunder when he was angered.

'Let him be, Marc,' the monk said. 'As we have just observed, he is too puny to do much harm. Mayhap he is a better cook than a swordsman.'

'Oh, indeed yes, lord.' Soraya grasped at the straw the holy man offered. 'Not only can I cook, I can prepare healing herbs for your fever and for your catarrh.' She tried not to grin. 'From the market-place in the village.'

The monk studied her for a long minute. 'Very well,' he said at last.

Her knight frowned at the holy man. 'But my lor—'

'What is it, de Valery?' the monk snapped.

Soraya started. The holy man's voice was even worse than thunder.

'My lor— Father,' de Valery pursued. 'I ask you to consider the danger.'

'Danger of what?' the monk scoffed. 'The boy wishes to kill you, not me. Anyway, he can do you no harm.'

The knight stepped close to the holy man and said something in a low voice, but the monk shook his cowled head. 'I order him to stay with us,' he said in a loud voice. With a hint of laughter he added, 'In God's name.'

De Valery clamped his lips shut, wheeled and tramped off toward for the harbor, leading his warhorse.

'The only question for you, boy—' the monk chuckled under his raspy breathing '—is, are you seaworthy?'

The ship was waiting, as Richard said it would be the night the king had confided his plan. A Genoese merchant ship. God's blood, Marc thought never to see such a welcome sight. He had always expected to die somewhere in the desert of Syria, and now, in the bustling harbor before him lay hope in the shape of curved timbers roped to the quay and swaying gently with the tide.

He gazed at the vessel so long his eyes watered. He was going home. Out of this desert hell to the heather-carpeted hills of Scotland. He would see his lady mother once more. And, if God had shielded his brother Henry from the infidel, one day soon Marc would dandle Henry's sons on his knee.

It fell to Henry, as the oldest son, to carry on the family name and govern the de Valery lands. Marc had never resented it. He had never wanted land or titles or riches such as other second sons coveted. His years in Outremer had taught him well: life itself was more precious than wealth.

He loved Henry. Admired him. Shared with him a bond no woman would ever understand, certainly not Jehanne, who waited for Marc at Rossmorven Keep. When he returned from the Crusade, he would marry his betrothed, as arranged by their parents many years before, and get a son on her. Perhaps many sons.

Ah, God, he had thought his chance to roam the hills and heal his wounded soul would never come.

With a start he realised Richard was speaking to him. 'De Valery?'

Richard cleared his throat and began again. 'We will not wait for nightfall. We will board now. Come.' The king moved his mount forward, toward the ship. 'Bring the boy.'

The lad went still as a post. 'Oh, no, lord. Onto a ship? That I cannot.'

Marc turned toward the stricken voice. God almighty, the boy's face had gone white as goat's milk.

Richard twisted in the saddle and peered down at the servant. 'Why can you not?' he inquired sharply.

Soraya froze. If she wanted to avenge Khalil's death, as she had sworn, she must board this ship. If she wanted to retrieve the dagger, as she knew she must, she had to board this ship. She shut her eyes tight.

'Move!' the holy man growled. 'Do as you are told.'

Her thoughts tumbled in her brain like drunken butterflies. She could not bring herself to walk onto the ship.

But she must. An oath bound her mortal soul.

Ahead of her, the monk dismounted, led his horse to the rough wooden gangplank and clattered up onto the ship. The Frankish knight pivoted and sent her look of such disgust Soraya shut her eyes. When she opened them, two bare-legged seamen sprang onto the dock and began untying the thick mooring ropes. A sail went up and the ship shuddered to life.

Her quarry was leaving! She could not let him escape, and besides he still had the dagger.

Without pausing to let herself think, she raced down the quay and leaped from the edge of the dock. Her fingers scrabbled at the ship's splintery wooden deck and the next thing she knew cold seawater was closing over her head.

So, she was to die then, her soul condemned. She opened her mouth, gulped in water. *Breathe! You must breathe!*

She bobbed to the surface to see hands reaching out for her.

'Vite! Vite,' a voice yelled. A rope sailed out and dropped onto the water. Soraya struggled toward it, looped it twice around her waist and held on tight.

Men towed her toward the ship. Her body bounced and scraped along the wooden siding until she flopped onto the deck and lay like a beached fish, spitting up seawater.

A swarthy, black-haired man stalked over, drew back his boot and kicked her hard in the ribs. He shouted something in a language she did not recognise, but when the holy man advanced and spoke some words in the same language, everyone fell silent. To her, the monk uttered a single sentence. 'Come. It is not your fault.'

She scrambled to the monk's side, clutched the coarse wool robe with both hands. He leaned down to her, but the Frankish knight snagged the back of her sopping tunic and slid her backward across the wet deck until she rested at his feet.

Soraya bit down on a scream. He would kill her now. He would have let her drown but for the holy man's interference. She glanced up in a kind of stupor, her eyes stinging from the seawater, her attention held by his hard gaze.

The holy man and the knight exchanged a long look, and then the knight yanked her upright before him. She cried out at the stabbing pain in her ribs, but when his dark, glittering eyes met hers she gasped with fear.

'Do not hurt me.' She tried to speak with authority, but her voice trembled. 'I am but a small and humble creature of God, and—'

'Hush,' he snapped. 'While you are on this ship, you are to remain quiet and out of the way. And stay away from me. I trust you not. And avoid him, as well.' He tipped his head to indicate the monk, who was turning away.

'Yes, lord. I will serve you well, I promise.'

'Your word is false,' he said. 'I need no servant. Especially one who has twice proved quick with a knife. And he—' the blue eyes flicked to the monk '—needs no boy. Do you understand me?'

Soraya gaped at him. She understood nothing, but the intense light in her knight's gaze warned her of some danger. Yet why would he be concerned? She was his sworn enemy.

The ship lurched under her feet. A sickening dizziness brought her hand to her mouth, and suddenly she didn't care what the knight was saying. She was going to be sick.

Chapter Six

The galley shuddered under Marc's feet, and the two horses, tied to the thick rail, snorted and stamped their hooves to regain their balance. He smoothed his hands over Jupiter's quivering hide and tightened the tether so he would not injure himself.

A seaman scampered up the mast to unfurl the single sail. On either side of the ship the rowers grunted and leaned into their oars. The vessel cut through the sea swells like a blade through a ripe melon.

Richard lounged at the far end of the desk on a makeshift pallet of hemp sacks that smelled of rotting fruit. 'Stop pacing and get some rest, de Valery.'

'I will not rest until we dock in Cyprus, God willing.'

'The Templars will offer us lodging,' Richard assured him with a crafty smile. 'Especially when the good knights learn who now holds the island.'

Marc need not ask who. On his journey to Jerusalem, Richard had overrun Cyprus—fortress, vineyards, Templar bank and all. What the king wanted, the king took. 'Why does control over that island matter more than a gnat's dinner?'

The king's gaze drifted to where the servant boy squatted

next to a bowl of herbs and wine he was warming over an oil lamp. 'I have my reasons.'

Marc grunted. Richard never did anything without a reason. He was a royal, and with Great Eleanor at his back, the king of England was invincible. Even his brother John feared him. But with Richard on crusade in Outremer, John's meddling fingers crawled greedily into the honey pot that was England. Richard had to stop him.

The servant boy rose abruptly, dashed to the rail and leaned his head over it. The choked sound of retching made Marc's own stomach clench. When the bout was over, the lad dragged his sleeve across his mouth and staggered back to Richard's bedside. The turban wound about his head had loosened; strands of straggly dark hair were plastered to the pasty forehead.

'Are you still seasick, boy?' Richard's meaty hand patted the thin arm.

'Aye, lord. I do not like ships or sailing.' The boy lifted the king's head and tipped a few spoonfuls of the herb concoction past his lips. Richard grimaced, swallowed, grimaced again, and the boy settled the empty bowl beside the lamp. 'Soon you will be well, lord.'

Again the lad rose and wobbled toward the ship's rail. 'I am in your debt,' the king breathed at his retreating back.

Marc pressed his lips into a thin line. 'I would have a care, were it my belly the boy dribbles his noxious mixture into.'

'I've been guzzling his potion since afternoon, de Valery. As you can plainly see, I am growing stronger by the hour.'

It was true. For the first time in a month the ailing king rested peaceful as a babe, and the flush of fever no longer coloured his cheeks.

'The lad has some skill in herbal brews,' Marc allowed. 'You have struck up some sort of bond with him,' he continued carefully. 'No doubt you are right—the boy wants only my life, not yours.'

'Ah, yes. I want to keep him close.'

Marc jerked at the word. He could not say why he felt the least bit protective of the thieving little wretch, but he did. Nor did he trust the innocent look in the lad's sea-green eyes. He would lay not a single farthing on the truth of anything the boy uttered. Still, he felt oddly protective of him.

Possessive, even.

'The lad is my servant, not yours. I would like him to stay near me after all. If he manages to stop trying to attack me, he could come in useful.'

Richard's eyes turned to steel. 'You are impudent, de Valery.'

'I am honest,' Marc countered. He turned away to his own pallet. 'As you well know.'

The sun dropped into the sea at their back, painting the cloud-splattered sky gold and then purple. Once more the lad left the rail, walked unsteadily to the king's pallet, his face grey as moldy bread. Almost at once, he pivoted and raced back to the railing.

'When the ship reaches Cyprus,' Richard said casually, 'we can turn the boy over to the Templars.'

Marc said nothing.

'Good herbalists are always welcome in a warrior stronghold,' Richard added.

Aye, so they were. Marc thought a moment, then dug into his canvas bag for the bread and cheese the boy had stolen in the village. Bless this food, Lord, and think not on how we came by it. While he sliced off slabs of cheese with his eating knife, he watched the lad hang over the side of the ship. By now the boy's belly must be empty as a Greek's wine jug.

Dusk fell, and still the boy retched. God, the lying little scamp was paying for his sins. He felt halfway sorry for the lad.

'You said you were seasick once,' Richard said without opening his eyes. 'When you were but a boy, you told me. Tossing on the Firth of Dornoch in a coracle, as I recall.'

Marc swallowed at the memory. 'True,' he grated. 'And when my brother Henry and I sailed for France for our fostering, our uncle said I looked green as river moss when we docked. Do not remind me.'

'With the boy ailing,' Richard continued with a chuckle, 'you can sleep tonight without worry. He is too sick to plunge a dagger into your gut.'

'Aye, that is true enough.'

'Tomorrow though, when he recovers, I will have need of him.'

Marc blinked but did not reply. We shall see. King or not, the devious lad was Marc's responsibility. And there was yet more, he admitted. Enemy or no, something in those green eyes pulled at him.

Soraya gripped the deck railing until her fingers went numb. The briny smell of the sea alone made her gorge rise; being tossed about on the blue-black swells was worse than dying. She flashed a look over her shoulder. Five more heartbeats and she would let go of the rail and try her legs.

The monk slept soundly, his breathing less raspy and his fever lessened, thanks to her tea of lemon balm and thyme. The other one, the knight de Valery, lay some distance away, but she could not tell whether he slept or not.

She watched the inky water below stir into a froth by the ploughing ship. Her chest muscles ached from throwing her stomach contents into the sea. She would not last in such misery until the ship reached Cyprus.

In Cyprus, once she felt better, she could get her dagger

back and then disappear into the populace and search out King Richard. The people spoke her tongue, as well as the mangled French of the Normans, even Greek. Sometimes she wondered if Uncle Khalil had chosen her at the slave auction for her skill at languages. Certainly it was not for her beauty; six years ago, when she was but ten summers, even the promise of beauty was a hazy dream on the far horizon of her life.

She uncurled one hand from the smooth wooden rail and flexed her stiff fingers. Slowly she lifted her other hand and stood swaying on watery legs. If she could manage to reach the holy man, she could lie down on those foul-smelling sacks and rest. She had always felt somewhat uneasy around men, probably because of her years sequestered in the zenana, but the old monk seemed harmless.

She could not say the same for the knight de Valery.

Halfway across the deck she dropped to her hands and knees and ducked her head. The queasy feeling flooded through her; bitter saliva poured into her mouth. She clamped her lips tight shut and waited, controlling her breathing. After a moment she crawled forward, toward the sleeping monk, and then hesitated, remembering the knight's words. Stay away from him.

It made no sense, but perhaps it would be better to lie on the other side of the holy man, near de Valery. And await her chance to seek revenge. Before this night bled into dawn, she would keep her vow and kill the Frankish knight.

Hunched on all fours, she reached his pallet, bent over him and surveyed the knight's supine body. Already he slept like a dead man, his mouth hanging open, hands at his side. But he was very much alive. His chest and belly rose and fell at each breath.

The hilt of a small knife protruded from his sword belt. God be praised, she could do it now!

Carefully she placed one hand on his tunic, then slid it downward, fingering her way inch by inch over the linen. Warmth rose from his body. He snorted suddenly, closed his mouth and rolled his head to the other side.

When she calmed her heartbeat, she moved her fingers onto his worn leather belt and groped for the weapon. It was not her jeweled dagger, but it was a blade at any rate. God willing, it would do as well. She prayed it was sharp.

She waited, caressing the small metal hilt, matching her breathing to his. In. Out. Then another sleepy snuffle.

Very slowly she lifted the knife away from his belt and moved her hand upward, toward his unshaven chin. Eyeing his neck where the tunic gaped open, she drew the blade toward herself and tested the edge with her thumb. Should she plunge the point into the hollow at the base of his throat? Or slice sideways from ear to ear?

The Frank drew in an extra-deep breath and flopped one arm over his head. The cords in his neck rippled and then relaxed. Soraya leaned closer and raised the blade.

A pulse throbbed in his throat. She watched his heart beat and rest…beat and rest. She could not take her eyes off that faint flutter of life.

She tensed her muscles, drew her arm back to give her added force when the blade bit into the skin. His heart pumped steadily on. She listened to his breathing, watched the air enter his open lips and whistle back out. In…and then out.

She shut her eyes, enacted each step of the deed in her mind to prepare herself.

Now.

Her muscles bunched. She ground her teeth together and bent forward, hand raised level with her head, and stopped her breathing.

To her horror she found she could not move. Some other-worldly force seemed to grip her arm and hold it motionless. Trembling, she sat back and lowered the knife. She could not do it. Lord have mercy. *I cannot take this man's life. I cannot.*

She stared at the blade. An eating knife, for cutting meat and bread. A simple, small weapon. She could easily toss it into the sea afterward.

But she could not kill him.

She closed her eyes in disgust. Am I then such a coward? I have not the heart of the weakest harem slave, the most spineless beggar in the market square. Lord, let me die now in shame.

She turned the blade in her hand, pointed it at her own chest, then lowered it until the sharp tip scratched her tunic just below her sore ribs. Above her head, the rigging creaked.

She clasped her other hand over the hilt to drive it deep, sucked in a shuddery breath and held it. She must be strong.

A fist shot out and grasped her forearm. The knife went skittering across the desk, and a cry of despair rose from her lips.

'You pesky fool of a boy,' the knight's voice hissed. 'What do you think you are doing?'

'I swore an oath,' she said, trying not to sob. 'I have failed.'

'An oath!' he snapped in a voice heavy with sarcasm. 'Think you that Allah hears an oath taken to commit a mortal sin?'

'I swore not to Allah. I am a Christian.'

'A Christian?' For an instant surprise showed on his face, then was quickly masked. 'All the more sinful,' he growled.

Soraya rocked back on her heels. He thought she had intended to take only her own life! He was unaware of her original intent.

The knight rose up on one elbow, still gripping her wrist. 'Do you imagine that God cares whether you live or die? What do you gain by sacrificing yourself? Honour? Wealth? Your name chiseled onto a stone in the desert?'

'I gain self-respect.' She spoke in jerky syllables, her voice clogged with hiccupy sobs.

He spat off to one side. 'Self-respect.'

Soraya clamped her jaw tight to stop her weeping. Her body shook violently, her limbs twitching as if she had contracted the plague.

She dropped her chin to her chest and let hot tears drip onto her tunic. Think! What should she do now? The knight released her wrist, and she heard him exhale with a catch.

'Aye, ye poor dumb lad. Come here.' A strong arm reached to her shoulder and tugged her forward, and she tumbled against his hard chest. Overcome by her cowardice, she felt worse than seasick.

With a gentle hand he pressed her head against his warm neck. 'Sha, sha, now. No one need know of your great failure.'

Soraya closed her eyes and breathed in the scent of his skin. He smelled of sweat and horse and a pungent spice, like cinnamon.

She swallowed, feeling a wash of heat course through her body. She wanted to taste him! Never before had she experienced such a strange feeling of excitement. Of... yearning.

She stiffened. He was a man. And a Frank.

She scrambled away from him, her heart beating like a caged bird inside her chest. Speechless, she stared into the knight's face, watching his eyes harden, then narrow with distrust.

'You are afraid of me.'

'No, lord. Truly I am not.''

'You need not fear me, lad. I will not harm you except to protect myself.'

'That is not why—'

But it was. She did fear him. More than any danger she had

ever faced, this man threatened her. He was dangerous simply because he was a man.

No, not just a man. Her throat tightened. This man.

Chapter Seven

By the time the ship docked at Paphos on the western coast of Cyprus, Soraya could scarcely stand. Weak from retching, saddened by Khalil's death and still stupefied at her inability to slay the knight de Valery, she clung to the railing watching the activity on shore.

Genoese merchants in flowing robes swaggered along the smelly quay, arguing with ship captains and food vendors. Templar knights with cross-emblazoned white surcoats surreptitiously eyed women who promenaded along the harbor walkway in provocative sheer caftans, their nails and cheeks painted red. Houries. The noise of the harbour gave her a headache. If she debarked, the crush of people at the dock would swallow her up.

'Move on, then, lad.' De Valery strode past her, leading his dark stallion toward the gangplank. 'You will recover your sea legs by suppertime.'

Her throat convulsed. The thought of food made her nauseated.

'Soray!' the knight shouted at her from the top of the gangplank. 'Make haste!'

Still, she could not let go of the ship's rail. She knew little of this teeming place before her, full of unbelievers. She belonged in Palestine.

But in Palestine the man who sent the message she now carried for Khalil would kill rather than have it fall into the wrong hands. She glanced back toward her homeland and shuddered.

She could not go back. Perhaps even now an assassin was tracking her down to slit her throat in some shadowed alley. She sucked in a lungful of hot air that smelled of fish and thought she would be sick again.

'Soray!' His sharp tone cut through the cottony feeling inside her head and she stumbled forward.

'Aye, lord, I am coming.'

De Valery tramped halfway up the gangplank, grasped the neck of her tunic and dragged her forward. 'Hold on to Jupiter,' he instructed. He thrust the animal's brushy tail into her hands. 'Now, lad, move!'

She took a single step, wobbled off to one side and would have tipped into the sea had she not accidentally stumbled against the horse's hind end. By some miracle the beast did not strike out with his rear hooves, and she staggered after the animal, acutely aware of the knight's quiet laughter.

So, he was amused at her plight, was he? He would be less amused if she tossed up her stomach contents onto his mount's beautifully plumed tail. Better yet, on his blue surcoat.

Her head spun as he stalked beside her.

'Steady, now. Move quickly, boy. We must not lose sight of the…monk.' He stretched out his long legs and tramped down the walkway so fast Soraya could not keep up.

She loosened her grasp on the destrier's tail and sped up her pace until she could touch the animal's withers. Biting her lip, she gazed at the stallion's saddle. Without thinking she flexed her knees, sprang upward and dug the fingers of both hands into the coarse hair of his mane. She clawed her way up into the saddle and clutched at the high pommel. Her brain reeled from the effort.

'God!' the knight muttered under his breath. 'You are part mountain goat.'

'Nay, lord, I am part lioness.'

Instantly she saw her mistake.

De Valery's face tipped up to look at her, his eyes questioning. 'Lioness? Not a lion?'

She shook her head quickly to cover her lapse. 'You know nothing of such matters,' she blurted. Another mistake, this time much worse. A servant did not contradict his lord.

He narrowed his sea-blue eyes. 'Nothing, you say?' His voice dropped to a menacing whisper. 'What do I not know, besides the impudence of a servant boy?'

His shadowed gaze caught hers and held it. With all her will she tried to look away, but she could not. It was as if he conjured away the noisy market-place, the cries of hawkers, the shouts of seamen until her senses swam in a giant cocoon of silence.

'I did but mean...' Her dry tongue stuck to the roof of her mouth. She looked away to the left where a huge fortress loomed, built of grey stone with crenellated walls and square towers. Some great lord must live there, watching over his ships.

'I see more than is apparent,' he grumbled. 'Things are often not what they seem, and Saladin is a master of such tricks.'

'The Christians, too, use tricks.'

'Yes,' he sighed. 'The Christians, as well.' He looked at her oddly. 'Not only have you an agile tongue but there is a quick intelligence hidden under your dusty head covering. How is it you were a mere servant to your uncle?'

The horse sidestepped to avoid a ripe melon escaping from a nearby cart, and Soraya swayed in the saddle. Dizzy, she clapped her hand over her mouth. She did not want to answer his question, so feigned sickness.

'Can you see the monk?' he asked.

'Yes, lord.' She spoke through her fingers, tight against her lips. 'He stops to mount his horse, and now rides on toward that fortress ahead.'

'Good.' Marc had feared the impulsive, headstrong king would pursue some military diversion in the city. Instead it appeared that Richard would seek shelter. God, he would bear close watching. A healthy Richard was harder to reason with than an ailing Richard. And there were those who would not weep to see him dead.

'Keep your eyes on him, lad. He can be more slippery than an oiled mackerel.'

'Yes, lord. But if I may respectfully suggest, if you mounted we could move faster.'

Marc grunted. 'If I mounted, you would then walk?'

The lad fell silent. Hah! Marc guessed the boy would rather concede the matter than climb down from his hard-won perch on none-too-steady legs.

Marc reached for the water skin, uncorked the vessel and took a long pull, then handed it to the boy.

'I dare not drink, lord. I fear I will not keep it down.'

'Better that than die of thirst. Such an end is not pretty.'

A drawbridge manned by an unseen guard blocked entry into the fortress. Marc stopped some paces away as a voice boomed from the narrow window slit in the square stone gatehouse. 'Who seeks entry at the gate of the Templar knights?'

'A friend,' Marc called. 'A knight of the Scots and a holy man of God.'

'What names?' the voice barked back.

'Marc de Valery and…' He hesitated. Would Richard reveal himself once safely inside these walls? If so, Marc would be caught in a lie.

'…and a monk lately come from Jerusalem. Simon the…hermit.' He ignored the king's choked protest behind him.

'Hermit, indeed,' Richard muttered. The boy, Soray, twisted in the saddle and shot an interested look at the cowled figure.

'He is not a hermit, then?' the lad whispered. 'I thought him one of those chosen by God.'

'You think too much,' Marc replied in a cold voice. Not only was Richard not a monk, he was most assuredly not a holy man. Not a man loved by the crusading barons from France and Germany.

'Yes, lord, that is true, I do think too much. I think about the moon and the stars, about the water that bubbles out of the desert, about—'

'Enough! Think instead where we shall sleep tonight if we are not welcomed by the Templars.' He eyed the gatekeeper's shadow behind the narrow window. 'We are godly men. We seek shelter and permission to hear mass in your chapel.'

'Christians, then,' came the voice. 'Of Rome or Constantinople?'

'We speak the words of God in humble Latin, not in Greek.' Behind him, Richard snorted in impatience and stepped his horse forward. 'Tell the fool we demand admittance. Tell the grand master that the conquerer of—'

Marc wheeled and gripped the king's arm. 'Quiet!'

Richard glared at him, his face reddening. 'You overstep, de Valery.'

'I am commanded to protect your person. It would be well to follow my lead.' Richard was brave, but he was arrogant. No wonder Leopold hated him.

'Ha!' the king shot. 'I am leader here.'

'It matters not who leads,' Marc asserted, 'but who survives. Let me negotiate our entrance, lest you nettle yon keeper. Warm honey works better than cold demands.'

Richard sat back in his saddle. 'Ah, the honeybee has a sting! Very well, de Valery, proceed.'

But already the grinding of the drawbridge over the wide moat sounded in their ears. The king turned his head toward Marc and grinned. 'You win. This time.'

Marc stifled an oath. Richard was more boy than man at times. How he loved a jest, a game of skill, even quarrelling with his sworn protector. How was it England had survived two generations of Plantagenets?

He led Jupiter forward over the heavy oiled planks, paused while the portcullis ratcheted noisily upward with the clanking of metal chain, then advanced into the outer bailey. Richard followed, mercifully silent for a change.

Once inside, the groaning drawbridge rose and the toothed portcullis wheel rattled its way twice around. Marc waited. He could smell the stables, the harsh scent of hot metal wafting from the smithy's shed.

De Valery peered up at her. 'Still seasick, are you, boy?'

She nodded, feeling tears sting against her upper lids. Her eyes burned when she retched so she knew what was coming. She clamped her lips tight together.

Just when she felt her control beginning to slip, squires tumbled out the inner gate, followed by four mounted knights armed with steel-tipped lances.

'What in God's name…' Marc pulled his horse forward to

shield the unarmed monk, then rode forward, his hand on the hilt of his sword.

'Hold!' The monk stood up in his stirrups and raised one arm above his head in an imperious gesture, as if he expected to stop the setting of the sun. A bold move for a man of God.

'Devil-blessed fool of a man,' the knight admonished. His eyes glittered like two blue jewels.

The monk swore. 'You are worse than Becket. Once appointed archbishop, he thought he was king.'

'Aye,' muttered the Scot. 'Beware of honest men.'

The monk spit out a laugh, but sank back in his saddle once more. 'So it would seem. An honest man would guard a life in spite of its owner. Your pardon, de Valery.'

Marc threw him a hard look and allowed the armed knights to form an escort around them. One of the men gestured, and the monk dismounted. They were moving toward the wooden steps leading to the heavy-timbered fortress when suddenly the holy man halted.

'Do not send the servant boy to the kitchen,' he announced. 'He comes with us.'

Soraya saw the muscles in the knight's jaw tighten. Before he could speak, she clambered off the destrier and slipped in between the monk and de Valery. They moved forward, the knight in front of her, the monk behind, until the armed guards wheeled their mounts away.

Squires came and took their horses away to be cared for, then the three of them clattered up the steps and were swallowed into the cold grey walls of the keep.

Chapter Eight

The vast timber-roofed hall echoed with the clank of wine cups and orders shouted to the table servants by the single burly figure at the high table. Hounds lolled on the rush-covered floor, snapping up dropped tidbits of meat and bone. The din was deafening, the sounds so loud and ugly Soraya clapped her hands over her ears. Had these Templar Knights no fine carpets or cushions on which to recline? No timbrels or lutes to calm the soul?

She watched Marc follow a servant to the high table, the holy man at his heels. Both were seated on either side of a heavyset man with sun-coloured hair. Suddenly she stood alone in the great hall that stank of sweat and wine.

'You there!' a pimply-faced youth yelled in the Norman tongue. 'Sit you at the end of the servants' table.' He pointed toward the back of the hall where a group of chattering boys sat at a trestle far back in the shadows. Some wore Arab-style tunics and head wraps. Others, younger and bareheaded, wore ragged shirts that hung down over skinny, hose-covered legs.

'*Merci,*' she managed. The air reeked of grease and offal, and as she seated herself on the long bench, her stomach erupted. No one paid her any attention! In the zenana she would have been cosseted with cool cloths and iced sherbet while slaves cleaned the floor. Here, the hounds made quick work of her disgrace.

She sank onto the rough plank bench and lowered her head. *God help me to endure this hellish place.*

Only the high table was covered with a cloth. The trestle where she sat was bare wood, stained and smelly from previous meals. The other servants were fighting over a haunch of roasted meat, knocking over wine cups and scattering a bowl of sugared nuts across the table.

'Better get busy, boy, if you want to eat.' The voice came from a chubby red-headed youth on her left.

She answered in the Norman tongue. 'I do not wish to eat.'

'Then you don't work hard enough,' spoke a deeper voice at her right. 'One day of service in this keep and you will beg for scraps.'

'I am not hungry,' she protested in a quiet tone.

'Eat!' he insisted. *'Mangez!'*

The others took up the cry, like a chant. *'Mangez... mangez...mangez.'* The noise made her head buzz.

'Let's have a look at you.' The red-haired boy prodded her shoulder. Instinctively she pulled away.

'O-ho, he's a shy one! And bony, too,' he said, pinching her arm.

She jerked free, then leveled her gaze at each of the shouting boys, now rhythmically slapping their palms onto the table top. *'Mangez...mangez.'*

'I will not.' Inside she trembled with fear, but she would never let it show. Khalil's training had taught her such control that she could endure a knife cut without flinching.

'Oh, aye, you will eat,' the deep-voiced boy next to her

rumbled in her ear. He jabbed her in the ribs with his sharp elbow. '*Mangez,*' he whispered. 'Now! Or I will cram it down your throat.'

Marc looked up at the sudden noise at the far end of the hall. Some chant or other at the servants' table. He scanned the benches until he found Soray, seated between a chunky-looking lad and a half-grown stripling with a mop of silvery hair and a curved back. As he watched, the taller boy jammed his elbow into Soray's side. Marc's hand closed into a fist.

The Templar grand master Giles Amaury leaned forward. 'You were saying, de Valery?'

'What? Ah, yes, the siege in Jerusalem. It goes badly for both sides. The Christian forces have scant food remaining, and the infidel has none, but he controls the water holes.'

He watched the white-haired lad again drive his elbow into Soray's side. Soray twisted away, then clenched both fists and rammed them hard into his attacker's groin. Marc winced. He almost pitied the boy.

The fat one on the other side edged away, then shot one hand out and flicked Soray's cheek. In the next instant that boy, too, bent groaning over his belly.

The other servants at that table fell silent. Then someone across from Soray reached to fill his wooden wine cup. But instead of drinking…

The grand master tapped Marc's metal trencher with his eating knife. 'You are distracted, de Valery.'

Marc jerked. 'My lord Amaury?' Out of the corner of his eye he saw Soray deliberately dump his wine cup into the lap of one of the injured lads. God! Small though he was, Soray was both brave and clever; the lad would have made a fine knight.

Giles Amaury paused to catch Marc's eye. 'And then that ninny Richard of England cut a swath through the enemy as if he were scything a wheat field. There were Christians among the Muslim ranks, but even so, he cut down every man. Christians!'

Marc sent a covert glance toward the monk on Amaury's other side. Richard's head was bowed. The robe-covered arm did not so much as twitch, but the fingers of the extended hand drummed rhythmically against the table covering.

'True enough,' Marc said slowly. 'England's king may be a better leader than a statesman. But, faced with an ambush of mixed troops, only a fool would stop to separate out the chaff.'

'The man is dangerous,' the grand master shot. 'A fool in fine armour.'

Marc set down his flagon of sweet Cyprus wine with a clunk. 'Richard may be many things, but he is not a fool.'

The king's fingers stilled. 'I think, de Valery, that your young servant needs rescuing from yon table.'

Marc strained his eyes but could see nothing further amiss. 'I think not. The lad has declawed the lions, both of them.'

Richard's penetrating blue eyes sought his. 'Look again.'

It was an order, not a polite request. Marc understood at once. Richard would be private with the Templar grand master.

'You are right,' Marc amended. 'Young Soray looks to be in need of…direction.' In truth, young Soray had things well in hand, but Marc quickly excused himself and started across the hall toward the servants' table.

'De Valery!' the grand master abruptly called at his back. Marc halted.

'I would not wish you to roam freely about this keep. My servant will conduct you to your guest quarters.'

A moment of silence, then the low murmur of voices resumed, the disguised king's and the grand master's. What mischief was Richard stirring up now?

A paunchy, grey-haired man in a white surcoat appeared out of the gloom, sidestepping both hounds and refuse without breaking his stride. 'This way, sir knight. Follow me.'

Marc stopped at the servants' table and spoke at Soray's back. 'Come on, lad. To bed.'

Soray scrambled off the bench, resisting the impulse to throw her arms around her rescuer. 'Oh, thank you, lord. Thank you!'

'That tired, are you?' he said, an edge in his low voice.

'Oh, no, not tired,' she blurted. 'But I have been…quite busy here.'

'Ah,' said her knight. 'Commendable aim you have.'

She gaped up at him. 'You saw?'

'I saw.'

Soraya flinched. His world, even the small part of it she had seen, was ugly beyond words, full of rudeness and noise and awful smells. She hated it.

But she did not hate him. On the contrary, she was beginning to like him. He roared and grumbled, but he did not strike. He fed her, warmed her at his fire, protected her from angry merchants…even laughed at her remarks. Apparently he found her acceptable company.

She followed him out of the great hall and up a winding staircase, the stone steps unevenly worn with long use. Up and up it went, curving always to her right. By the second landing, she was so dizzy she feared she would stagger off the edge. Blindly she reached out toward her knight, caught a handful of his tunic and held on.

'Better than the tail of a horse, is it?' he said over his shoulder. The amusement she heard in his rough voice made her grin.

'Much better, lord,' she said at his back. 'A horse could never climb such steps as these.'

He chuckled and shortened his steps. 'But a horse has no need for guest quarters in a Templar keep.'

They both laughed.

On the next landing, the grey-haired man led them down a short hallway, through a wooden door that screeched on rusty hinges and into a small chamber with a single window cut into the stone wall.

'Here it is, my lord,' the man puffed. 'Fine view. See all over the city, you can.' He surveyed Soraya with a measuring eye. 'Mind you don't lean out too far past the shutters, boy. Many a young page has found himself swimming upside down in the moat.'

She stared at the window and fought down a shudder.

'Anything you be wantin' from the kitchen my lord?'

'Hot water and soap,' de Valery replied.

'I'll send it up with a page. Don't think I can manage this climb more than once a night.'

Water and soap? 'You would bathe?' she blurted. Here, in front of her?

'I would,' he snapped.

'Now?'

'Aye, lad, now,' he growled with impatience. 'What better time?'

The old man started for the door. 'You'll be wantin' a large tub for the likes of one tall as yerself. I'll see to it.'

From the rank smell of bodies in the dining hall, she knew that knights did not bathe often. She caught her lower lip between her teeth. In a few moments de Valery intended to disrobe; as his servant she would be expected to help him shed his garments and then...

She swallowed hard. She had never before seen a full-grown man naked.

'What ails you, lad? Help me get these boots off.'

She ducked her head and tugged at the spurs and the tarnished buckles on his blackened leather boots.

Chapter Nine

It took seven buckets of steaming water to fill the wooden tub. The last servant, panting from his exertions, set a bowl of soap, a cloth and a towel on the floor next to the tub, and by the time the door closed after him, the knight was shrugging off his tunic.

'Open the window. I smell like no rose.'

'Oh, no, lord, you smell just as you should!' The words spattered out of Soraya's mouth like sand blown in a windstorm. 'You need not bathe at all. You smell…just like a rose. A musky one, like the pink rose my uncle Khalil trained over an—'

'Enough!' he roared. He began stripping his legs free of the mail stockings. Soraya looked everywhere but at him, the fireplace set deep in the thick stone wall where lazy flames threw out a flickering light; the simple rope chair upon which he draped his discarded garments.

'Don't stand goggling, boy. Give me a hand with this mail and my hauberk.'

Soraya stepped forward. Don't think. Just do as you must. Three hard tugs and the mail shirt rolled off his torso with a soft crunch. Then she untied the laces of the padded hauberk underneath.

'The window,' he reminded, his voice tight.

She swung the shutters as wide as they would go, gulped in the soft, scented night air. Below her, the moat gurgled as if in warning.

She was his servant, but she could not look at him. When she finally gathered her courage and turned back to the knight, he stood before her completely naked. She caught her hand to her mouth.

His body was beautiful, his chest hard-muscled, his waist narrow. His entire form looked lean and hard, as if chiseled out of stone. In spite of herself, her gaze drifted lower, to his battle-scarred thighs. And his…

Oh, my. Her breath whistled in through her teeth. That, too, was handsomely formed.

She looked away. 'My uncle Khalil has a fine house,' she stuttered. 'In Damascus. With fine carpets and hammered silver chests, and the linen always spotless. And—'

'What on earth are you chattering about?'

'I was speaking of my uncle's house,' she said quickly. She knew she was talking nonsense to a knight who cared nothing about the house in Damascus, but it was all she could think of to distract herself. 'I had a private bathing pool in my quarters. Heated. I bathed ev—'

'You had your own quarters, did you?' he said, his voice sharp. 'A servant? Huh! You are a skillful liar, boy, but you do not fool me.'

He made a half turn away from her and lifted one bare foot into the tub. She forced her gaze to the floor, inspected the bowl of soap, the linen towel. She heard a splash and a groan of satisfaction, and she could not resist raising her head.

He was leaning back against the edge of the tub, eyes closed, a tired smile on his lips. 'Start at my neck,' he said in a drowsy voice.

Soraya went perfectly still. He wanted her to…touch him? Touch the naked flesh of a man?

'Soray?' came the grumbly voice. 'Make haste, lad.'

She knelt quickly beside the tub, reached for the cloth and lifted the bowl of soap. It was runny and smelled of sheep fat. She looked at his chest, at the bulges of muscle, the sprinkling of black hairs around his flat, brown nipples, his bare forearms resting on the tub edge. A peculiar feeling lodged deep in her belly.

'One moment, lord,' she murmured. She could not sully his wondrous body with soap such as this. She set the wooden bowl down. Yanking open the leather pouch she carried under her tunic, she poured in half a palmful of aromatic rosemary leaves, then plunged her hand in the mess and squashed the herbs into it. When it smelled fresh and pungent instead of rancid, she scooped up a glob with two fingers and dribbled it onto his bare skin.

'Ah, smells good,' he said.

'So will you within the hour,' she said without thinking.

'So I do stink, do I?' He laughed softly. 'Small wonder. One Christian legion could flatten an entire army of Saracens just from the stench of our bodies.'

He did not stink. He smelled of sweat and leather, and his breath, when he blew it out, smelled of wine. But he did not stink.

He smelled like a man.

Marc did not open his eyes when the soap drizzled onto his chest. It smelled different, spicy and pleasant. He smiled to himself and began to let his body take its ease. He had managed to get King Richard safely to Cyprus. Also, after months of drinking sour ale, he was tasting good wine. And the soothing attentions of Soray, scrubbing gently at a month's caked filth, were calming.

He opened his lids. 'War is a dirty business. A warrior fights not only the enemy, but heat, desert sand, exhaustion, thirst, even hunger, while kings and princes negotiate behind each other's backs and make secret bargains. Grasping power-seekers, the lot of them.'

'Saladin is reported to be honest,' the boy ventured. 'And chivalrous.'

Marc huffed. 'Saladin wants to hold Jerusalem at any cost. He is like a patient desert ant—truce or no, he will find a way, through force or chicanery. Or both.'

His servant uttered not one word. The rough cloth traveled back and forth across his chest, and when he leaned forward, it slid up and down his back from neck to tailbone. The lad might be unfamiliar with the ways of knights and armies, but he understood something about bathing. Marc turned one ear toward his bent knee to allow the boy to scrub his scalp and again he closed his eyes.

He was more tired than he had thought. So tired his brain was muddling things together, the scented soap, the sweet, warm air flowing in through the open casement, the feel of a hand other than his own giving attention to his body. It was soothing. Almost caressing.

He sat upright with a groan.

'What is wrong, lord?'

'Nothing,' he grated. 'Everything. I have been months without a woman.'

The washcloth halted and Soray sat back suddenly.

'A woman?'

'Aye. You are too young to know of such things.'

A look passed over his servant's white face. 'I have heard that other warriors, Christians, take Saracen women.'

'Aye. They say such women are soft-skinned and perfumed. And skilled in dancing. And other things.'

'And are they?' came a small voice.

'I would not know, lad. I have never taken one.'

'Never?'

Marc ignored the question. Now he felt the sharp prick of desire, and it brought another groan from his throat. 'Come, boy. Hurry it up so the water will still be warm for you.'

The boy's breath sucked in and again the gliding cloth halted on his shoulder. 'For me!'

'You said you bathed, did you not? Or is it just hands and face you wash?'

Marc drew the washing linen out of the boy's hand and scrubbed his belly and his privates, then his legs and feet. Soray hunched beside the tub, his eyes on the floor.

Marc dunked his head into the tub and came up shaking off the water like a hound. He stood up, turned toward the boy and lifted his arms. Soray stared at the rivulets of water dripping from his hair onto his chest, but the lad did not move.

'Well, towel me off,' he barked.

The servant bit his lower lip and began mopping at Marc's wet skin, careful to touch no lower than Marc's waist. God, the lad was an innocent.

An irrational feeling of protectiveness washed over him. He must guard the lad from predators until he was old enough to…

Absently he took the linen towel from Soray's hand and dried his torso, a scar making him think suddenly of his older brother.

'Henry, my brother…'

Unaware he had spoken aloud, he blinked when Soray softly inquired, 'What about your brother, lord?'

'We are very close. We were fostered together, with my father's older brother in France. Henry won his spurs when he was eighteen, and then he took time to tutor me in the tilt yard. I still bear this scar on my chest from a badly deflected blow. There was lots of blood and Henry laid me down on the grass and wept.'

'You love your brother,' Soray said quietly.

'That I do. I pray nightly that I will see him once again soon, God willing.'

The lad moved away and stood with one hand on the door bar. 'Shall I fetch a page to empty the tub?'

'What? No, do not. Use the water, lad. Strip and soak yourself.'

Soraya's heart skipped once and stumbled to a stop.

Strip herself? 'I thank you, lord, but…I…'

The knight turned toward the huge curtained bed, and Soraya swore he was hiding a smile. She was dirty and smelly, but… She glanced down at the inviting bathwater. Oh, to soak the filth off her body.

But she dared not. Unless…

She studied the blue damask curtains tied back with a thick red cord, then let her gaze drift to Marc, who was nearing the bed.

'I wish you a peaceful rest, lord.' She waited, heard the whisper of the straw mattress as it took his weight.

'Peaceful it will not be until our friend the holy man is safe in his…monastery.'

Soraya did not reply. Instead, she stood motionless, listening to the knight's gradually slowing breaths. When air gusted out of his open mouth with a hoarse after-sound, she sneaked a final look at him.

He lay spread-eagled on the fur coverlet, arms flung

outward, his mouth sagging open. Asleep, she prayed. She tiptoed forward.

'Lord?' she whispered.

No answer, only a grunt and more steady breathing.

She tore off her leather sandals, her tunic, her belt with the precious pouch of herbs and her bag of gold coins, well wrapped in silk to prevent their clinking. Last she stepped out of her wide trousers and unbound the headpiece and the strip of linen confining her breasts.

Keeping her back to the sleeping knight, she noiselessly slid first one leg, then the other, into the lukewarm water. She dropped to her knees, tipped her head under the surface and soaped her thick curls. Every few moments she craned her neck to watch the figure on the bed.

Yes, he slept on. She took her time sponging her body, then rose, stepped silently out of the tub and wrapped herself in the still-damp towel. Just as she moved toward the pile of garments she'd left on the floor, someone began pounding on the chamber door.

'De Valery, wake up! Open the door!'

God save her, it was the holy man with the voice of thunder. She froze in the center of the room, afraid to utter a sound, afraid to move lest the knight wake and notice her. She hugged the linen towel tighter around her body and flinched as the pounding boomed again.

'De Valery, I bring news!'

The knight on the bed groaned and flung one arm over his face. 'In the morning,' he muttered. 'Go away.'

'Open this door at once!'

De Valery rolled heavily toward the edge of the bed and raised his torso up on one elbow. Soraya spun away, putting her back to him. Out of the corner of her eye she watched him lurch off the bed and stagger, still half-asleep, toward the chamber door.

Her heart leaped. Her tunic and trousers and the strip of linen she used to bind her breasts lay directly in his path. Trembling with fear, she waited.

The groggy knight stepped over the pile of clothes and slid back the bolt. Just as the door scraped open, Soraya clutched the towel to her bosom, darted behind de Valery to snatch up her clothes and leaped onto the bed.

Huddling in the center, wrapped in the towel, she waited until the holy man pushed through the doorway, then hurriedly yanked one of the bed curtains closed. The damask hanging zinged along the wooden rod, screening her from view.

De Valery's sleep-muzzy voice spoke. 'What news?' he demanded.

'Something has happened.' The monk was breathing so heavily Soraya guessed he had climbed the three floors at a run. Frantically she wound the linen strip around her upper body, and was just tugging her tunic over her head when she heard the holy man stride across the room.

'Have you some wine?'

'No.'

'Well, get some, man,' the monk shouted. 'We must talk.'

'Soray,' the knight ordered. 'Go down to the kitchen. Ask them to send up food and wine.'

She scrambled into her trousers, slid off the far side of the bed and scooped up her sandals. Then she ducked past the holy man and sped down the hall to the stairway.

On the way back up from the kitchen she heard men's voices drifting along the corridor and she hid in a garderobe to listen.

'He would sell it?' one man grated. 'To the Templars? But where would we get such a sum for the purchase?'

'Look in your vault, Giles. More than enough gold is hidden there.'

'Damn the man!'

'The English are not patient, Giles. We must pay.'

Soraya curled her toes but made no sound. As soon as the voices faded, she fled.

When she returned to the chamber, the bathtub was gone and a flagon of wine, a round loaf of bread, a saucer of greenish olive oil and some cheese sat on the crude wooden table against one wall. De Valery was half-dressed in a long, loose shirt, apparently one he found in the wooden chest at the foot of the bed, the lid of which now stood open. The holy man paced back and forth in front of the casement.

'Do not argue, de Valery. It is done.'

Soraya edged around the perimeter of the shadowy room, staying out of the holy man's path, until she reached the bed. In one bound she sprang behind the still-drawn curtain.

'It will be dangerous,' the knight snapped. He slammed his wine cup onto the table, and Soraya winced.

'It is already dangerous,' the monk shouted. 'We leave before lauds. Get some sleep.'

Footsteps, and the chamber door creaked shut.

'God deliver us from England,' the knight muttered. He padded to the window and she heard the shutters squeak. When she risked a peek around the bed drape, de Valery was leaning his forehead against the upper part of the frame, his arms braced against the rough stone wall on either side.

'God,' he whispered. 'The scheme is mad. And he is mad, as well.'

Soraya hunkered down on the warm spot she'd made on the bed. She didn't understand what was happening, but it mattered not to her who bribed whom in this uncivilised place.

Let the Frankish knights squabble among themselves. Uncle Khalil's message, the secret communication she now carried for the English king, was safe enough, borne as it was on the body of the knight de Valery, though he did not know it. Soon she would get it back and then make her way to find the English king.

But first, she must discover where England's king was hiding before the enemies of Saladin tracked her down. They would kill to destroy that message.

Aye, God, she was trapped two ways. If she failed, Saladin himself would never let her live, and the Saracen leader had spies everywhere. He would slice her head from her neck with his own scimitar and then call for figs and sweetmeats.

In the ominous quiet she curled into a ball, let her lids drift shut and tried to sleep.

Chapter Ten

After the king banged the chamber door shut behind him and stormed away, Marc puzzled over his final words. Get some sleep. But keep your sword near. He paced about the small room, something uneasy in his belly, then acknowledged Richard's advice. He must sleep. He settled one knee on the straw mattress but jerked back when a large lump lodged against his thigh.

God's teeth, there was the boy, curled up at the foot of the bed, sound asleep. Marc laughed softly. It was a bold servant who claimed space on his master's sleeping place. Instead of prodding the lad off onto the bare plank floor, he grudgingly made room, too tired for one of the boy's clever arguments.

The next thing he knew, something woke him out of a dreamless sleep. An odd, ruddy light flickered through the chamber and Marc bolted to a sitting position.

Fire! The fortress was burning! They were three stories above the ground floor. Trapped. He nudged the boy with his foot. 'Wake up, lad.'

Instantly the boy sprang up. 'What is it, lord?'

'Trouble.' He didn't know what, exactly, but he could guess.

Very likely the enraged Cypriots would not accept Richard's impulsive secret sale of their homeland to the Templars.

An ugly roaring noise rose from the inner bailey below, and Marc strode to the open window. Soray was there ahead of him. The lad must have ears like a hunting hound.

'Look,' the boy whispered. Marc peered out the casement.

A mob of people swarmed over the courtyard, blazing torches gripped in their hands, clenched fists punching the air. Over the stench of unwashed bodies and smoldering pitch, Marc could almost smell the fury of the crowd. Merchants, Muslims, Jews with black skullcaps and churchmen—not Templars but those of the Greek faith—poured like a flaming tide over the fortress grounds. The black smoke billowed upward.

Someone had let the news of the king's bargain with the Templars slip across a careless tongue. Richard was brave but maddeningly shortsighted. The townspeople, the landowners, the religious scholars from many countries would all revolt before they let the Templars rule them.

He'd seen enough. 'Quick,' he ordered. 'My hauberk and mail.'

The boy's fingers were fast and efficient, though Marc noted how they trembled as they tied the lacings of his padded undergarment. When the mail shirt and leggings were in place, Marc grabbed up his sword belt and stuffed his feet into his boots.

'Make no noise,' he commanded. 'Not a sound. Enemies surround us.' He snatched up the dish of unused olive oil left on the table and slathered it on the rusty hinges of the chamber door.

'Come.' Cautiously he inched the door open. When it swung wide in silence, he breathed a sigh of relief, but the rising whine of the mob below sent a shiver up his backbone. To escape, they must reach the ground floor before the angry rioters broke down the door.

'Stay close and be quiet,' he ordered. Drawing his sword, he started down the twisting staircase, his booted feet pounding on the stone. Behind him the panting boy tried to keep up, but to his credit voiced no complaint. At the bottom, Marc halted so suddenly Soray bumped up against his back. Richard was standing there waiting for them.

'Get to the stables!' the king's raspy voice announced.

'Through the scullery!' Marc shouted. Once on the ground floor, they raced for the half flight of steps leading down to the kitchen. Just as they thudded past the huge firepit, Marc caught the choking scent of smoke, then heard the sharp sound of cracking timbers. The main entrance had been breached. The maddened Cypriots were swarming into the great hall and torching the place.

Marc whirled, caught the boy around the waist, tucked him tight under his free arm like a side of venison and plunged through the narrow doorway with the king at his heels.

They dashed into the shadows next to the inner curtain wall and began to edge around the perimeter toward the stables. Fifty paces beyond the stable building lay the postern gate. Pray God they could slip through it unseen.

'Is there a ship?' he murmured to Richard.

'Aye. Genoese. Two masts.'

Marc grunted softly. How had Richard persuaded Guy de Lusignan to procure a ship? Or had he simply bought it, captain, crew and cargo?

They reached the stable door and plunged inside. In the thick blackness, Marc whistled for his mount and when Jupiter appeared, he released the boy, scrabbled for the bridle and flung the heavy saddle onto the animal's back. Richard had not yet located his horse.

'Do not mount,' Marc called softly.

'Aye,' said Richard. Then, as if by magic, there was the king at the stable exit, leading a grey gelding. Marc frowned. The horse was not Richard's, and he dared not ask why it was already saddled. So, the king had anticipated trouble.

Marc led them to the little-used postern gate and wrenched the iron grill open when a knot of men brandishing torches poured from behind the armourer's shed. With screams of fury, they launched themselves at Marc and the king.

God! Surely they could not know that the monk was King Richard in disguise! In the next sickening second, the truth dawned. It was not the king they sought, but Marc himself. The mob took him for a Templar!

He shouldered the king through the gate, then drew his sword and turned to face the crowd. The sight that met his eyes turned his legs to water.

Soray had planted himself in the path of the shouting men. The lad stood alone, feet splayed apart, a length of sturdy bow-wood in his hand. Stolen from the smithy, no doubt. Marc's heart swelled at the boy's foolhardy bravery.

A black-robed man lunged forward and Soray delivered a crack across his shins that brought him to his knees. Marc stepped up beside Soray, and without a word they faced the attackers together. Soray struck at the legs, and when a man buckled, Marc slammed the flat of his sword against his unprotected head. Men dropped like sacks of grain and lay groaning at their feet.

'Fetch my horse!' he shouted. Soray darted away, and when the next screaming man staggered backwards from a broadsword smacked across his belly, he felt Jupiter's breath gusting at his shoulder. Soray shoved the bridle lead into his hand, and Marc mounted and clattered out the gate.

The boy hesitated, then dashed after him, clanged the gate shut and used the length of ash to jam it closed. It would hold but a moment or two, but it bought precious time.

Marc turned Jupiter in a tight circle around the boy, and somehow Soray scrambled up behind him and flung both his slim arms around Marc's waist. How the lad could fly!

They galloped to the edge of the moat. 'We swim,' he called to Richard. He plunged his mount into the oily-looking water.

The king splashed into the brackish, smelly ditch after him, and in silence the two horses ferried their riders to the opposite side. When his mount struggled up the bank, Marc spurred him on in a desperate race for the ship and safety. Soray hung on tight. Richard pounded behind them.

Three two-masted ships floated side by side in the harbor. The horses clattered along the curving quay until Richard gave a yell and pointed. A gaggle of barefooted seamen on the smallest ship shouted in vulgar Italian and banged down a narrow gangplank. Both horses clambered up the wooden walkway and trotted onto the vessel.

From her perch behind the knight, Soraya spied another black-haired captain, another stack of rotting fruit sacks, and—God preserve her—another sail flapping to life above her head. Her heart sank all the way to her sandals. At the briny smell of the sea, her stomach began to heave.

But they were safe, the holy man and herself. And, most important of all, her knight.

Five days later they docked at Talamone, near Tuscany. The air smelled of sea water and smoked fish, and the harbor was alive with activity. Hordes of merchants clamoured for passage on the ship. Fishermen, their faces tanned to the colour of ripe plums, unloaded nets of squirming sardines. A monkey capered at the command of a gaudily dressed minstrel.

A single mounted knight waited at the end of the quay, armed in chain mail but carrying his iron helmet under his arm. Marc and the holy man slowed. As they debarked the ship, the man dismounted and advanced toward them.

'De Valery!' He saluted, then pulled Marc into a bear hug.

'Roger de Clare! What in God's name are you doing here?'

De Clare paid no attention to the monk, but sought Marc's gaze with a steady, sober look. 'I came to find you, my friend.'

'And so you have. But why? How did you know where to look?'

'The Templar master, Giles Amaury, told me your destination. My ship landed yesterday. I have been waiting for you.'

A thread of apprehension wound into Marc's belly. 'Why?' he demanded. His voice sharpened. 'Why?'

Roger reached one hand to Marc's shoulder. 'I bring news that concerns you.' He gestured for Marc to step to one side with him, out of hearing.

'What news?' Mark asked. He did not like the flat tone of his friend's voice. A dark apprehension flooded through him.

De Clare remained silent, his earnest brown eyes sombre. Then he reached out and gripped Marc's shoulder. 'News of your brother.'

Every instinct told him to stop de Clare's words, to refuse to listen. Refuse to believe. 'Henry is with Philip of France, at Ascalon.'

'He is no longer.' Roger spoke gently, but his words enraged Marc just the same.

'He is, I tell you. He fights at Philip's side.'

Roger hesitated. 'He does not, my friend.'

It was not true. Marc closed his eyes. 'You lie!'

'I wish that were so, Marc. You know I do not lie.'

Ah, God, no. He turned away from the stricken look on Roger's open, honest countenance. No!

'He is buried at Ascalon,' Roger said in a low voice. "There is a Christian cemetery.'

Marc wanted to strike out at something, pound his fists until they were bloody.

'There is more, my friend, if you would hear it.'

'No more,' Marc choked out. 'I will hear no more.' He stumbled off a few paces, heard Roger speaking quietly with Richard, and something inside him crumbled.

Someone mounted a horse near him, and he heard the metallic chink of mail. He stumbled forward to find his friend, Roger de Clare, and the king riding on either side of him. Jupiter snuffled at his back.

Marc willed himself to feel nothing.

'An inn lies near,' Richard said. He pointed down a narrow street where the tall buildings on either side leaned toward each other. 'We shall lodge there for the night.'

Marc nodded. His limbs felt heavy, his mind fuzzy as a ball of his mother's spun wool. He craved sleep. And more—he wished never to wake up.

The boy, Soray, moving quietly by his side, slipped his small hand into Marc's and held it tight.

'You must eat, lord.'

The soft voice spoke near Marc's ear, but he could not open his eyes. 'No.' He rolled over on the narrow cot.

'You must, lord.'

'Do you give the orders, now?' he said in a tired voice. 'You are but my servant, Soray. I am not hungry.'

'True, lord. But if you die, I shall be your servant no longer.'

'I will not die. I cannot. I am needed in Scotland.'

'There are some ripe melons here, lord. I "borrowed" them from a very fine fruit vendor in the market square.'

In spite of the cloud of misery that hung over him, Marc smiled. No market-place was safe from Soray's clever fingers. He opened his grainy lids to see the boy's clear green eyes peering into his.

'I will eat later, perhaps.'

'Now,' the boy insisted gently.

Marc let his gaze travel about the small whitewashed room. 'Is the monk nearby?'

'The holy man rests in the chamber next to this one. Your friend, Roger de Clare, dines with him.'

Marc groaned. Sooner or later Roger would recognise England's king. The whole of the crusading army would soon know of the Lion Heart's absence, and what would follow after that, he willed himself to not think about.

He tried not to think of Henry, as well, but it was no use.

In his mind's eye he looked back to his boyhood—saw his brother positioning Marc's hand on a lance, or sharing a stolen peach with him, juice dripping off his chin, his eyes gleaming with triumph. God, God, I will never see his face again.

Without thought, Marc began to talk. 'I remember the honey cakes we stole from the kitchen. And the pranks we played on our fellow squires.'

'Was that not wicked, lord?' Soray said.

'Wicked? No. We played such tricks on each other, as well. Henry could keep a perfectly straight face while I struggled to separate my bootlaces from my bridle reins, or found the front of my braes sewn shut.'

The boy laughed softly.

'Aye, I laughed, as well. I always gave the game away by laughing. Henry was clever at everything.'

Soray cocked his head with apparent interest. 'Tell me more.'

'More. Yes, there is much more. Henry could gentle a warhorse with a few words whispered in its ear. And he could do the same for a comely serving maid in the time it took to fill a wine cup. Ah, God, I wish I did not remember.'

Marc turned his face to the wall. Henry. My God. Henry.

A soft tap sounded at the chamber door. With a concerned look at Marc's face, Soray scrambled up to answer it.

Chapter Eleven

A young woman stood in the doorway, an extremely pretty girl about Soraya's own age, dressed in a gown of patterned red silk covered by a short, sleeveless surcoat of yellow trimmed in narrow bands of red brocade.

'*Kalespera,*' the girl said.

A Greek, then. '*Yasas,*' Soraya returned.

'*Poene andros?*'

'Man?' Soraya replied in the girl's native language. 'Where is what man?'

The Greek girl studied her. 'Yes, the man. I am sent for him. I am called Irena.'

Soraya opened her mouth and instantly closed it. This Irena was sent for de Valery? Her knight? Hot fury smoldered in her chest.

'I do not believe so,' she said as politely as she could manage.

The girl's wide red mouth spread into a smile. 'But I do believe so, yes.'

'No.' Soraya looked her in the eye. *You cannot have him. He is mine.*

Irena was very beautiful, a face of sculpted ivory and lashes that fanned her cheek like black silk fringe. A courtesan, but clean and well-dressed. Soraya glanced down at her dirty tunic and worn trousers.

'Who sent you?' she demanded.

Irena laughed softly. 'Why, the holy monk in the next room. I was instructed to comfort his friend, in all ways. Through the night,' she added with a suggestive purr in her voice. Her gaze hovered on Soraya. When she had given Soraya a slow appraisal, she added, 'And you, as well, my young friend. If you wish it.'

The woman gave a little push on the door and swept inside past Soraya. The scent of flowery perfume floated after her.

Ugh. She smelled like an overripe orange. She glided to the cot and leaned over the sleeping knight, the folds of her red undergown wafting the scent behind her.

'Ah, so handsome he is. His name?'

Soraya clenched her fists. 'His name is Sir Marc de Valery.'

Irena frowned. 'A Templar?'

The temptation to say yes was overwhelming. Templars did not take women to their beds. But she could not speak the lie. 'No. Not a Templar.' Her voice came out uneven and she cringed inside.

Why am I feeling such anger? I have no say over what sins this man commits.

Irena bent again over Marc's supine body and smoothed one soft, white hand over his brow. Soraya studied her own hands. Sun-browned, her palms and forefinger calloused from years of practice with her bow. Not soft or elegant. Not graceful or soothing, like the courtesan's. Lord in heaven help her, she truly was beginning to look like a boy.

Irena's hair flowed loose down her back in dark waves, held at the crown with a narrow jeweled circlet. With a sigh

Soraya reached up to touch the turban covering her own short, clumsily cropped hair.

'Waken, my fine fellow,' the courtesan murmured in a silky voice. 'See what delights I bring you.'

Soraya could not bear to hear more! She fled out the open doorway and knocked at the holy man's lodging next door. 'Forgive me, lord, but I am not needed—' I am not wanted! '—by my master at the moment. Perhaps I may be of service to you?'

The monk welcomed her with a wide smile. Behind the holy man, Marc's friend Roger laughed aloud.

'Silence, de Clare,' the monk growled. The monk drew her inside, fed her cheese and fine-grained bread, and while she ate, he sat across from her cushion and, of all things, began to sing. Something about a lovesick prince, she thought. The words, in the language of the southern Franks, had slurred, lazy endings.

When he ended the song, the monk leaned toward her and laid his large hand on her knee. Soraya jerked and scooted backward until she bumped into Roger de Clare's booted foot.

'Leave the boy be,' Roger said in a low tone. Behind her she heard the hiss of his sword against its scabbard.

'I take no orders from you,' the holy man barked. Then he dropped his voice. 'I would not harm him, de Clare. I wish only to be friendly.'

'You will do nothing at all.' At the knight's gesture, Soraya curled up on a pallet and tried not to listen for sounds from the adjoining room.

She spent a most uncomfortable night; Roger tossed and snored where he lay between herself and the slumbering monk, who was equally noisy.

In the morning, she lay still, pretending to be asleep until long past dawn. When she rose at last, she found herself alone. She tiptoed to her knight's room and peeked around the corner of the open doorway.

'Where have you been?' a voice grumbled from the cot. The clear blue eyes sparkled with anger.

'In the next chamber, lord. With the holy man and—'

'What?' He jerked upright on one elbow.

'For certain, lord, I could not stay here.'

'Why could you not?' He snapped out the words like a shower of hot stones.

'Because.'

'Because?' he thundered. 'Speak straight, boy!'

'Because it would have been…crowded.'

'Crowded!' He shook his head, eyeing her slantwise. 'Crowded with what?'

Soraya began to sweat under her tunic. 'With her, lord. The girl, Irena.'

'Ah, Irena.' He sent her an odd smile.

Soraya pressed her lips together. She hated hearing even her name on his tongue. Hated the smell of her perfume rising from the bedding. Most of all she hated the thought of her knight disrobing in front of the courtesan, being naked with the Greek girl. And more. She drew in a shuddery breath and turned away.

'Look at me, boy.'

Her insides jumping, she pivoted to face him.

'You are not too young to know of such things, lad. What do you think happened here last night?'

More than she could bring herself to think about. 'I do not know, lord. I do not care to know.'

Marc stared at her. 'Nothing happened here last night. The woman, Irena, lay beside me while I slept, and this morning she kissed me and was gone. I had no carnal knowledge of her.'

'But why not?' Soraya blurted in amazement.

Marc didn't answer. Instead he swung one foot to the polished stone floor. 'Are you hungry?'

'No, lord. I am not,' she lied. If she put anything into her stomach it would come right back up.

'Well, I am. Come. We're going to the market-place.' He began buckling his sword belt over his wrinkled surcoat. Soraya noted that he was no longer wearing chain mail.

'Will...' She cleared her throat. 'Will she—Irena—be returning?'

Marc stopped with his sword halfway into the hardened leather scabbard. 'What? Oh, you mean the girl. I think not, lad. We parted friends, but...' His voice halted. 'That much you need not know. Besides,' he added with a chuckle, 'the girl was a gift to me, not to you.' He reached out to pat Soraya's head, but she ducked away.

'Next time,' he said.

Next time! Such an event would happen again?

'I do not like sleeping close to the monk, lord.' She hadn't meant to say that, but it just popped out of her mouth.

Marc frowned. 'Praise God for that. Come. I smell sausages!'

The market-place was jammed with people and carts so closely packed it was difficult to thread one's way to the stalls. The cobbled stone square throbbed with movement and colour and exotic smells.

And the noise! Soraya thought her ears would burst. She and de Valery communicated using a sign language; it was easier than shouting at each other across a cart of grapes.

She skirted a table of dried fruit and sweetmeats, and signaled to him a question: Some of these?

In answer, his hands outlined a rounded shape in the air and he pantomimed a snorting animal of some sort. Aha. Sausages.

She shook her head, but he trod on past the sweetmeats. At another display he shaped his hands into a circle. A melon?

She nodded, pointing to a sagging table of fruit a few paces behind him.

This time he nodded, as well, and turned toward the display, just as the holy man and de Valery's friend Roger appeared from behind a canopy-covered stall. She watched the two men slap Marc on the back with apparent goodwill, but she could hear nothing of their conversation.

All three moved slowly toward the melon stand, and Soraya darted toward them. What did Frankish knights know about choosing melons?

The monk trod around the display, thumping the melons and talking to Roger. Marc held up a mottle-skinned fruit for inspection, and she moved closer, pointing at the melon. At that same instant she caught sight of something out of the corner of her eye—a blur of movement, followed by a gutteral shout.

Marc looked up at the disturbance, dropped the melon and twisted his body toward the holy man. He tackled the monk, throwing himself on top of the robed figure.

Soraya stumbled into the solid body of Roger de Clare, who grabbed her arm and yanked her down onto the paving stones next to him. People began to scatter, shouting and trampling each other as they fled.

A dark figure whirled toward her wielding a glittering curved sword, and she opened her mouth to scream. A wash of air swept over her back, and a sharp, stinging pain bit into her skin. For a moment she heard nothing but the buzzing inside her head, then Marc's voice.

'Run! Follow me!'

The knight and the holy man streaked away down a narrow alley. She leaped up and raced after them, Roger pounding at her heels. Around a corner, across another, smaller square and into a long, shadowed street with bright-coloured houses on both sides. At last they emerged into a tree-shaded clearing on the opposite side of the harbour.

Roger threw himself down under a plane tree, followed by the monk and Marc. Soraya dropped at Marc's feet, gasping for breath.

When they could speak, the men pulled themselves into a loose circle.

'Did you see his face?' the monk queried.

'No,' Roger answered. 'But he wore a brown robe and was armed.'

'The robe was black,' Marc countered.

The holy man snorted. 'I thought it a colour like mud, part brown, part black.'

Soraya rolled her body into a sitting position. 'Forgive me, lords, but you are all mistaken. The man wore a tunic, like yours—' she pointed at de Valery '—but the colour was green, very dark, like cypress needles. And it was mud-spattered. Did you not notice? The man's legs were wrapped in black.'

The men stared at her in silence. 'You are sure of this?' Marc ventured.

'Yes, lord. I saw him clearly. And his sword… The blade was curved.'

'Ah,' said de Valery. 'A Saracen weapon.'

'Aye, lord. But I could not see his face clearly for the wrapping about it. His eyes were very dark. A Turk, perhaps. A Kurd. Even a Nubian. I cannot be sure.'

'But a Muslim,' Marc said.

'Probably, lord. Though there are some who are both Arabs and Christian. Maronites. And the Copts.'

'Which of us was the intended target?' the monk asked.

Marc scoffed. 'You mean which one would a Saracen want to kill? All three of us!'

'Not so,' said Roger in a thoughtful tone. 'Look.' Gently he grasped Soraya's upper arm and turned her so her back faced the men.

De Valery swore.

Soraya twisted her neck to see over her shoulder. 'What? What is it?'

'The back of your tunic is sliced to the skin, boy. Did you feel nothing?'

'Only a wind and then a needle prick that stung like the bite of a desert ant.'

De Valery took hold of her shoulder and inspected her back.

'It was no ant, lad, but a sword.'

Soraya's head spun. 'But why me, when you are all…all…?'

'So obviously Christian?' the monk supplied, his voice raspy. 'Two knights and a monk to choose from, and the swordsman picks an Arab boy?' He folded back his hood and held de Valery's eyes for a long moment. Soraya could swear some communication passed between them. At last, her knight touched her shoulder once more and she turned to face him.

'Either a bumbling swordsman who missed his kill—' he spoke the words slowly, as if weighing each syllable in his mind before it passed his lips '—or an expert swordsman who meant only to warn.'

Soraya's belly turned to ice. She knew she was the target of the Arab with the curved sword.

'Damnation,' the holy man spit out. 'The boy is not important! It is I who—'

Marc's harsh voice cut him off. 'I would not speak so freely if I were you…Father.'

Roger looked from the holy man to Marc and back again,

his eyes narrowing. 'By all the saints…' Abruptly he shook his head. 'Who knows of this?' he snapped.

'None but de Valery,' the monk said quietly. 'And now you.'

Roger made as if to kneel before the holy man, but de Valery barked an order. 'Do not!'

Roger stepped back a pace.

'We are overlooking something,' Marc said. 'If it was not the monk this Arab's blade sought but the boy, the question is, why?'

Three pairs of eyes turned on Soraya, boring into hers like a blinding shaft of light. De Valery planted his tall, muscular body in front of her.

'Why?'

Chapter Twelve

The knight de Valery thrust his menacing face a finger's distance from Soraya's, the muscles in his jaw working as he clenched and unclenched his teeth.

'Speak, you little thief!'

'I c-cannot explain, lord,' she stammered.

'Cannot?' he barked. 'You mean you will not. By God, I should—'

'Leave the boy be,' Roger said, his voice calm. 'He has done no wrong that I can see.'

Soraya was about to breathe a sigh of relief when her eye caught the monk's gaze. He studied her, a frown drawing the heavy red-gold eyebrows together. 'That we can see,' he echoed. 'But God knows what lies under this one's skin.' His thick wrist shot out to grasp the neck of Soraya's tunic, and with a low growl he jerked her forward.

She stumbled headlong into a surprisingly hard body beneath the holy man's moth-eaten black robe. He brought his scowling, sun-reddened face close to hers, his eyes hard. 'Have you indeed done no wrong, boy?'

Before she could answer, he spun her around and twisted

one arm up against her back. She yelped as the muscles in her shoulder knotted. The holy man yanked again on her pinioned arm and a sharp pain, like the point of a hot knife, shot from her neck to her elbow. It felt as if her sinews were ripping.

I will not scream. I will not. The monk yanked again, and a moan escaped from her throat.

'Let the boy go,' de Valery challenged.

'Why?' the holy man replied, his voice hard as stone. 'A little discomfort—' he tugged her arm upward again '—is most effective, I have found.'

'It becomes you not,' the knight answered. 'Even a Saracen does not hurt a child. Let him be.'

Instead, the monk tightened his hold. 'The boy knows something,' he growled. 'I can smell it.'

De Valery's face changed. He moved closer, reached past Soraya and seized the holy man's shoulder where it joined his neck. 'Release him,' he ordered. Soraya saw his forearm flex as he squeezed.

'De Valery,' the monk murmured, 'I am unarmed.'

'That you are not.' The knight tightened his grip until the knuckles on his large hand whitened. The monk tried to twist free, but Soraya blocked the way.

'Marc,' Roger said, his voice flat and even. 'Think what you do, man.'

'Yes,' the knight snapped. 'I am thinking.' Sweat stood out on his forehead, but he did not release his hold.

With a little grunt, the monk abruptly eased the tension on Soraya's bent arm and released her. It hurt to unkink her elbow, and straightening it out was agony.

She stepped well away from the holy man, then pivoted to face him. 'Thus am I repaid for easing your fever? What kind of man are you?'

De Valery caught her shoulder and dragged her to his side. 'A powerful man, boy. Have a care.'

The holy man spit at her feet. 'I would know why an assassin seeks you, rather than me.'

She could never explain why the Arab attacker had singled her out, not without revealing that she now carried the message for the king of the English. The message Saladin had originally entrusted to Uncle Khalil. But all at once an idea popped into Soraya's brain and bloomed like a desert thistle opening to the sun. Maybe there was a way of telling the truth. Yes! It was clever. So clever it would have made Khalil smile. At last it would give her the excuse she needed to demand her dagger back from Marc.

'I will tell you what you wish to know, lord.' She spoke not to the monk who had hurt her but to her knight. 'Because it is a sin against God to speak a lie.'

The monk rolled his eyes, and Roger, behind him, choked out a laugh. De Valery said nothing but turned penetrating blue eyes on her and waited. His gaze was so clear and unguarded that for an instant she imagined she could see into his very soul. The flutter of warmth in her belly came so unexpectedly she bit back a gasp.

'I am not what I seem,' she said simply. 'I am not a slave. Or even a servant.'

'Oh, aye,' her knight scoffed. 'And I am good Saint Ninian.'

The holy man stepped toward her. 'What then are you, boy?'

'That I will tell you truly, if...'

'If?' the monk spit at her.

'If you promise not to beat me.'

'Beat you? Nothing would please me more, but...' He glanced at Marc and raised his hands, palms up. 'It seems you have a champion.'

'Two champions,' Roger de Clare called out.

The monk chuckled. 'Surrounded, then, am I? Very well, I shall not beat you.'

Soraya took her time, weighing how much she should reveal. Just enough to ensure her own safety but not enough to arouse suspicion.

'As I said, lord, I am not what I seem. My uncle Khalil— may he rest in peace—is…that is, he was a spy. For Saladin.'

The holy man gave a whoop of laughter. 'For Saladin, you say? *Certes,* that is a large bone to swallow.'

Good. He does not believe me.

'I travelled always with my uncle. When he was…when he lost his life, his mission passed to me.'

'And wh-what "mission" was that?' The monk spoke jerkily between bursts of choked-down laughter.

'To deliver a message.'

The monk drew in a gulp of air. 'And to whom was this supposed "message" to be delivered?'

Soraya almost smiled. 'To the king of the English.'

The holy man guffawed, joined by Roger and de Valery. Then her knight suddenly sobered and peered at her through hard, narrowed eyes. 'You lie,' he said softly.

'Nay, lord, I do not.'

'You have lied before.'

'True. This time I do not.'

'Such a story is too preposterous to believe. You are a thief and a teller of falsehoods. *Djinn* tales, to entertain children.'

'No, lord. Believe me.'

'You are what you are, an Arab boy who serves me. And I am the king's man. Do not forget that.'

'Oh, aye,' she mimicked. 'And do not forget that I am Saladin's messenger.'

'Wait, de Valery,' the monk said. He turned to Soraya. 'How will you find the English king?'

'I do not know. My uncle came to the Frankish camp with the message to give to a certain man who would take it to the king, but he…' She shot a glance at De Valery. 'My uncle was slain before he could deliver it.'

De Valery snorted. 'You are the most imaginative tale-spinner I have ever encountered, boy. You will entertain us richly, all the way to France.'

Soraya smiled with secret delight. None of them believed her. If they did, they would stop at nothing to get their hands on the message.

'And so,' the monk wheezed between chuckles, 'you say someone does not want this "message" to reach the king.'

'And because, as you say, your uncle is dead,' Roger interjected, his voice rising, 'this "someone" now searches not for your uncle, but for you?'

The monk stopped laughing. De Valery stared at her until she thought his eyes would kindle into blue flames. He spun her around, ran his hand across the rent in the back of her tunic. 'What if these wild tales are not lies?' he said in an odd tone.

'*Et alors.*' Roger dropped the phrase into the sudden pall of silence, 'We must, er, then find the king.'

'No!' de Valery shouted. 'We must send word to the king…in Jerusalem.'

Roger sent him a puzzled look.

'Exactly so,' the monk said quickly. 'In Jerusalem.'

Soraya hesitated. 'Then, lords, I must part from you and set sail for Jerusalem at once.'

Again, three pairs of eyes settled on her. 'You cannot,' de Valery breathed.

'Ah, you will miss me, will you?' she teased. 'But you yourself can learn how to pick out a ripe melon, lord. And even—' from inside her tunic she pulled a flat loaf of bread and a handful of dates '—how to "borrow" more substantial food.'

'God's teeth, let's have that!' De Valery reached for the loaf and tore off a chunk. 'I am near starving.' As he chewed, he exchanged a long look with Roger de Clare.

Roger bowed his head. 'Aye. I suppose I must return to Jerusalem, as well,' he said slowly.

'And when you reach Jerusalem once more,' the monk said, enunciating each word with care, 'convey my greetings to His Royal Majesty.'

De Valery stepped nearer to the holy man. 'Our disguise may protect the king, for a time,' he murmured close to the cowled head. 'But it will not protect the boy. I wager it is not the king they want, but the message.'

Both men settled their gazes on Soraya. 'The message,' the knight said in a quiet voice. 'Where is it?'

'Here, lord. With me.'

'Where?' he said more insistently.

'I will not tell you. I must deliver it to no one save England's king. Lion Heart, they call him.'

Behind her, the monk grunted. 'We have ways to force you to speak.'

'Do you think me a fool? You can torture me unto death, but I will not play my master false.'

'Brave talk,' the monk scoffed. 'For a small, weak boy in shabby garments and no weapon.' He pinned her arms to her sides in a brutal, suffocating hug.

'Truly, I am not brave,' Soraya whispered. 'But my heart is true.' She flicked a surreptitious look at de Valery. 'Foolish, perhaps, but true.'

'I believe the boy,' Marc said quietly into the monk's ear. 'It is true, his uncle was killed…accidentally, an act which grieves me to this day and for which I will forever pay penance. The rest is a tale too far-fetched for a sober man to ignore.'

He moved to stand before her. 'Do you trust me, lad?'

'Aye, lord. Up to a point.'

'How if I told you a truth in exchange for yours?'

At once the holy man released her and coughed loudly. 'Have a care, de Valery,' he muttered.

'Think, man,' Marc snapped. 'The king is not safe if he ignores what intelligence is sent to him. We must have that message!'

The holy man's eyes flashed fire for an instant, then closed. 'Do what you must, de Valery. But if the boy proves false, I will slay both of you.'

'Come, lad.' De Valery turned back toward the town. 'I have something to show you.'

'Marc!' Roger shouted after him. 'Stop! It is but a fool's errand.'

'We shall see,' Mark muttered over his shoulder.

The holy man huffed in frustration. 'Let him go, Roger. The boy will never believe it, even if he sees it with his own eyes.'

'He might. He is canny, that one.'

'Huh!' the monk spit out. 'He steals bread in the market-place, a child's game. He tosses sand in our eyes to save his miserable skin.'

De Clare grinned at the holy man—Richard. 'The boy misses nothing. I will wager my horse on the matter.'

'Done!'

At the inn, Marc went straight to his cot, lifted the mattress and drew forth his hemp supply bag. The boy looked on, his features impassive. Behind him, Roger de Clare and the disguised king crowded in and leaned their backs against the wall, watching what Marc was about.

When he found what he was looking for, he glanced at Richard, then drew out a small object wrapped in white silk. Carefully he unrolled the fabric. Into his waiting palm dropped a small metal object.

'The privy seal of the English king.' He held it out to Soray. The boy leaned over, inspected it from all angles, hesitantly laid a forefinger on the seal and turned it over.

'A face,' he said, his voice hushed. 'With a crown on his head.'

'A king,' Marc corrected. 'The insignia of Richard Plantagenet.'

Soray's questioning green eyes met Marc's. 'It is not the same image displayed on the banner over the largest tent in the Frankish camp. It is not a lion.'

'You have a good memory, lad.'

Roger nudged the monk's shoulder. 'And keen eyes,' he murmured.

The king gestured to the metal seal. 'What do you make of this, boy?'

Soray lifted his head and gazed straight into Marc's eyes. 'The knight de Valery is a greater thief than I.'

'Ha!' Richard chortled. He nudged Roger's shoulder. 'So, boy,' he said slowly, 'if, as you say, you are not spinning a spider's web of half truths, let us see this message you carry.'

'No. I cannot. It is not for your eyes.'

A silence like an enveloping carpet fell over the tiny room.

'You see, Roger,' Richard said at last. 'It was a bluff after all. There is no message. The boy is but a servant, with an overactive imagination. Not a spy.' He jabbed his finger into Roger's chest. 'You owe me your horse. Pay up.'

De Clare groaned at his defeat. Richard merely chuckled, pleased with himself and his wager. Marc, however, watched Soray, who studied both men, then caught his lower lip between his fine, white teeth and smiled.

'Believe me, lad,' he said in a quiet voice. 'The Lion Heart is close by.'

'Where, then?'

'Here. With us.'

'How should I believe this?'

'Because it is I who say it to you. And, as you say, it is a sin to lie.'

'Then—' the lad's voice dropped to a whisper '—one of you is the king himself.'

Very deliberately Soray moved toward Marc and reached out for the jeweled dagger in his belt. Marc caught the boy's hand in his, then jerked it back. Something in the boy's touch, the softness of his skin, unnerved him. Made him want to enfold the small body in his arms and protect it.

He stood motionless, watching Soray's strong brown fingers touch lightly on the leather and draw the blade forth.

What ailed him? He stood like a rooted tree, unable to move while Soray's slow, deliberate movements held him spellbound. The boy's strange eyes seemed to laugh at his discomfort, then darkened into something else. Something that was not laughter.

The boy raised the weapon. It did not even occur to Marc to duck away; some unspoken bond between him and the lad assured him there was no danger.

Soray smoothed one hand over the jeweled hilt, made a quick, hard gesture and twisted the ruby away from its setting. A tiny scrap of crumpled vellum dropped into the boy's small hand.

Richard and de Clare hissed in simultaneous breaths. Soray

smoothed out the fragment and, without looking at it, passed it to Marc.

The writing was in graceful curving Arabic. "'To Richard of England in brotherhood,'" Marc translated aloud, turning towards Richard.

The king stiffened and stepped away from the wall. 'Read on.'

Marc squinted at the tiny, perfectly formed letters. "'Beware the eagle that lies with the lily. You are in imminent danger.'"

'Ah!' Richard burst out. 'The eagle of Austria and the lily of France. Leopold,' he rasped. 'And Philip of France.'

'There is a signature,' Marc said into the heavy quiet. 'Saladin.'

'It is a ruse,' Roger blurted. 'The Saracen commander does not send love notes to his Christian enemy.'

'Ah, but he does,' Richard murmured. 'Saladin is a Saracen, yes, but he is chivalrous like no other knight I have known. Also, he and I had made truce together, before we sailed from Jaffa.'

'If it is not a ruse,' Roger sputtered, 'then the boy truly is a spy for Saladin.'

Marc watched Soray. By the saints, the lad's face was an impassive mask. But he did not deny it.

'Come,' he ordered the boy. 'Outside.'

In the arched corridor Marc crouched before his servant, confronting him at eye level. 'You will answer me some questions.'

'Yes, lord.' The large green eyes looked boldly into his.

'And you will speak only the truth, or I will kill you with my own hand.'

'Yes, lord.' The young voice was clear and steady. God knew, Marc liked the lad. The little scamp had somehow wormed his way into Marc's heart. It would be hard to kill him.

'First, who are you? And do not say you are a servant. You are no servant.'

'True, I am not. Arabs stole me away from my parents and then killed them. They brought me to Damascus and sold me into the sheik's harem. My uncle, Khalil al-Din, bought me at a slave auction at the zenana where I was raised when I was but ten. He trained me as a spy.'

'Then he was not truly your uncle?'

'In truth, no. In life, yes. Khalil was kind to me. I never knew an hour of hunger in his house.'

'You tried to kill me. Was that your uncle's wish?'

'No. I tried to avenge his death, but in the end…in the end, I found I could not do so.'

'Why not?' Marc held his breath waiting for the answer.

'For many reasons. Because it would not have returned my uncle to life. Because holy writings teach that it is wrong to take a life. And because—' the boy's gaze dropped to his leather sandals '—because you also were kind to me. You are weary of war, sick with killing. That is a good thing. I have grown to like you.'

Marc rocked back on his heels. 'Why did you not take the message your uncle carried straight to the king?'

Soray's eyes glinted. 'Think, lord. You had possession of my dagger, which contained Saladin's note. Therefore I had to follow wherever you went. And I could not ask you for my weapon as it would have aroused your suspicion. You thought I wanted to kill you.'

Marc thought for a moment. 'That Arab swordsman, the one in the market-place. He wanted to stop you from delivering this message to the king. Did you recognise him?'

'No. But Arab assassins are everywhere. They are easy to hire.'

'The eagle and the lily,' Marc murmured. 'No doubt whoever wishes to stop this message will try again. No one knows the king is here, in disguise.'

'Thus my mission is completed, God willing.'

'Not so. There are men who would kill to stop such a message. They will assume it has not been delivered to the king. You are safe nowhere.'

'How if I return to Jerusalem? With your friend, de Clare?'

'How,' Marc blurted, 'if you stay here, with us? When the king is safe in England, Saladin's message will no longer matter. Now there would be great peril in your returning to Jerusalem.'

In truth he did not want the lad to leave. Now that his brother Henry was dead—his mind stuttered at that black thought—Marc struggled daily to survive the agony of his grief. The only sunlight warming his shadowed spirit these past weeks had been Soray.

The closer Marc came to his family home in Scotland, the more he would need the cheering distraction his intriguing servant offered.

Soray's clear-eyed gaze met his. 'Do you wish me to leave you, lord?'

Marc shook his head. 'I do not.'

A flash of delight flared in the boy's eyes, but in the next instant he dropped his gaze to the stone floor. 'Are you not wary of one who once desired your death?'

'Many men desire my death, boy. Normans. Saracens. Even Scots of rival clans, especially now that I am to be laird of Rossmorven. The world is not a safe place. You, lad, are the smallest and most insignificant of such threats.'

Soray pulled himself up as straight and tall as he could. 'Insignificant?'

Marc laughed. 'Worry not, lad. You will grow.'

Aye, Soraya acknowledged. That is what I fear. Each day her waist narrowed and her swelling breasts pushed against the linen binding. She knew instinctively it would be dangerous to travel as a woman in these foreign and wicked lands where holy knights betrayed their vows and women sold themselves in the market-place. She would attract too much unwanted attention.

At times she had disturbing feelings, feelings evoked by the presence of the knight who now stood in the corridor, facing her.

Her knight reached out and tipped her chin up with his finger. 'The choice is yours, lad.'

Ah, no. Her choice had long since been made. Marc de Valery moved always at the back of her mind, even when he was angered at her. Frankish knight that he was, she could not bear to leave him. She would never leave him.

'Soray?' His voice, close to her temple, turned gentle. 'What would you?'

She would do what her heart dictated. But she could never, never tell him why.

'I would stay with you, lord. If it please you.'

Chapter Thirteen

Marc studied the crowded lane they had left behind and gauged the foot traffic around the little clump of trees where the four of them had gathered. 'We are wasting time.' He flicked a glance at the still-disguised king.

Richard set his jaw. 'By the legs of God, de Valery, let us rest!'

'I cannot. We must leave tonight, and we must not be seen.'

'Pah! The gate will be closed when the sun sets. How are we to get our mounts outside the town wall? Fly?'

'We will wait here until dusk, then slip through the gate just before the keeper shuts it.'

Richard grumbled but settled himself under a plane tree a short distance from Marc, Roger and Soray. They waited, not talking, until the bloodred sun arced overhead and slowly descended behind the town gate at the west end of the marketplace.

Marc delayed until it was almost dark, and then he signaled to Roger and the king. In silence, he and the other two men led their horses down the shadowed lane until they were within a stone's throw of the west gate. Soray walked beside him, his hand gripping the wide sleeve of his surcoat.

Two turbaned stragglers, travelling merchants with bulging panniers on their foot-weary mules, tramped in through the guarded opening in the wall. Marc slowed until the merchants clip-clopped down one of the twisting streets that opened onto the paved market square, then hurriedly motioned Richard and de Clare to move past him. Roger would be first out the gate, then the king. Marc would be the last one through.

The watchman started to swing the gate shut, the huge iron hinges creaking in the still air.

'Hold!' Marc shouted. The man paid no attention, but bent his back to the struggle with the heavy barrier. One more foot of closure and the huge warhorses could not fit through the opening.

He tugged his mount forward, swearing under his breath. They weren't going to make it.

Suddenly Soray released his sleeve and darted forward and Marc swore again. Would the boy never learn restraint?

He dropped Jupiter's lead and pounded after him. Desperate to stop the lad, he flung his arms about Soray's small body, his hands chest-high. Under his palms he felt something soft and rounded. Almost like…

Like a woman's breasts!

Soray emitted a yelp and Marc snatched his hands away. Dumbstruck, he stared after the boy, who plunged onward, reached the gatekeeper and began to tug on his skinny arm.

The old man made shooing motions. *'Vatene, furfante!'* Soray held on and began communicating to the keeper in a spur-of-the-moment sign language.

Marc stared at the tunic covering the slim figure, noting how the dark silk pulled tight when he moved, revealing softly rounded hips and a hint of a narrowing waist. How had he not noticed these things before?

Because you never bothered to look closely. What man studied the physical form of a mere servant boy?

The argument between Soray and the gatekeeper went on and on and Marc grasped what the boy intended—a diversion so that Roger and the king, and he himself, could slip through the gate. Soray cajoled and gestured until the old man threw up his hands in defeat and pushed the gate wide again.

Richard twisted toward him. 'The boy has cleared our way,' the king hissed. 'Allons!'

Marc could not move. He stared at Soray, transfixed by the supple body underneath the tunic. God, he could strangle him—her—for such a deception!

Richard frowned at him. 'What ails you, man? You look pale.'

'A…slight pain only.' Unconsciously he placed his hand over his heart.

'Ignore it,' the king growled. 'Use the legs God gave you and move!'

Marc strode forward, reached the still-open gate just as Soray bid farewell to the keeper and skipped through ahead of him. Shaking with rage, he stalked after the slim figure. Soray was a girl. A female! He had been duped. Lie after lie had slipped like silk from those lips. Damn the boy! He had trusted Soray.

And he had worried about the boy, about not letting him get too close to Richard, about protecting the lad's innocence! He gave a harsh laugh. The lad had endured heat and dust and thirst with him. Laughed with him. He had spoken to Soray about his brother's death. God's teeth, he had grown to like the boy!

What a fine joke on himself. In his mind's eye he saw the small quick hands tugging off his boots, tying the laces of his gambeson, helping to buckle on his sword belt.

Sponging off his naked body with scented soap.

They had bathed in the same room. Even slept in the same bed! *Christ and the saints, I must have been blind.*

Darkness closed around them, so thick they stepped the horses slowly in the direction Marc pointed. North. They dared not lose sight of each other lest they become separated.

For one shameful moment Marc thought about leaving Soray in the hills of Umbria, abandoning him. Her. It was a notion unworthy of a knight, but in his present state of fury at her deception, to say nothing of the added responsibility of travelling with a female…in his befuddled brain the idea held some appeal.

'We will reach Montiano by dawn,' he grumbled to Roger and the king over his shoulder. 'We will sleep the day, and travel again at night.' When he would not have to look at Soray. When he could redirect his mind away from the young servant he had grown fond of.

He set his jaw and scanned the blackness ahead. The ruins of an old fortress wall loomed some yards ahead; he released Jupiter's lead and grasped Soray's arm. Motioning Roger and the king to ride on, Marc roughly dragged the boy off the road. He was so angry he was afraid of what he might do.

Part of Marc's heated mind had to admire the courage and resourcefulness of the boy, even if he was a motley quilt of falsehoods. The rest of him wanted to punish the little scamp until he begged for mercy. Until *she* begged for mercy.

In the darkened shadows of a crumbling stone wall, he forced Soray to face him. Never had he seen such defiance in a pair of eyes, blazing with pride and arrogance. He advanced a step toward her, but she did not flinch. He took hold of the turban and yanked it off; the short black curls sprang to life. Still she did not move. He reached out, touched one small, soft breast, then jerked away, his hands trembling like wind-blown leaves. To hide them he jammed his thumbs into his leather belt.

'So. You are not a boy.' He could scarce keep his voice steady.

'I am not.'

Marc gritted his teeth. 'What is your name, then?'

'My name is Soraya.' Then, before he could blink, she drove her knee into his groin, and when he doubled over she jabbed her fist into his Adam's apple.

'Do not touch me again. Ever.'

Marc gasped in agony, hearing her voice as if from a long way off. 'I could kill you for this,' he choked out. 'It is within my rights.'

'Kill me for what?' she challenged. 'For protecting myself? Or for duping you? Is your pride so great, de Valery, that you cannot swallow down a morsel of humility?'

He straightened and took a long look at her. 'Do not dare to speak to me in this manner. You are but a servant.' Cursing, he turned his back and cradled his throbbing balls in both hands.

'I am not your servant.' Her words were scarcely audible, and so full of hatred the air between them seemed to shimmer. Marc groaned with the sickening ache in his crotch.

'I have a potion that will ease—'

'A plague on your potions!'

All he wanted to do was get away from her. He stumbled toward his horse, mounted gingerly and spurred the animal forward until he drew abreast of the king.

'It is a soft night,' Richard remarked. 'And quiet.'

The urge to laugh nearly overcame him. This night was anything but quiet. With a groan, Marc turned Jupiter toward the north star. Instantly, Soray—Soraya—scrambled up behind him and slipped her slender hands into his sword belt. He began to sweat until the neck of his tunic was damp.

They rode in silence until the moon rose, and abruptly

she leaned forward. 'I hear something, lord,' she whispered. 'Horses.'

'I do, as well,' he replied, keeping his voice low. God help him, now he felt doubly responsible for her because she was female. He hesitated a moment, then pulled the jeweled dagger from his belt and passed it over his shoulder.

'Take it. You should be armed. You should have your knife back. If all else fails, the gem will purchase protection for you.'

'I am grateful, lord,' she whispered. She drew away from him to stow the knife inside her tunic, then tightened her grip, lifted her face to clear the high cantle and rest her cheek against his surcoat. It felt like a small, hot sun burning into his back.

He wrenched his thoughts free of her and gave a soft whistle. Roger dropped back beside him.

Without slowing his pace, Marc leaned toward his friend. 'Someone is following. Veer to the east with Richard. I will ride north and meet you tomorrow in Montiano, at the monastery of San Stephano."

'God willing,' Soraya murmured in his ear.

'And may it please our holy lord Jesus, as well,' he muttered. He watched the king and Roger move away until they dissolved into the dark, wincing at the noisy jingling of their bridles, the creak of hardened leather saddles. Sounds that could easily be heard.

Behind him, Soraya cocked her head and suddenly nudged him.

'There are but two riders, lord.'

Two only. Marc sighed in relief. But what two? A Frank would be after the king. A Saracen would want Soraya, or Saladin's message. Or both. Two riders, if well armed, would be difficult with the girl at his back.

'I believe they are Franks,' Soraya whispered. 'Arab riders

travel silently. Franks ride as you do, lord, all jingles and hoofbeats.'

'Your ears are sharp,' he grumbled.

'I wish to live,' she said simply. 'And you, as well. The assassins of Saladin are as quiet as moon shadows.'

'May it please God, we shall both live. We will shelter ahead, at that ruined well.' Without breaking his slow, steady pace, he guided the horse to the right. Galloping would make too much noise.

The well, what was left of it, was nothing but a pile of salt-frosted stones. Marc dismounted and led Jupiter to the far side, where Soraya slid off. He forced the horse to kneel, and then to lie down. He shoved Soraya down to her knees and crouched beside her against the warm animal.

'We will wait.' He strained his eyes into the darkness. No movement, but as he listened a soft *ching* carried on the still air. Soraya's head came up at the sound, and in an instant, Marc clapped his fingers over her mouth. 'Speak not,' he murmured.

Her lips moved against his skin, full and soft as flower petals. With a guilty start he snatched his hand away.

The jingling grew louder, and then a man's voice rumbled close by. *'Beeilon sie sich!'*

Soraya shrank against Jupiter's rounded belly and Marc pressed her head down, his hand grazing the headpiece she wore. Jesu, even the soft turban scorched his fingers.

One of the approaching riders began to sing in gutteral German, the words obscene, something about a starving knight and a peasant girl's milk-white breasts. The refrain, shouted in lusty rhythm, heated his face with embarrassment. Marc prayed Soraya did not understand the language.

But her shoulders were twitching. She did understand! She was silently laughing at the bawdy lyrics.

He brought his mouth close to her ear. 'If you make a single sound, I will throttle you on this spot.'

She nodded her head, but her slim torso continued to shake. Marc held his breath while the two travellers plodded past, moving at such a slow pace he feared his hammering heart would be audible. At last, the only sound was Soraya's hiccuping laughter. They were safe.

'There is no art in a Frankish song,' she announced. 'Only crude words. No poetry at all.'

He stood to urge Jupiter onto his feet. 'Poetry! What would you know of poetry?'

'A great deal, lord. Ovid, and Omar Khayyam, even the song of King Solomon.'

'You lie,' he barked.

'I do not lie. "Behold,"' she quoted, '"thou art fair, my love…thou hast dove's eyes, and thy—"'

'Enough! How is it you are educated far beyond a servant's need?'

'Do not ask,' she replied, her voice oddly quiet. 'But know this—I am servant only to you.'

'Saracen spies are well schooled, then?' He heard the angry edge in his voice but made no attempt to curb it.

'Aye, lord. If you believe so.' She mounted behind him, holding herself away from him in rigid silence as they rode.

Hours later the sky began to lighten to the grey of dawn. Marc clenched his jaw. If they were fortunate enough to reach Montiano and the monastery, he would demand answers to his questions.

Chapter Fourteen

Soraya let her forehead droop against Marc's back and closed her eyes. Her arms were stiff from long hours of riding with her thumbs hooked over his broad sword belt, and her stomach clenched with hunger. The scent of the sea faded into the earthy smell of vineyards and olive trees as they turned inland, skirting sleeping villages and driving off the occasional curious hound who bounded out to sniff at their heels.

They passed a small building of dark stone, a wine press she guessed from the rich, musty scent. It made her mouth water; her throat was parched for liquid.

The night air smelled of dust, and near the towns the breeze carried the disgusting odor of rotting rubbish. A cold wind came up, gusts buffeting Soraya's back, only thinly covered by her cotton tunic. She shivered and her teeth began to chatter. Clamping her mouth closed tight, she pressed her icy nose against Marc's warm neck.

Instantly his spine went rigid. 'Do not be alarmed,' Soraya murmured. 'I will not sully your fine surcoat.'

His body quivered. Was he laughing at her?

She lifted her head. 'What do you find on this cold, windy plain that is so amusing? Surely not my wet nose?'

'Nay. It is not your nose I feel pressed against me,' he blurted. 'Now that I know what secrets you hide beneath that filthy tunic, it is hard not to imagine what pokes me. And it is not your nose.'

Soraya shrank away from him. 'Do not think on that matter,' she said quickly.

He gave a weary laugh. 'A thirsty horse will drink.'

'You are not a horse. Besides, I could not possibly poke you, since I bind myself with a length of—'

'Would to God I were a horse, then, and not a man. A man can imagine.'

Despite her shivering, she grinned at the picture that formed in her mind. Her knight was conscious of her! Of who she was. Or at least what she was. It sent an odd jolt of excitement to her belly.

'Aye,' she agreed. 'You are a man.' By St. John, she still burned with fury at de Valery's assault on her person. True, she had kicked his manhood hard for his effort, but somehow it wasn't enough.

'I want to tell you something,' she said. 'I felt your power over me when you touched me. I could do nothing to stop you since your strength is greater than mine. But I was so angry I wanted to kill you.'

'You were not injured, Soraya. I was.'

'But it made me think. You could break my limbs, crush my head with the hilt of your sword, ride your great warhorse over my helpless body and trample me into dust. Against you I have nothing to fight with but my intelligence and…'

And what? What power could a woman have over a man?

Marc shifted in the saddle. 'A woman's power lies in areas other than brute strength.'

'Oh?'

His breath rasped in. 'For the love of God, cease your chatter.' And then he was silent for so long she wondered if he had forgotten her question.

All at once she knew. He himself had given her the clue—a man imagines things... A woman's power was simply being a woman!

She couldn't help smiling. She now knew something that affected him, and it was something she controlled. From this moment, she would be unable to resist pricking his pride, his male arrogance with an art she had not remembered she possessed—being female. She would pay him back for what he had done at the well.

'In the zenana,' she began softly. 'In the zenana where I spent ten summers, the other girls were taught certain things, the power of honeyed words and silken touches. I was not included in those lessons, so they meant little to me then. But now...'

Marc jerked upright.

Soraya laughed. Now she understood something else. Now she sensed an instinct within her she had not recognised until this moment. A hunger.

God help her, she hungered for this man's touch. A double-edged dagger, her tutor had cautioned. *Take care you do not feel its bite before you have entwined your prey.*

And so she would.

'We are not far from shelter,' he rumbled. 'Montiano lies at the far end of this valley.'

She peered past his shoulder but could see nothing other than the thick, black shadows of night. 'Can you then see in the dark?' she asked.

'I know this road. I have travelled this way before.'

'And your king? Does he know it, as well?'

Marc pushed out a tired breath. 'Aye, he does. Provided he keeps his mind on his business. His sister, Joanna, is Queen of Sicily—Richard cares for her. And his wife, Berengaria, is there, as well. Two doves in a cage of hawks.'

'Ah, I know how that feels. In the zenana I was a bird among cats. Except that the eunuchs have no—'

'Stop!' Marc ordered. 'For the love of God, button your lips closed.'

'Do not order me about. I am not your slave.'

'As long as you are with me, Soraya, you will do as I say.'

She loosened her grip on his sword belt, moving her fingers along his lower ribs. 'Of course,' she said in her softest tone.

'You are impudent,' he snapped.

'Yes. But, as you have discovered, I can also be…surprising.'

His shoulders hunched. 'You try a man's patience, Soraya.'

'Yes,' she said again. 'I was trained to do so.'

Marc kicked the horse into a canter and she had to grab hard about his waist to keep from toppling off the animal.

'Up ahead,' he gritted. 'The monastery. Beyond those trees.'

At last. Sanctuary from the cold and the wind and the gnawing ache of her thighs. She needed respite from the discomfort of travel. Respite from him. Alone, she might bathe her dirty skin and smelly hair, and unbind her breasts, which swelled painfully against the silk wrapping.

A grey stone wall rose before them, silent and dark. It looked like a brooding animal, an owl, crouched against the dark sky. A single black iron gate shut out the world, or perhaps shut the inmates inside.

Soraya sniffed as they drew closer. The wall was plain, un-embellished with the patterned arabesques incised on the walls of eastern holy places. Did not these monks honour God with the gift of artistry?

'I do not like this Romish land,' she breathed. 'Their villages stink of rotten food and their buildings are uninspired.'

'You know nothing,' Marc grumbled. 'Rome is the seat of the holy empire.'

'Constantinople is the seat of the holy empire,' she challenged. 'This place is foreign.'

'To a Christian, this place is the center of the universe.' He nudged Jupiter toward the monastery gate, reached out and pulled the bell rope.

'The center of the universe indeed,' she scoffed. 'Even the earth we stand upon is not the center of the universe.'

'Christians believe so.'

'Educated Christians do not believe so.' Again she felt his shoulder muscles tighten.

'What would you, a mere girl, know of the universe?'

'In the zenana, I was taught—'

'Enough about your zenana,' he roared.

'You think me an infidel, do you?'

His hand that held the reins twitched. 'And are you not?'

A grate slid back with a rasp and a face appeared behind the iron lacework. 'Peace be with you,' a voice said.

'And with you,' Marc responded. 'We are travellers seeking a night's shelter.'

'How many are you?'

'Two.'

'Very well.' The gate rattled and then swung open. 'Enter in peace. I am Brother Andreas. Other travellers such as yourselves occupy one guest chamber. But there is another...

Marc jerked. 'Have you not two chambers?'

The monk eyed Marc and frowned. 'We are not a wealthy

order, *signore.* We have one chamber only. Sufficient for you and…' His pale blue eyes studied Soraya, mounted behind him. 'And your servant.'

Marc stepped his horse through the opening and the monk clanged the gate shut behind them. Marc repeated his question to Soraya in a low voice. 'You are not an infidel?'

'I am not,' she murmured close to his ear. 'My parents were Christian. I was educated as a Muslim because my tutors were of that faith. But I have always been a Christian.'

Marc sucked in his breath. 'Aye, I forget you were sold into slavery.'

'I have always felt alone, even in the zenana where I was surrounded by others. I…did not fit in.'

Marc stared ahead at the austere walls enclosing the San Stephano monastery. *I have always felt alone.* Her words drove a spike into his chest. He thought of his dead brother. For as long as he could remember, Henry had kept him company. Henry had taught him to ride, to train a falcon, even how to speak to a noble lady. How to laugh.

He would never see his brother again. Now he, too, was alone. He walked his warhorse forward a few steps, feeling a knot pull tight in his chest.

A fierce urge to keep Soraya from harm swept over him. He'd felt it once before, on the ship to Cyprus, when he knew her only as Soray, the servant boy. Something about the plucky lad had invited his grudging admiration and sparked a concern for his welfare.

Her welfare. God's teeth, a net was tightening around his heart. He could no more abandon her than he could have abandoned Henry after a rare fall from his destrier. Or abandon Richard, his liege lord, on his journey home to England.

The white-robed monk stood aside, watching Marc's horse

clop into the courtyard. Still clinging to Marc's wide leather belt, Soraya nodded at the man as they passed and his shaggy eyebrows shot upward.

He turned to motion them forward, and she noted his visage…round and shiny as the moon. She noticed his hands, as well, the skin pale, the fingers long and very clean. She knew that holy brothers shared the work of tilling the soil and gathering in the harvest, yet this round-faced monk looked like…well, not a farmer, but a man who worked inside, out of the harsh cold in the winter or the hot summer sun.

A whisper of unease tickled the back of her neck. Something about Brother Andreas, as he called himself, was strange—perhaps the sweet, almost childlike expression on his face. Or the fact that he kept studying her with such curiosity in his eyes.

'The stable is that way, *signore.*' The monk gestured with his white-cowled head. 'Already two fine mounts are housed inside, but there is one empty stall remaining.'

'My thanks, Brother Andreas.' Marc unclasped Soraya's hands from around his waist and let her slide to the cobblestone paving, then swung himself out of the saddle. Under his breath she heard him chuckle and then mutter to himself. 'A fine mount? That spavined beast I bargained over for Richard?'

The holy man lifted a small candle lantern made of punched-out metal. 'Come.' He padded softly across the cobbled courtyard to a ramshackle wood structure nestled near the west wall that enclosed the monastery buildings. The double-wide door creaked open and Marc and Brother Andreas disappeared inside.

Soraya surveyed what she could see of the dark monastery buildings. A timber-roofed arcade bordered the square inner courtyard where she stood. Doorways opened off the walkway, and the sound of men's voices chanting holy songs drifted on the still air. How peaceful it was. At last, they were safe, protected from bad weather and bandits.

But when Marc emerged from the stable with Brother Andreas trailing at his heels, his mouth was pinched, his expression full of fury.

'Your chamber lies this way,' Brother Andreas announced. 'Next to you are lodged the two travellers who arrived before you.'

'I would speak with them,' Marc announced.

'What, now? It is past lauds. Good Christian men will be fast asleep.' The monk paused at a rounded wooden door, pushed it open and raised the lantern.

The room had only one narrow bed, with bits of straw poking out of the tick. A simple chest of dark wood sat along the opposite wall.

With a sweet smile, the holy man set his lantern on the chest and gestured them inside. 'God give you good rest, *signore*.'

Chapter Fifteen

The chamber door swung shut with a solid thump. Soraya eyed the single narrow cot, then glanced at Marc's glowering face. 'What is wrong?'

He moved to the barred window, his quick movement guttering the flame of the candle Brother Andreas had left. Looking out into the blackness, he muttered two words. 'The horses.'

'What about them?'

'Brother Andreas spoke truly, both are fine beasts. But neither belongs to Roger de Clare or to the king.'

Soraya sucked in a breath. 'But they sleep in the next chamber! How could they reach this place without—'

Marc frowned. 'They did not reach it. They are lost or delayed or... The travellers lodged next to us are strangers.'

'How can you be sure? Just because their horses—'

'God help me, what have I done? I swore an oath to protect the king!'

He strode past her, banged open the door and entered the darkened arcade. She heard his boots thud against the courtyard paving stones. 'Where are you going?' she called after him.

'To saddle my horse. I must find Richard.'

She stood uncertainly in the doorway. Was it true? The king and Roger had not arrived? Nonsense. Marc was mistaken. He must be mistaken. Surely his friend and the king slept next door?

She would prove it before Marc's overburnished sense of honour got him killed. She tiptoed toward the adjacent chamber door and studied the simple latch. One quick motion and she could open it. She laid her hand on the thick iron bolt and noiselessly pushed it to the left until it gave a sharp click.

'Who's there?' a thick voice thundered. 'Show yourself!'

A second voice shouted something in German.

She slammed the latch home and darted back to her chamber. Marc had been right after all. Neither man was King Richard or Roger de Clare.

A faint light floated across the inner courtyard. A shout, then hoofbeats clattered across the stone and she heard the monastery gate rasp open. He was gone. A fool's errand it might be, but she was beginning to better understand this man she felt so drawn to. He would risk his life to honour a pledge.

She lay awake, waiting for him. Hour after hour passed and still he did not return. Finally, toward morning she heard the entry bell at the gate ringing. He was back!

She tumbled off the straw mattress, threw open the wood shutters and peered through the window bars.

The first horse through the gate was the sway-backed mare the king usually mounted. But it was Marc who sat astride the animal; Roger and the king followed on the two warhorses. Of course. If they were attacked on the road, Jupiter would carry the king to safety.

She bit her lip. Had Richard been accosted? She raced out into the arcade and across the courtyard. 'Mar—' She caught herself. The king and Marc's friend, Roger, still thought her a servant boy.

'My lord, are you well?'

Her knight swayed, then slipped sideways off the sorry-looking mare. He was not well. Wounded, perhaps. Or ill. She knelt where he lay motionless on the stone paving. 'My lord?'

Her gaze moved from his sword belt to his chest to his neck. No blood. Tears burned under her lids. 'Marc,' she murmured. She looked into his face and their eyes met.

'Found him at a tavern, with his hand down the alewife's—' He bit off the rest. 'And Roger…like the good Norman that he is, lay drunk under the table. What a pair.'

Soraya laughed, partly in amusement, partly in relief. The king was found and Marc was unhurt. His mouth softened into a smile that gradually widened into a grin as they looked at each other. But, she noticed, he did not get up off the cobblestones.

'Why did you fall off your horse?' she asked. Surely he must hear her heart hammering in her chest.

'My hands are so cold they cramped, and I couldn't grasp the reins. Only by the grace of God did none of us freeze to death.'

Soraya glanced over her shoulder at Roger and the king, still mounted but drooping over the necks of their mounts. Richard had a happy, befuddled expression on his angular face. Roger looked green as stagnant water.

'Drunk,' Marc murmured. 'Both of them.'

'Where will they sleep? The chambers are all full.'

'In the stable. They smell like a barley wagon left out in the rain.'

She watched round-faced Brother Andreas lead the two warhorses, their riders still mounted, through the yawning stable door. Quickly she gathered up the mare's reins and followed.

Marc sat up slowly, listening to the hooves clip-clop into the stable. He steeled his nerves to cut through the fog in his sleep-sodden brain and take himself to bed. He was so angry with Richard he didn't dare speak to him, but in the morning he would give the king something to chew on.

He yawned, stood up and took three wobbly steps toward his chamber. A slim figure garbed in shirt and wide-legged trousers slipped under his shoulder to steady him.

'I must bathe, Soray,' he muttered. 'I am crawling with tavern fleas, and you—' he passed a heavy arm around her shoulders '—you smell like a wet sheep.'

'No doubt I do. But an ewe,' she whispered. 'Remember, I am not a ram.'

He snatched his arm away and cleared his throat. 'Aye, I remember now. Would to God I did not.'

'Here, lord.' She pushed him through the doorway into their chamber. Marc took one look at the cot, stumbled toward it and with a groan stretched his body out full-length on the straw mattress.

So, she smelled like a sheep, did she? And he had forgotten she was a woman! Had called her 'Soray' as if she were still his servant boy. God in heaven, he scarcely looked at her! Was this the brave knight she admired? She was no more significant to him than a marrowbone swimming in a pot of soup!

She stared at the sleeping man until her eyes burned. And she had thought to conquer him with her newfound feminine power. Were all females such fools?

So be it, then.

A metal wash basin dangled from a nail in the chamber wall. She had glimpsed a fish pond at one end of the courtyard; surely God's creatures would not begrudge her one pan of water for scrubbing her skin clean? She snatched the basin off the wall.

The pool was icy, but she scrubbed and splashed in the

shadow of an ancient cypress, using her silk chest-wrapping as a washing cloth. Shivering in the shadows, she knelt by the pond, eyeing the pair of gleaming gold carp that darted under a lily pad, unwrapped her head covering and dunked her hair into the pool.

The water was so cold it made her ears ache. She had no soap, but merely rinsing away the travel dust made her scalp feel clean and tingly. Her hair had grown longer; soon she would have to cut it off again, as she had before she and Khalil had left Damascus on their mission.

She grabbed her curls by the fistful and squeezed out the water. At least smelling like a fish was better than smelling like a sheep.

At the chamber doorway she halted to study Marc's motionless body on the cot. One arm was raised, the elbow bent to cover his eyes. His chest rose and fell, air whistling out through his open mouth. She could dance barefoot on his belly and he wouldn't waken.

Between his next two breaths, she made her decision. 'Move your noisy self over,' she muttered, then climbed onto the cot, rolled so her back was to him and snuggled her spine against his warm chest.

Her mission for Saladin was completed, though the Muslim leader would not know of it until Richard stood on English soil. Nevertheless, she had fulfilled her duty. Did it make sense to continue this miserable journey with a man who thought first of his king and last of a woman? Already he had forgotten that she was not a servant boy, but a girl. Forgotten that she was educated. Or perhaps that did not matter to him.

'Tomorrow,' she murmured to herself as her eyes drifted shut. No matter how much she had come to like 'her' knight, tomorrow she would ask Roger de Clare to take her back to Jerusalem.

* * *

Marc dreamed of his brother. Henry was hurt, lying alone in a dry desert wash, and Marc reached out to hold him, to soothe away the pain and keep him from dying. He wrapped both arms around his brother, but Henry's body began to grow lighter and lighter and then floated out of his grasp toward the sky.

'Wait,' Marc choked. 'Wait!'

He woke with a shout, his limbs trembling, his heart thudding against his chest wall. Henry. God in heaven!

A dream only. He lay still until the banging inside his rib cage eased, then shifted to his side.

Something soft and warm was stretched out next to him and he stifled a yelp, then rose up on one elbow. Soray. Curled up beside him, his slim back curved against Marc's belly.

God's feet, it was not Soray who lay asleep beside him! A mass of dark curls tumbled over half her face, and the scent that rose to his nostrils was fresh and faintly sweet.

Soraya. It was Soraya who lay next to him!

With a groan he peered down at the unmistakable form of a woman. The curve of her breasts pushed the damp tunic into a gentle swelling, and her neck was bent forward with one hand tucked against her chin, exposing her nape. The skin looked pale and smooth. Unblemished.

He leaned closer. The little indentation at the top of her spine was so small, so unprotected. And, oh God, she smelled so…female.

Her mouth had fallen slightly open in sleep. Her exhaled breath smelled of mint and something darker. Sweeter. An odd catch formed in his throat, like a sob that begged for release.

He studied her features, the fringe of black lashes against her creamy cheek, a mouth that looked soft as the flesh of a ripe plum. One small, perfect ear poked through the tangle of black hair. Under the layers of dust and desert sand she was a beauty.

Moving with deliberation, he stretched his body out on the cot once again and stared up at the timbered ceiling. He had no right. No claim. A woman as desirable as Soraya would be spoken for a hundred times over in Damascus.

Slowly he turned halfway toward her and gently settled his arm across her waist. He must keep her safe. Safe from cold and disease. Safe from bandits, safe from Saladin's assassins.

With a low moan he closed his eyes. Safe from himself.

Chapter Sixteen

Soraya leaned forward and spoke into Roger de Clare's ear. The knight huffed out a laugh at her words. 'Impossible,' he declared. 'De Valery has pledged to keep the king safe. You understand that, don't you, boy? It is a matter of honour for a knight to keep his word.'

'But…'

'De Valery cannot do this alone, no matter how brave he is in battle. I cannot leave him, lad. It will be difficult, dangerous even, to reach England with enemies anxious to do Richard evil. What Marc has sworn to Richard, I have sworn to Marc. I will not return to Jerusalem until the king rests safe on English soil.'

Soraya unclasped her hands and nodded. 'I understand. I will ask again, when it is timely.'

'When we reach England,' Roger gently corrected. 'You are part of it now. De Valery serves the king, and you serve de Valery. He would not do well without you.'

Soraya's mouth fell open. 'He has need of me?' she whispered. Her heart lifted and soared off into the ether. 'Do you truly think so?'

Roger patted her shoulder. 'You keep his spirits up, Soray. I do not know how you do it, but since you joined him he has laughed more than he did during all his black months in Outremer. Even at the death of his brother, Marc has not sunk into the foul-tempered mood I saw after Acre. You are good for him, boy. We are in your debt for this service.'

Soraya stared at the knight. She was good for Marc? She truly mattered to him?

'I will take you back to Jerusalem in the spring, if you still wish it. Provided any of us are still alive.'

'Are all knights thus? Pledged by oaths of honour?'

'Yes.' Roger massaged his temples. 'It is the way of civilised Christian men.'

She sat back on her heels and studied him. 'I have herbs that will ease your headache. Shall I brew you a—?'

'God, no,' Roger exploded. 'You are a good lad, Soray. A fine, plucky boy. But deliver me from your remedies. Richard still complains about that tea you brewed for him.'

'But it cured him, did it not?'

'Well…yes, so he says. But after last night my belly is not steady enough to keep anything down.'

Marc stared bleary-eyed at the empty space beside him on the cot. God help him, she was gone! But where? To steal bread and cheese from the refectory breakfast table?

He shook himself fully awake. She was not stupid enough to leave the monastery unaccompanied. She was, he acknowledged with a growl deep inside his throat, not stupid at all. She was too clever for her own good. Ignoring his boots and mail shirt, he made for the chamber door.

Once out in the courtyard, the morning air was so cold his lungs burned. The stable. No doubt she would go to the stable to 'borrow' a horse. He yanked the door open and squinted into the gloom.

King Richard sat spraddle-legged in the straw, cradling his head in his two large hands. Roger did likewise. Beside him, revealed in a wedge of greyish light from the open door, knelt Soraya, her hair hidden once again by the thick turban and her chest flat as a trencher.

She scrambled to her feet and stood beside Roger, but she stared at the floor. An unreasoning anger surged through Marc. Why had Soraya sought out his friend?

'And what conspiracy have we here?' he said, his voice dry.

'Keep your herbs, boy,' Roger murmured. 'And I will keep the other matter to myself. Now, help me to stand.'

With Soraya's help, he struggled up on wobbly legs and cautiously turned his head. 'No conspiracy, Marc. Just a sorry man with a splitting headache.'

'And another sorry man with the same,' the king's voice grated. 'Shut that door, de Valery, before the light blinds me!'

Marc kicked the stable door closed. 'We must talk,' he snapped.

The king flinched. 'Quietly, man. A boar is trampling my brain.'

'Huh! No boar, sire. Only too much serving wench and wine.'

'Do not shout, damn you! And for God's sake, do not remind me.'

Marc sent a blistering look at Richard. 'It was a foolhardy act, stopping at a common tavern. Dangerous.'

'Nonsense!' Richard rasped. 'I spoke not one word to anyone other than the maid I was busy—' He shot a glance at Soraya. 'I was busy with.'

Roger stepped away from Soraya. 'It will not happen again. I swear it.'

Marc turned away, paced back and forth in the musty straw. 'A "monk" does not dally with women. An onlooker would wonder at such activity, and that would be dangerous.'

'Oh, aye,' Richard snarled. 'I must be celibate, then, all the way to England? Who gives orders here, me or you?'

Marc swore under his breath. 'I do.' He kept his tone even. 'You entrusted your life to me, my lord. I will do what I must to keep you safe, whether you—'

'Whether I, what?'

'Forgive me, Your Grace. Whether you like it or not.'

Richard bounded up with a bellow of pain and clapped one huge hand across his eyes. The other he laid across Marc's shoulder. 'You are a good man, de Valery.'

Marc rolled his eyes toward the stable roof. 'Can you ride?'

'Yea,' Roger answered.

'Nay,' the king grumbled at the same instant.

'Saddle your mounts,' Marc ordered, his voice deadly quiet.

Roger frowned. 'Do we not break our fast?'

'We do not.'

The king shook his head. 'Mayhap the boy, Soray, could…?'

'Commit thievery for the comfort of your belly? I think not, sire.' He turned to catch Soraya's eye. 'Besides, he is…'

He was going to say 'my servant.' Instead he stared at the space where she had stood. 'Gone.' Where had she slipped off to now?

An hour later, the three men led their saddled mounts through the stable doorway, their horses' hooves clicking across the frost-slicked courtyard into the weak sunlight. Marc patted Jupiter's flank, then ran his hand along the animal's muscular neck.

Where was Soraya? He could delay mounting only so long.

Richard hauled himself awkwardly onto the sway-backed

mare, then clutched his head with both gloved hands. Roger tried three times to stuff his left foot into the stirrup, retching after each attempt.

Still no Soraya. Marc smoothed his hand over Jupiter's nose. At each exhaled breath, vapor puffed out of the animal's nostrils. Where the devil had she gone?

The sound of men's voices chanting matins drifted from the sanctuary at the back of the courtyard. It had been a long, dry time since he had heard Mass. He considered it when he received news of Henry's death, but somehow he felt he didn't have the right. The hideous massacre at Acre still stained his soul.

Now he felt even less deserving since he found himself lusting after a woman. A maddening, unpredictable girl masquerading as a boy, but a female nonetheless.

He tipped his head to hear the monks' singing. As he listened to the soaring melody an ocean of loneliness washed through him. His soul was no longer at rest in his warrior's body; he hungered for something. The simple touch of a comrade-at-arms. A word, a gesture, even a clap on the shoulder—just something to tell him that he mattered. That he was worthy of having life and breath in the midst of mutilation and death.

He hungered for human connection.

Brother Andreas appeared from the stable yard, leading a healthy-looking pony. Behind him danced Soraya, smiling as if she had just dined on cakes and cream.

'Look!' She pointed to the small brown horse. 'Is she not handsome?'

Indeed, the animal looked sleek and well cared for. 'Too small a mount for Richard, so why—?'

'She is mine,' Soraya announced with pride.

Marc snorted. 'Won it in a game of dice, did you?'

She sent him a look that would curdle milk. 'I bought it.'

'Oh, aye. I am to believe that? Bought it with what? Or have you sold my chain mail?'

'I bought her,' she returned, her tone icy, 'with good coin. One gold bezant.'

Marc studied the stubborn tilt of her chin. He did not believe her for one instant, but he knew better than to challenge her. She would spin some lively tale and the king would take her side, and Marc would look a fool. If only he could leave her here, at the monastery. She would be safe. Protected.

And out of his mind.

Soraya stepped away from Brother Andreas, tipped her head up to meet Marc's gaze. 'You must admit, lord, it is better than sharing the same mount?'

He stared down at her. 'Aye, it is,' he conceded. 'Where did you steal the gold bezant to pay for the animal?'

'I do not steal, lord.'

'Ah, I forgot. You "borrow." You are worse than a plague of locusts. I wish you had remained—'

At the king's interested look he stopped himself with effort. He wished she had remained in Jaffa. He wished she had remained a boy.

'We cannot go back to the way it was before,' she said in an undertone.

Marc shook his head. 'We must.'

'We will be companions, then. As before. That is why I purchased the pony.'

He leaned toward her. 'You could stay here, at San Stephano,' he said softly. 'You would be safe. I would leave money for your care.'

'I would rather be your companion,' she murmured. 'On my own pony. Which I have purchased for our travels.' She sent him a slantwise glance. 'Have I not been a good companion?'

He blanched at the word. Be truthful, man. Did he feel like her companion?

God's eyebrows, he did that, and more. He had grown fond of Soray before he knew his servant was a girl. Now it was worse—he was still fond of her.

More than fond. Part of him wanted to be rid of her, leave her here at the monastery and forget the strange pull she had on him. Another part of him wanted never to be without her.

He stifled a groan, mounted and reined his horse away toward the monastery entrance. Brother Andreas gestured for Soraya to mount her pony, then hurried ahead to open the gate.

'Godspeed,' the monk shouted. He pressed a canvas sack of food into Marc's hand, and the three men walked their mounts out of the monastery grounds. 'Godspeed!'

Soraya settled herself on the folded wool blanket that served as a saddle and took up the rope reins Brother Andreas handed to her. She glanced down at his smooth, sweet face. 'Thank you for our lodging, Brother Andreas.'

A beatific smile broke across his shiny round countenance. 'God give you safe journey, lady.'

She went absolutely still. *Lady?* Brother Andreas knew she was not a servant boy! But how?

She kicked her heels hard into the pony's side, bolted through the gate and caught up with Marc at the narrow wooden bridge over the river. 'My lord!'

Marc glanced back over his shoulder, then halted. The king and Roger clattered onto the bridge ahead of him.

'My lord,' she gasped, drawing her mount to a halt beside his. 'Brother Andreas! He knows what I am!'

Marc frowned. 'Of what significance is that?'

'Something is wrong,' she said carefully. 'I can feel it. If

Brother Andreas knows one of us is not what we seem, might he not suspect the same of another? Of the king?'

Marc's blood ran cold at the possibility. And then from the centre of the arching bridge, Richard's rich voice rose in a lai. For the love of Christ, he sang in the Languedoc tongue, a ballad from the court of Aquitaine.

Instantly he scanned the pine-dotted countryside. Far to the north, snow-capped mountains loomed. Here in the flat green valley there were no hiding places from which an enemy could launch an ambush. Even so, he wished Richard would not sing.

'For all his kingly virtues,' he muttered, 'Richard is but a playful boy.'

'A mischievous boy,' Soraya agreed. She kicked the pony to keep pace with Marc. 'Richard is playing with you. He waits to see how you will smuggle him back to his kingdom under the noses of his enemies in France and Austria.'

Marc grumbled under his breath. 'If I have to, I will bind and gag him and toss him over the back of his horse.'

Soraya's mouth sagged open. 'You would dare assault the person of the king?'

Marc rode on, looking straight ahead, his face set. 'I swore to protect him, and that I will do.'

'Are you not divided against yourself, then? Does not your duty to your liege lord oppose your honour as a knight?'

He made an exasperated sound. 'You think too much.'

'Aye, I do. Uncle Khalil said so quite often, but underneath he was pleased. My education and knowledge made me more valuable. Khalil's main fear was that no man would want such a woman as a wife.'

'You talk too much, as well.' Marc had lost sight of Roger and the king, who had descended to the far side of the arched bridge. Quickly he guided Jupiter onto the wooden structure.

Soraya caught up to him and sent him a covert smile. 'But talk passes the time, does it not? Sometimes it even makes you laugh! Would you wish to ride in silence all the way to England?'

'I would wish…' He bit his tongue.

'I know what you wish,' she said quietly. 'You wish to be the king's man and an honourable knight. You wish to return to your own homeland. And,' she added with deliberate slowness, 'when you reach the land of the Scots, you will wish to marry.'

'God's eyes, what gives you that idea?'

'You are a man, are you not? Besides, Sir Roger told me of your betrothed, who waits for you.'

'I have not laid eyes on Jehanne of Chambois since we were pledged as children.'

'And now she is a woman. And you, a man with duty stitched across your heart, will want to honour such a pledge.'

'It is not as simple as that.' He thought of the Greek girl, Irena. He had not taken what she offered and that was because…because…

Not because of Jehanne. It was because he felt nothing for the courtesan. Irena offered only her body. After Acre, and the lingering sickness of his soul in which he spent dark nights searching for what was real and true in a man's life, he knew only one thing. Possessing a woman's body was not enough.

God help him. He dared not think further on it. Not until he had safely delivered the king to Great Eleanor and the English throne. Without Richard, France would nibble away the Angevin lands, and the king's grasping brother, John Lackland, would suck the English people dry.

And well Marc knew that John had his greedy eye on Scotland. England, and Richard, must be saved at all costs.

Soraya rode in silence until they reached the center of the curved bridge, and then her back stiffened. Richard's horse, ahead of her on the bridge, veered suddenly to one side. The king leaned sideways at an odd angle, then toppled off his mount and splashed into the river.

Roger heard the sound and turned back, but Richard had disappeared beneath surface. An expression of disbelief flashed across the knight's narrow face.

'The king!' he shouted. 'In the river!'

Marc spurred his horse forward, surging past Roger before he could turn his mount.

'Hurry, man! The great fool cannot swim!'

Chapter Seventeen

Marc dismounted, splashed into the icy river and managed to snatch Richard's black robe just as he went under for the third time. Grasping the coarse linen at the neck, he hauled the heavy monarch to shore.

The king lay on the riverbank like a beached whale, the monk's habit plastered to his powerful limbs. Water trickled from his nose and mouth, but he did not move.

Marc thrust Soraya to one side, rolled the king's body over onto his belly, and plopped himself down on the broad back. 'You cannot die!' Pressing his fists alongside Richard's spine, he rocked his weight forward. 'Breathe, damn you!'

Water gushed out of the king's mouth.

Roger appeared at his elbow. 'He must have fallen asleep on his horse, slipped into the river before I could reach him.'

'Can't swim,' Marc snapped. 'The drunken fool can't swim.' He rocked forward again.

Richard coughed and made a gurgling sound. 'Watch your tongue, de Valery,' a weak voice ordered. 'No one calls the king of England a drunken fool.'

Marc heaved himself off the sodden form and walked away.

His hands were shaking. Richard's safety was his responsibility. He must keep a closer eye on him.

He turned to see Roger and Soraya strip off the wet robe and dry the shivering king with Soraya's horse blanket. Under the monk's robe, Richard wore knee-length chausses, dripping river water down his knees.

'F-find me a t-tunic, I'm freezing!'

Marc pivoted to face the king. 'No tunic. You could be recognised. Wrap yourself in this.' He heaved the damp saddle blanket into Richard's waiting arms. 'I will build a fire.'

Soraya had already gathered an armload of dry pinecones and a few dead tree limbs. By the time flames curled around the fuel, Richard's teeth were chattering. She fed the fire and brewed a hot herb tea which the king drank in greedy gulps while the monk's robe steamed on a makeshift frame of woven branches.

'Look not so gloom filled, Marc,' the king said affably. 'It is but a small delay.'

Marc swore under his breath. 'Look at the sky,' he barked.

Black clouds were spilling over the snow-capped mountains to the north. In the distance the boom and rumble of thunder signaled a storm, and the billowing mass was heading across the flat, tree-dotted plain toward them.

'Get dressed,' Marc ordered. 'We ride on.'

Rain pelted down on Soraya's head, soaking her turban, her tunic, even her trousers. The wind rose in icy gusts that chilled her already shaking frame. The three horses ahead of her plodded on through mud and marshy spots, even rivulets of water that sluiced across the flat stones of the old Roman road that led north.

No longer could she feel her fingers. Or her nose. Even her

ears had numbed in the bitter cold. Her hands gripping the damp rope reins cramped in position as she struggled to keep up.

What was she doing here on this miserable, sloppy road in this miserable land of…Umbria, was it?…on this most miserable of mornings? She hated this place. Why, why must she care for a man who preferred a harsh northern clime instead of the hot, dry desert?

Ahead of her, Marc drew up his huge warhorse, twisted in the saddle and called out something. The noise of the pounding rain was so loud she couldn't hear, but she watched his lips move and tried to puzzle out his words. Putting one hand to her ear, she signalled she didn't understand.

In answer, he made a circling motion with one raised arm. Hurry up, she guessed. She glared at him. She could move faster if freezing water were not blowing into her eyes and up her nose.

Marc stared at her for a long minute, then shrugged, dropped his arm to his side, and moved on. Dear God, if it please You, make the rain stop and the sun break through those black clouds ahead.

Just when she thought she couldn't stand the wet for one more minute, the rain turned to snow. A thick fog of pristine white flakes swirled down, slowly blanketing the road, the pine trees, the farmers' fields, her pony's neck and withers, her hands, even her eyelashes. She had to blink every few heartbeats in order to see. Would she ever feel warm and dry again?

The world was silent except for the jingling of harnesses and the smack of hooves on slushy stones. A velvety layer of white covered everything.

Marc was cold to the bone and famished. He glanced back at Soraya, still mounted on her snow-dusted pony. She looked like the snow queen his mother told him about when he was a boy; if you dared to touch her, you turned into a statue of ice.

She was shivering, and kept her head down against the wind. Her feet, clad in those light sandals, were turning blue. How they must ache!

He wrenched his gaze back to a sparse scattering of thatched huts ahead. Snow piled up on the straw roofs and wisps of faint grey smoke curled out of some, but no sounds of life, human or animal, broke the eerie stillness. With a groan of frustration he rounded a corner and found himself in a crude but protected market square. Deserted.

His stomach grumbled its disappointment. He had not eaten since yester-eve when he and Soraya had shared a round loaf of gritty black bread and some goat cheese. He didn't ask her where the food had come from.

He glanced back at her once more. Her pony plodded ahead more slowly, and her hand fluttered toward her mouth. By the devil's horns, she was eating something!

Hot fury raged through him. The little sneak had stolen food from the monastery. Damn her thieving hide!

He pivoted his mount and blocked her path. 'You lying vixen!'

Soraya halted her pony. Slowly she raised her gaze to meet his, her eyes snapping green sparks. 'How dare you accuse me of lying! I have not lied to you for three whole days!'

'How dare I?' Marc scoffed. 'Christ, but you are a piece of the devil's work.'

Soraya stepped the pony to her left, leaned toward him and smacked her half-frozen hand smartly across his cheek. 'Do not blaspheme.'

He rubbed his hand over his face. 'What are you eating, then?'

Soraya sent him the most venomous look she could manage with her eyebrows frozen into a line. 'An apple.' She gritted the word at him through clenched teeth. 'I plucked it from a tree growing just past the bridge. You would be eating one, as well, had you thought ahead when we passed the orchard.'

'What orchard?'

'The orchard of apples we passed after Richard fell into the river.'

Marc stepped his horse backward. 'Ah. I was distracted. Your pardon, then, if I accused you wrongly.'

'If? If!' She spit the word at him, hoping it would freeze his ears off. Ah, no, she did not wish that; her own ears ached from the cold, the pain so sharp it made her head buzz. She glared into his face, watched his mouth tighten into a thin line.

Coward.

But he was not a coward; that she knew from watching him risk his life to rescue the king. She waited to see what he would do next.

Without a word, he plodded through the empty market square and around a corner. Soraya clamped her jaw shut and followed.

A long time later, Marc again turned in the saddle. This time he grinned at her and pointed down a narrow lane. A hut! Apparently empty, since no smoke rose from the thatched roof.

Snow covered the steep roof and piled up against the sagging plank doorway, but beggars could not choose. Praise the saints, they had found any shelter at all! Soon she would be warm. Soon she could devour another wrinkled apple for her supper.

Just as she turned into the street after him, something caught her attention. A man, bundled from head to boots, slouched in a doorway holding a fiddle. He wore knitted gloves cut off at the fingers, and as she stared at him he lifted the instrument and tucked it under his chin.

As if by magic, a tune rose and danced over the quiet street. Then the grey scarf wound about his chin and neck slipped down, and Soraya sucked in her breath. The man's round, shiny face wore a familiar sweet smile. Without slowing his busy fingers, he dipped his head in a nod. His eyes were the same milky blue as…

She kicked the pony forward. The music faded as she caught with Marc, who stood motioning for her to dismount.

'Shelter,' he said. 'In there.' He gestured toward the squat doorway.

'That m-man,' she stuttered.

'The musician? What of him?'

'He— He looks just like Brother Andreas.'

'Your brain is snow-addled. Brother Andreas is leagues from here, at the monastery. Go inside and get warm.'

She stepped in close to him. 'Marc,' she said in a low voice. 'Listen to me. Brother Andreas is not at the monastery. He is here, playing a fiddle in a doorway.'

He looked her full in the face. 'You are having visions. Either that or you are—'

'Do not say it,' she snapped. 'Do not dare.' She drew herself up as straight as she could with her back and leg muscles cramping from the cold.

'Aye, I will say it. You pluck apples off trees no one else notices. You conjure up a friar far from an abbey that lies leagues to the south. What next?'

Soraya thrust the rope reins into Marc's chilled hand and stalked toward the open doorway of the waiting hut. But instead of entering, she spun in her tracks to confront him.

'If you are to protect our monk-king, Sir Short-Sighted, I suggest you pay attention to intelligence that comes your way, by whatever means.'

'You speak like a woman, imagining ghosts in every garderobe.'

'I speak as a spy,' she said, her voice tight with anger. 'I do not imagine even you are foolish enough to ignore what I see with my own eyes.'

Marc's body jerked. 'I do not ignore you! God, it is all I can do to keep my hands—' He stopped abruptly. 'I will go and see for myself.' He brushed past her.

'I shall wait for your apology!' she called after him. She would anticipate it with relish.

Inside the rude dwelling Soraya found King Richard and Roger puffing in vain at a dying fire. Smoke billowed from the hearth in the centre of the room, but no flames licked until she shut the door and air began to flow through the hole in the roof.

Huddled by the hearth to get warm, she watched in disbelief as the king of the English unceremoniously stripped off his monk's robe and damp underclothes and paced about the small hut in nothing but his ruddy skin.

He tossed the sopping bundle onto her lap. 'Here, Soray. Hang these to dry near the fire.'

She kept her gaze on his bare feet. 'Yes, lord.' But she was unable to avoid seeing his lower anatomy. Her cheeks heated.

'What are you blushing about, boy? Have you never seen a naked man before?'

Soraya swallowed. A vision rose of Marc's unclothed muscular form, his expressive mouth, his eyes lit from within by some amusement. His generous male endowments.

Fingers of heat licked her body. Her breasts swelled under the constraining silk wrap, the woman's parts between her thighs beginning to tingle in an odd way, as if a butterfly were beating gossamer wings against her flesh.

'Soray!' the king thundered. 'Move yourself and dry out my garments!'

She jumped to her feet, draped the damp robe and chausses over a low roof beam. When she reseated herself by the fire she kept her eyes downcast.

'Just look at the lad, de Clare. Shy as a virgin.'

Roger looked over at her with a chuckle. 'No doubt the boy is a virgin, sire. And not likely to learn the ways of lusty men traveling with Marc, I would wager. Ever since Acre, our Scot shows no interest in even the most willing female.'

'Hah!' Richard scoffed. 'Gelded him, did it? The killing, I mean.'

'I think,' Roger said carefully, 'it unmanned him in another way. Blunted his spirit more than his prowess.'

'Ah.' Richard nodded. 'Poor man. A fine warrior in battle, the best! But cursed with a conscience.'

Roger's thin face went purposely blank. 'The Scots are a mystery. Half poet, half raving berserker.'

Richard gave a bark of laughter, then dropped his forehead onto his palm. 'My head spins like a windmill.'

'You need food,' Soraya ventured. 'We all do. The marketplace is deserted, but I could…' Inside Soraya blanched at the thought. Another hour in that grinding cold and her toes would drop off.

Marc saved her by charging through the doorway carrying a coarse string bag of cloth-wrapped items, a thick fur cloak and a child's heavy woolen stockings.

'Food!' the king chortled. 'I smell cheese!' Roger fell on the bag. 'Wine! And bread—four loaves! How did you come by all this?'

'I bought it. From a peddler.' He smiled at Soraya with sharp blue eyes and a flush of warmth bloomed all the way to the backs of her knees. She held her breath, waiting for his apology about Brother Andreas.

'These stockings are too small for me, de Valery,' the king said.

'They are not for you, sire.'

'But the cloak…' Richard made a grab for the soft brown fur, and Marc jerked it out of his reach.

'That, too, is not for you, my lord. It is meant for Soray.' He caught her gaze and in his eyes she read an unspoken entreaty. *Forgive me.* He all but spoke the words aloud.

Something scratched at the door, and the men froze. Silence spread over the hut. Then more scratching, this time accompanied by a low moan. Soraya sprang forward.

'Don't,' Marc shouted.

Too late. She flung the door open and peered out.

A small black dog with matted hair and soft brown eyes shivered on the threshold. With a whine he bounded inside and headed straight for the fireplace, where he shook himself thoroughly. Water droplets sprayed from his shaggy coat over the king's bare backside.

'Damme,' he yelped. 'Get rid of this mutt!'

Marc reached for the animal, but Soraya got there first. She hunkered down over the dog like a mother hen protecting a new-laid egg.

'Out!' Marc ordered.

'No,' she returned calmly. Cautiously she ran her hands over the animals small form. 'He is cold and wet, but not injured or sick. At the worst, he is hungry. And…' she laid her cheek against the dog's wet curly hair '—he is soft.'

'We cannot feed another mouth,' Marc said in a quiet voice.

Soraya kept her head pressed against the shaggy animal. 'You cannot have him.'

The king waved one large hand in their direction. 'Let the boy feed the damned dog. That won't last long when the lad's own belly begins to growl.'

'My lord,' Marc began, his tone exasperated. 'You do not know this boy as I do. Soray will likely give his own supper—'

'God's eyes, man, let the lad keep the mutt. I order it, de Valery.'

Soraya scooped the ball of wet, floppy curls into her arms and squeezed. A rough wet tongue licked her chin, then her nose, and she laughed. She would call him Saqii. In Arabic, the word meant frost.

Chapter Eighteen

The goatskin of wine traveled around the small circle warming before the fire three times before King Richard tipped it upside down and sucked air. Not one drop trickled out and the king gave a heavy sigh. 'Mayhap I could venture out and find another peddler?'

Marc laid one hand on Richard's freckled arm. 'Do not, my lord. You could be recognised.'

'In this garb?' The king lifted the skirt of his monk's robe. 'You jest, de Valery.'

'Not on this matter.' Looking after the king was like trying to catch an industrious bee in one's fist. Richard's quick mind, his energy, his impulsive urges forced Marc to think ahead, anticipate his next move. By the time they reached England, Marc's hair would turn grey.

If they reached England. He couldn't erase from his mind Soraya's suspicion about the minstrel she'd seen. Brother Andreas, she insisted. Yet when he had retraced her steps, the squat wood houses lining the narrow street were dark and silent. He heard no music, saw no one, much less a fiddler.

Still, something niggled at his brain. She would not make

up such a tale. He was learning not to discount her observations, or her intelligence. He should have listened to her. Trusted her words. But his first impulse was to ignore what she was saying.

Why was that?

Partly it was habit. Partly because just hearing her voice quickened his desire. No matter what the words were, the low, slightly throaty tone made his body react. Just the sound of her speech made him stiffen. Was he war-addled, then?

Nay. He swallowed a laugh. He was woman-addled.

He studied her now, where she sat wrapped in the fur cloak, nibbling a morsel of dark bread. He wondered that neither Roger nor the king saw what he saw—a lithe, graceful creature with eyes like green jade and an unusual chiseled face. By the saints, he should be glad Richard spared no more than an occasional glance in her direction. Soraya was beautiful.

And Richard was Richard.

Roger was courteous and kind, but he did not really look at a servant. Roger took things at face value.

The king stretched out before the hearth, propped himself on his elbows and stared into the flames. Idly he plucked at his freshly donned black robe. 'You must shed your clothes, lad. Hang them to dry as I did.'

'Yes, lord.'

'Strip, then,' Richard ordered. Marc opened his mouth to protest, but shut it when he caught Soraya's warning glance. She made a tent of the fur cloak and ducked beneath it. Almost at once the tent started to ripple as she apparently wriggled out of her tunic. More mysterious jerking and flopping, until a slim hand thrust two wet garments out from beneath the fur.

Underneath the cloak he imagined Soraya's naked body, long-legged and soft, so soft, like the finest silk. And her breasts… Ah God, her breasts and thighs would be the colour of rich cream. And inviting. His hands clenched.

He turned away to hide his arousal. Richard stood, scooped up her garments and draped them over the same roof beam Soraya had used. Marc choked back a laugh. He was witnessing the king of England, in disguise, playing maid to a maid, also in disguise.

The fur tent jerked once and went still. Richard's thick, red-gold brows went up. 'You, too, de Valery. We are all of us vulnerable to lung fever. Best get dry and stay so.'

Marc kept his eyes on the soft pile of fur in the center of the hut while he shed his surcoat, shrugged out of his mail shirt and untied his gambeson and leggings. Now he, too, was naked. It was of no significance to Roger, curled up in a corner and already snoring. Or to the king, who was now preparing for sleep in the other corner.

But it was of great significance to himself. And to Soraya. She knew he was unclothed. And she knew that he knew she was in the same state. His groin tightened.

Stalking to the low beam, he draped his damp garments next to Soraya's tunic and trousers, then settled himself near the lumpy cloak and began polishing his chain mail with a scrap of leather.

The hearth fire burned low. Shadows deepened. Richard lay on his back and began to sing softly. *'M'amie, j'noublie rien.'* My love, I regret nothing.

The tiny movement under the tent caught Marc's eye. A small hand crept out, holding a bit of cheese. The mongrel dog she had adopted over Marc's objection bounded forward, gobbled down the morsel and snuggled his way under the fur.

Mark told himself he was jealous only of the warmth, but in truth he wished he could be as close to her.

The mail shirt across his lap slipped to the packed earth floor. Marc leaned forward, burying his face against his knees.

Richard began another verse of the ballad. His eyes were closed as if in sleep, but his lips moved and the suggestive words floated out. 'For your kisses I would gladly die…'

Marc tried not to think of Soraya. Of her mouth, her hands. He shut his eyes and tried to block his ears, as well.

The hearth fire guttered, and the room darkened. He lay down next to Soraya's cloak, curved his body around it. At once he felt the soft fur being gently drawn up over his shoulders.

He stretched out his arm and laid it over the breathing girl next to him. He thought fleetingly of positioning himself across the doorway to stop intruders, but with his next indrawn breath, bringing the scent of her hair to his nostrils, he admitted he could not move away from her.

The mutt growled. Marc smiled into the dark.

Soraya felt his hand, heavy and warm, settle over her rib cage and suddenly she wanted to weep. There was something sweet in his gesture. Something caring and gentle. Yet he could be stubborn and razor-tongued in anger. Exasperating. Even pigheaded.

I hate him.

I love him.

God help me, I would die for him.

Marc woke to a throbbing pain. He jerked to consciousness to find Soraya's dog gnawing contentedly on his thumb. 'Leave off, you little cur!'

He felt Soraya's frame under the cloak shake with laughter. She reached out her hand, lifted the animal away and cuddled him close to her body.

The pup made a satisfied smacking noise. 'Are you injured?' she murmured over her shoulder.

'My hand is yet whole,' he breathed. 'It is my pride that smarts.'

'I am glad,' she whispered.

'For my hand? Or my pride?'

Again her shoulders shook with laughter. 'Your pride, my lord, needs no help.'

'God,' he whispered. 'You are a saucy handful. More trouble than you are worth.'

She rolled partway toward him. The mutt came with her, edged toward Marc's belly, sniffed once and growled low in his throat.

'You are wrong, Marc,' she said at last. 'I am worth more than you can imagine.'

Her breath caressed his neck. He wanted to kiss her. He wanted to crush her in his arms, bury himself deep inside her and claim her as his own. His body trembled with desire. He wanted to possess her. All of her.

Soraya lay beside him, breathing softly, while Roger and the king slept on. Slowly, Marc moved his warm, gentle fingers to touch the back of her neck. She held her breath, felt her heart stop. How glorious, to be touched by a man.

Wanting gnawed at her like a sweet pain, penetrating her blood and bone, making her skin burn with desire. She lay still, listening to the rhythm of their irregular breathing. His thumb moved back and forth just at her hairline, then purposefully stroked the shallow indentation at the base of her neck. Waves of sensation, like hot, sweet honey, spread over her belly, her thighs.

The place between her legs throbbed, as if her flesh were crying out for something. His fingers circled the shell of her ear, tangled in her hair, and his soft breath shuddered against her skin.

'Soraya,' he whispered.

And that was all. Just her name and his breath and his voice, but it was enough. More than enough. It told her of his need and of his carefully restrained passion. She rolled onto her back, then turned toward him. His hand touched her cheek, and she—God help her—she moved it down to her breast. He lay motionless, then gently leaned toward her to press his forehead against hers.

'Soraya.'

'Yes, Marc.' He did not move, and she understood. Roger or Richard could wake up at any moment.

The recognition of what simmered between them was blinding. She slid her hand to his mouth, felt his ragged breath flow between her fingers. He did not need to touch her; they were connected all the same.

It was the most ecstatic moment she could ever remember.

Toward dawn, Soraya dressed quickly in her dry tunic and trousers, then opened the hut door a crack and peeked out. A world of white lay before her. Village dwellings were scarcely recognisable under drifts of pristine snow; little hillocks had built up against the doors.

Above her the sky blazed blue as the sea, the thick clouds scudding like whitecaps. Roofs sparkled in the sunshine, and the intense light hurt her eyes. She shoved the door outward, smashing through a pile of snow that had built up on the threshold during the night.

The clear morning air, bitter with frost, turned her nose and ears to ice. The thought of finding some sheltered place to lower her trousers and do her morning business sent a shiver along the length of her spine. Just a small patch of earth would do—a courtyard garden, a secluded animal pen. Anything would suffice.

She skirted the horses and her pony, which Marc had turned toward the hut wall away from the wind, and found a small nook where two walls met at right angles. Her cold-stiffened fingers fumbled at her trouser waistband.

Just then a shadow moved across the corner of her vision. Then another. She looked up and screamed.

Two figures in black robes stood before her, swords drawn. She cried out again, and then they were upon her.

'Kill her now,' a voice said in gutteral Arabic.

'Not now, you fool.'

One man yanked her upright. She clutched at her slipping trousers, managed to pull them up over her hips but could not retie the waist string. The man pushed her forward, ahead of him, and she stumbled, holding the garment in place with one hand. The other, taller and leaner than the first, strode in front.

'Marc,' she screamed. Instantly a hand covered her mouth, and shoved her head into the folds of the voluminous robe. She gagged at the suffocating smell of strong herbs and smoke.

The tall man grasped her arm and shoved her around a corner, down a long lane, around another corner into the deserted market square where a pair of horses stood tied to a post. Then she was hoisted onto one of the animals, belly-down like a sack of wheat.

'Let us go!' the tall man said.

'Why not kill her now?' the other asked. When he received no answer, he mounted behind her and dragged her upright onto his lap. 'She is worthless to us.'

'In good time. First she will tell us what she knows.'

The instant he removed his smelly hand from her mouth, she screamed again for Marc.

Something slammed into the back of her head, and she sank into blackness.

Chapter Nineteen

Marc jolted into consciousness. He sat up abruptly, felt freezing air blow onto his neck. The mutt poked its cold, black nose into his bare belly, gave a half-hearted growl and rolled into a ball against him.

'Soraya?' he whispered.

Her tunic and trousers no longer hung from the roof beam, and his gaze went to the door. Had she gone out?

The minutes dragged by and he rose and began to pace back and forth in front of the hearth. Damn the woman, why did she not return?

The king yawned, stretched, then crawled to the opposite corner of the hut and drove his bare foot against Roger's backside. 'I'm hungry.'

'Go to the devil!' Roger mumbled.

'I would rather send Soray out to "borrow" something to break our fast,' Richard proposed with a chuckle.

That must be it, Marc reasoned. She is foraging for food. God knows she'll find the pickings sparse on a morning this cold.

The little mongrel dog nipped at his bare feet. 'Get away, you demon.' He scooped the animal off the floor and lobbed him onto the fur cloak. The dog's soft brown eyes looked at him reproachfully, but he settled down on the cloak, his black head resting on his paws.

Marc could stand it no longer. He caught up the fur wrap, dumped the mutt onto the floor and flung the door open. A blast of frigid air swept over him.

'Shut the door man,' the king yelled. 'It's freezing!'

'Cover yourself, then,' Marc snapped.

Richard bolted upright. 'What ails you, de Valery?'

'The servant, Soray. He went out earlier and has not returned.'

'Forget him. He is but a servant. Let us be on our way.'

'No,' Marc said quietly. 'Not yet.'

Richard's face reddened in fury. 'No? No man tells the king of England "No." Come, de Valery. I say we will ride on.'

Marc shot Roger a look. 'I cannot.'

The knight's smooth brow wrinkled into a frown. 'Think, man,' he said in an undertone. 'You swore an oath to the king. Your duty is clear.'

Marc turned away from his friend. Aye, my duty lies with the king. But, God forgive me, my heart lies with Soraya. Hurriedly he pulled on his clothes, then stepped out of the hut and closed the door. 'Soraya,' he called.

Silence. On foot he searched the quiet lane, inspected every structure, however rude, looking for some sign. Undisturbed snow was piled up in front of each hut; at each doorway Marc scanned the white-coated ground for any sign of disturbance—a footprint, anything.

He heard no sound in the bitter morning air, only the drip-dribble of snow melting off thatched roofs. Irrationally, he thought of Soraya's feet in her leather sandals, then of the warm woolen stockings he'd snatched from some washerwoman's drying pole. He hoped she was wearing them.

She was clever, he reminded himself. Resourceful. But he remembered the assassin in the market-place at Talamone; the marauding Saracen's sword was meant for Soraya, not the king. It was not Richard's back that was sliced, but hers.

He stopped short. Soraya was at ten times the risk Richard was. At once realisation sank in and he knew what had happened to her. A cold fury filled him. If one of Saladin's assassins harmed her, Marc swore he would ride back to Jerusalem and slice the Saracen leader's head from his shoulders. If she was in the hands of an assassin, God have mercy on her.

He found a mushy area torn up with the prints of boots and two horses; one of the images stamped in the snow was very small. The path led away toward the crudely piled stone wall surrounding the village.

He pivoted, floundered through the snow-clogged lanes back to the hut. Every moment of delay clanged a death knell in his heart.

He burst through the doorway. 'Get dressed,' he shouted. 'Now. Mount and follow me!'

Richard, lounging by the hearth, frowned. 'I think not, de Valery. We have not yet eaten—'

'Move!' Marc thundered. 'Soray has been taken.'

'Taken?' The king stood and leisurely ambled toward the now-dry monk's robe, hanging overhead. 'No matter, Marc. You will find another servant in the next town.'

Marc began to sweat. He struggled into his mail shirt and grabbed up his hemp supply bag. 'I will ride ahead.'

'You will not,' the king ordered. 'You will ride with me. You swore to protect me, and so you shall.'

Roger sidled close. 'You have no choice, Marc,' he murmured.

'Aye, I do,' Marc said under his breath. Betray the king and be dishonoured, or obey and lose… No man should have to make such a decision.

Somehow he prodded the king into dressing without feeling the nick of Richard's sword. Outside, he mounted Jupiter and started down the lane.

'Slow down, de Valery,' the king shouted. He brushed the dusting of snow off his mare's sunken back, slapped on his saddle and mounted. 'We will take Soray's pony with us. Too small a mount for me, but mayhap we will find another servant before we leave Italy. A girl, this time.'

Marc choked back a cry of rage. Roger stepped his horse toward him. 'Wait,' his friend said softly. 'So the king—' Roger blew out a long breath and shook his head '—will keep his mind on his own troubles.'

Marc delayed until he could stand it no longer, then wheeled his stallion and trotted down the lane and into the deserted market square, studying the snow-coated cobble-stones. The king and Roger appeared at the far edge of the square, moving at the pace of a tortoise. Soraya's little black dog trotted at their heels.

'This way!' Marc shouted. He pointed north, in the direction the hoofprints led, and kicked Jupiter into a canter. The dog romped ahead, sniffing at everything in his path—a pile of manure, an abandoned wheelbarrow, Marc's leather boots. Even a discarded eggplant, half-rotten and worm-eaten.

'Go away,' Marc warned. The small animal wagged its black tail and barked once. But it did not obey. It tagged along behind him, occasionally straying off to one side to smell a snow-swathed bush or a hay rick, then returning to his post with a sharp yip. Nothing deterred the stubborn mutt—not shouts or threats or even the occasional dropping of horse dung. The dog investigated, barked and fell into line again.

160   *Crusader's Lady*

The animal was a lot like Soraya, Marc thought. An ache swept through his chest.

'It appears you have been adopted,' Richard called with a laugh. Marc gritted his teeth and spurred ahead, out of earshot of Richard's jeering.

He guided Jupiter through the sleepy village, past thatched cottages hugging narrow, meandering lanes. When the huts thinned out, Marc rode through the north gate and on into rolling hills still lightly covered with snow. He must hurry; the snow would melt under the sun's rays, obliterating the already fading tracks he followed.

The trail of hoofprints suddenly split, one set veering east, the other continuing north, toward the mountains. Marc narrowed his eyes against the blinding sun and studied the snow-covered foothills ahead.

It would be more direct to follow the tracks leading north, ride north across the jagged peaks. But that would also be more dangerous. Bandits, for one thing. A blizzard, perhaps, judging from the roiling purple-black clouds hanging over the highest mountain. Which way would an Arab go?

He reined Jupiter to the east and prayed to God he had guessed correctly.

A cord bound Soraya's hands behind her back, but at least she was warm. Fire smouldered in a brazier at her side. She huddled close to it, then noticed a thin-bladed dagger stuck in the coals. The blaze, then, was not for cooking.

'I ask you again,' the rough voice said in Arabic. 'Where is the English king?'

Soraya shook her head. She was not gagged, but she knew it would be useless to scream. The thatched hovel she and the Arab occupied was hidden in a dense stand of scrubby pine trees. And the man had carefully swept away the horse tracks.

'Where is King Richard?'

She was silent.

'Save yourself pain.' He jerked upward on her bound wrists. 'Where is the king they call Lion Heart?'

'I travel with only plain knights,' she said, her tone pinched. 'Two knights and a simple monk. A holy man.'

'And four horses?' He jerked her hands upward again. 'Where is the message your uncle was sent to deliver?'

Soraya moaned with agony. She must protect the king, must keep his presence secret until he, and Marc, were safe in England.

Another jerk. Her shoulder sockets felt as if hot coals had replaced the joints.

'Where is the message? Where?'

She could not take much more. And if he used the heated knife…

Her throat closed. She could scream all she wanted; no one would hear her.

'May you have ten daughters—' she spoke each word directly into his face using slow, careful Arabic '—and may they all marry well.'

The man spit in disgust and picked up the dagger.

Chapter Twenty

Marc spurred his mount forward, then heard the king's tired voice behind him call a halt. God's blood, it was too early to stop. Darkness was an hour hence, but at the back of his brain nagged a compulsion to press on, to not lose the track of the horse ahead of them.

He studied the marks cut deep into the melting snow. Too small for a warhorse; the imprint was almost delicate. An Arab mare, then. Moving fast.

He pretended he had not heard the king and rode on. 'De Valery!' Richard thundered. 'Where are you going, man?'

Marc clenched his jaw until his teeth ached. To hell, Richard. I am going to hell. I am in hell every moment not knowing what has happened to Soraya.

'To shelter, sire,' he called instead. 'Follow me.' He glanced back to see the little black dog still trotting at Jupiter's heels. Saqii, Soraya called him. Frost. Odd name for an animal darker than Welsh coal, but the girl had a liking for things that were not what they seemed. He caught his breath at the pain searing through his chest. Soraya. Please, God, let me find her.

'De Valery,' the king bellowed. 'Stop! I command you.'

Marc drew rein. Just as he turned to face the king, the mutt, Saqii, streaked off into the brush.

Richard motioned for him to dismount. Marc slid off his horse with a weary sigh, and then Saqii was back, nipping at his boots. He kicked at the animal, but it bounded out of reach, then slunk back and sank his teeth into the hem of Marc's surcoat. Growling, the dog tugged at the fabric.

'Be off!' He tried to shake the creature loose, but the little beast flung himself at Marc's feet and again grabbed hold of the blue linen. 'Let go, you pesky devil!'

The king and Roger guffawed as the annoying ball of floppy black hair bit and pulled and growled. 'Stand still,' the king roared through his sniggers. 'It thinks you are a tree trunk!'

Marc ignored the king's mocking advice and the mongrel began to bark, a high, excited *yip-yip-yip,* pulling Marc forward by the now ragged hem of his surcoat.

A high, thin cry cut through the air, and the hair at the back of Marc's neck prickled. Then another scream tore into his gut. Marc started toward the sound, Saqii racing ahead of him. Another cry, and suddenly he understood.

'*À moi!*' he shouted. 'To me!' He began to run.

Richard's laughter ceased, and he spurred his horse after Marc. Roger overtook the king, his sword already drawn.

Half-hidden in a copse of scrub pine, a crude hut butted against a low hillock. Marc crashed through the flimsy door and crouched at the threshold, sword in hand.

The turbaned figure inside spun in surprise, snatched up a dagger and started toward him. The knife blade glowed red. With sickening clarity, Marc understood what he had interrupted.

Soraya was crouched on the earth floor beside a brazier, but when she saw the Arab lurch toward Marc she twisted her body to throw herself into the man's path.

Marc raised his sword, but the man feinted to the left and stumbled out the door. Before he took two steps, Richard's blade cut him down.

Marc dropped his weapon and gathered Soraya into his arms. Her hands were tied at her back and she trembled violently. On the skin of one wrist Marc spied an angry scarlet burn mark. What had he done to her?

His eyes stung. 'You are safe now,' he murmured against her temple. 'Safe.'

Soraya couldn't speak, just gulped in air and clung to Marc's surcoat.

The king burst into the hut. The cowl of his monk's disguise fell back, revealing a ruddy face creased with worry. 'How is the boy?'

'Alive,' Marc said dryly.

Richard took a step toward him. 'Was it me that devil wanted?'

Soraya shook her head.

'What, then?'

She tried to answer but her shaking voice was almost unintelligible. 'He want…wanted the message to Richard from Saladin. I would not reveal the content.'

Richard reached out a large hand and ruffled her hair. 'You are a brave lad, Soray.'

She turned her face into Marc's neck, and he made a half turn to expose her tied wrists. 'Cut the binding, man.'

The king slit the leather cord and Marc gently massaged her raw wrists. He swore when he noticed another angry burn mark.

'It's all right now, lad,' Richard boomed. 'I've taken care of that scoundrel.'

Marc hesitated. 'There was another man, as well, sire. Two horsemen rode out of the village ahead of us. The

tracks of one led north. The tracks of the other—this one—
turned east.'

'Where are we now?' Richard snapped.

'Umbria.'

'We dare not turn west,' Richard muttered. 'Philip will be
setting snares all over France. I say we skirt those devil mountains ahead and travel east, toward Ravenna.'

Marc blanched. 'Think, sire! Ravenna brings us closer
to Austria.'

'Huh! The king of the English fears no Austrian. I fear
Philip of France more than that sot Leopold.'

'Granted. But travel to Ravenna is still unwise.'

'You say I am unwise?' Richard roared.

'Not unwise, my lord. But reckless.' Marc longed to
keep Soraya cradled safe in his arms, but he knew he had
to let her go lest the king notice that he held the 'boy'
overlong. Gently he lowered her until her feet touched the
bare earth.

The king chuckled. 'Reckless, am I?'

'Aye, Your Majesty.'

Richard clapped Marc on the shoulder. 'You are a coura-
geous man, de Valery. Not many would speak so bluntly to
Richard of England.'

'I am truthful, lord.'

'Aye,' the king muttered. 'To a fault.'

Soraya's hand touched Marc's elbow. 'What is needed,' she
said, steadying her voice and looking at no one in particular,
'is cleverness. Neither Philip nor Leopold will expect you to
travel north, over the mountains, in winter. Perhaps we should
do exactly that.'

'Hah!' Richard shook his head. 'I don't fancy freezing in
a blizzard. Besides, I want to see those onion-top churches in

Ravenna.' He mounted his mare and folded his huge arms across his belly. 'Bring the Arab's horse with us.'

'And?' Marc prompted.

Richard smiled. 'We ride to Ravenna.'

Ravenna had more than onion-top churches. The city was busy, the market square overflowing with butcher stalls, lace-making displays, tables of herbs and healing powders cluttering the narrow streets. Soraya wrinkled her nose. The place smelled worse than Baghdad. And was far more noisy.

Richard insisted on studying the oriental roof-line of each church they saw, as well as visiting every tavern in the city to sample the wine. Soraya laughed at the strict order of the king's travels: church, then tavern. Church, tavern. Now they sat at a sticky-topped table in La Bella Putta.

Dizzy from the pungent, smoky smell of incense in the churches and too many sips of wine from the taverns, Soraya hunched on the splintery bench between Marc and Roger, whiling away the time while the black-robed Richard dallied. Clothed in the monk's disguise, the king apparently felt himself to be invisible. Soraya watched in horrified fascination.

The knights of Ravenna were pigs, with dirty surcoats, rusty chain mail, and loud voices, most often raised along with overflowing tankards in an earthy song that made her ears burn. Christians in this land were worse sinners than the crusading knights at the gates of Jerusalem! They drank at daybreak, prayed in the afternoon, fornicated at night.

'How I love this city!' the king exclaimed from a knot of revelers. His monk's cowl slipped back from his face and Soraya exchanged a glance with Marc. Roger rolled his eyes heavenward.

'We must get him out of here,' Marc muttered.

Roger nodded. 'Out of the tavern? Or out of the city?'

'Out of Italy altogether. He's enjoying himself too much. Monk or no, he is attracting attention.' He watched the king plop himself down on a table top and shout for more wine, then challenge a burly Swede to a drinking contest.

Roger sniffed. 'And how do we convince the king of England to do what we want?'

He stopped speaking while the tavern maid plunked down a slab of hard cheese and a round loaf of bread. Marc broke off a chunk of the cheese and handed half to Soraya, who was beginning to nod over her wine cup. The little black dog snoozed on her lap.

'Tie him hand and foot?' Marc suggested.

Roger shook his head. 'Trussing up Richard would be treason.'

'Tell him that his brother John and Philip of France are going to war against him.'

'Good.' Roger grinned. 'And it is no doubt true. No king tolerates insubordination, especially not from a crown-hungry brother.'

'Why not tell him,' Soraya ventured, 'that there is a great tournament and market fair awaiting him in… What is the next city to the east?'

'To the east lies Venice. But we cannot take Richard to Venice! Venice is more debauched than Ravenna!'

Roger thumped his cup onto the table. 'It must be Austria, then.'

'Impossible,' Marc blazed. 'Leopold is duke of Austria. Richard made a capon of Leopold at Jerusalem, and the duke will have a long memory.'

Soraya raised her head. 'I have noticed that Richard likes to gamble. Why not make him a wager?'

Marc stared at her. 'Aye, he does. What kind of wager?'

'A wager that he must leave Ravenna in order to win.'

'He likes horses, too. And warfare.' Roger gazed across the smoky room at the tall, jovial monk who was apparently besting the Swede in the drinking contest. 'And wine.'

'Richard likes winning,' Soraya reminded in a soft voice. 'Wager him that he cannot ride two hundred leagues in three days. Then he will not choose a slow mountainous route but will ride for the plains.'

Marc smiled and shook his head. 'He will turn north, to Venice.'

'There is plague in Venice,' Roger murmured. 'I heard it from that merchant over there.' He tipped his head toward the corner table where a stout man in a fur hat sat slurping up a bowl of lumpy-looking stew.

Soraya studied the man, and a lance of fear poked her belly. Even from the side, the merchant looked like…

'Brother Andreas!' she gasped. 'That is no merchant, that is Brother Andreas.'

'Nonsense,' Roger scoffed.

Marc held his tongue and inspected the man. Smooth, pink skin. Rounded head. He grabbed the bread and cheese and jerked to his feet. 'Soray is right. Come on!'

Roger sat goggling at him, but Soraya scrambled off the bench, hauled Saqii into her arms and ran for the tavern exit, keeping her head down, her cheek pressed against the dog's curly black coat.

Marc picked a path through the drunken knights surrounding the king, stepped in close and murmured a single word into his ear. 'Spy.'

Richard jumped as if bitten by a scorpion. Without a word he shoved his way past the unsteady Swede, ploughed through the group of fellow revellers and tramped out into the cold night air.

Roger had collected their horses from the sheltered tavern yard; Soraya was already mounted on her pony, which was prancing and shaking in the icy wind.

'Ride!' the king shouted.

Marc heaved his body onto Jupiter's back. 'De Clare!' he shouted.

'Behind you' came a calm voice. Roger was already mounted.

The king's sway-backed mare clattered off down the street toward the square stone church of San Giovanni. For a moment Marc thought the king meant to seek sanctuary in the house of God, but Richard rode on, past churches, taverns, inns, off-centre timber houses, even a nun's hospice.

'Get out of the city,' Marc yelled.

Roger leaned forward in his saddle. 'Too late. The gates will be locked.'

'We must try anyway. Head north.'

The north gate was not locked, but a split in the heavy log barrier had jammed it partway shut. The chink of space between the iron-reinforced oak gate and the stone wall where the beam should have touched looked wide enough for only a small man on a small horse.

Marc groaned. Soraya's undersized pony could get through the gap, but not the king's mare, much less two huge warhorses. The Arab's horse had been left at the tavern yard. A shivering guard huddled near the gate opening. He twisted toward them as they approached but did not rise. The king called out something, but the sleepy-eyed man spoke no French. No English. Not even Greek. Only Italian. Soraya tried sign language, but still the guard blocked the way.

Suddenly she began to sing a lilting verse in Arabic. The startled guard began to smile, then bobbed his head in time with the music.

From the shadows the king spoke, his voice low. 'The boy's efforts are wasted. No matter how much the guard loves a tune, none of us can fit through that opening.'

'Soray could,' Roger said thoughtfully.

The guard kept grinning and nodding, and when Soraya brought the song to a close, she dismounted. The man gave the 'boy' an elaborate bow, and she squeezed herself and the pony past him and out the gate.

They waited. For how long Marc did not know, but an instinct told him Soraya would think of something, and it would happen soon.

True enough, after more agonizing minutes a high, clear voice called out from behind the wall. *'An hahr.'*

'Quoi?' Richard and Roger said in the same breath.

'Get to the river,' Marc said. 'The bridge over it should be just a short distance from the east gate.'

By the time they found the east gate the approach was clogged with people staring at flames that lit up the sky outside the city walls. Shouting men thronged at the heavy plank barrier until finally the gatekeeper emerged from his small cottage. He took one look at the glowing sky and began to draw the timbers open with a chain and pulley.

Marc and the king pushed through the crowd until they stood directly in front of the barrier. The instant the opening was wide enough for his horse, Marc plunged through, then twisted to make sure the king was behind him.

Richard swore under his breath. 'Look at that!'

A floating tower of fire drifted slowly down the river. Tongues of orange flame licked at the old Roman bridge arching over the water. Through the smoke Marc glimpsed a burning boat, a fishing craft. Unmanned, thank God.

But that fiery escapade must have cost Soraya another gold bezant! Unable to suppress a smile, he spurred Jupiter forward and over the bridge.

Chapter Twenty-One

Still mounted on her pony, Soraya waited on the opposite bank of the river, her turban mud-streaked, her tunic ripped at the side, but grinning. Richard reached her first, leaned out of his saddle and clapped her shoulder as he rode by. 'Good lad!' Roger gave her a salute of knightly honor, his palm raised chin high.

Marc was the last to greet her, and by the saints he wanted to dismount and kneel at her feet! But that would pique Richard's curiosity, and God knew they had troubles enough.

He pulled his mount up beside hers. 'Well done,' he said quietly.

Her grin widened. 'It was, was it not? And so simple. Except at first I could not find a cookfire to light my brand, and then a kind old woman invited…'

Her dirt-smudged face had never looked more beautiful. He wanted to kiss her so much he fought to keep his hands on the reins. 'Sometimes I think you are almost too clever.'

Soraya looked him in the eye, and her smile wobbled. 'Ah, no, lord. I am just clever enough to keep you interested.'

'Come with me to Venice,' he blurted. It was unnecessary to ask the question, but he wanted to say it aloud, hear the words of invitation hang in the air. There were a thousand other things he might also say…. Come with me to my bed. Come with me to Scotland, to my life.

But he could not. His first duty was to the king, not his heart. She held his gaze and with a jolt of warmth he realised they needed no words to know what the other was thinking. Their eyes said everything.

'I will come,' she said. 'Wherever you lead.' She turned her pony and kicked it into a trot behind Roger and the king.

They rode all that night, Richard so wine-addled he could barely stay in the saddle, Marc and Roger bleary-eyed with exhaustion. Soraya clasped both slim arms around her pony's neck and drooped along its withers. The burns on her wrist stung and every muscle in her body ached—her back, her shoulders, her thighs.

But she wanted to be with Marc, no matter the cost.

Venice was a disaster. Richard's horse went lame when they first entered the teeming city and he insisted on having a new mount, a fine young stallion fit for a duke.

Marc argued himself hoarse. 'You no longer look like a humble monk, sire. On such a noble horse you look like a king, badly disguised as a monk. It is dangerous.'

'All life is dangerous,' Richard thundered.

'And so,' Marc reminded him, 'winter hammers us whichever way we turn. Snow and rain slow us down. Our money runs out with our next meal. And the English king is longer incognito.'

Marc's hands tightened on the reins. And sleeping in stables, as they had for the past three nights, was dangerous for another reason. Sooner or later the sharp-eyed king of the English would guess Soraya's sex. Plantagenet men had a keen appreciation of women. More than keen—notorious.

At dusk that evening still another problem loomed. Once again Soraya caught sight of Brother Andreas playing his fiddle, this time in St. Mark's square; Marc was now certain they were being followed. He did not fear Brother Andreas himself; he feared the man, or men, Brother Andreas might speak with when he wasn't posing as a minstrel.

The next day they rode out of the beautiful city. Before they had travelled a league, a storm blew over the Alps to the north, pelting the countryside with sleet that stung their muffled faces and hail the size of small onions.

'No farther,' Richard announced when they arrived at a crossroad.

Roger eyed the king. 'Back to Venice?'

Marc bit back a laugh. Richard had spent their last denier on a skin of wine, drank most of it himself and vomited all night.

The king sent Roger a sour look. 'Don't remind me of that place. Bad wine. Cold lodgings. Undigestible food—ortolans…ugh! And…no women. How is it Venetians are so numerous if there are no women to be found?'

He rode ahead, grumbling under his breath. Marc gazed after the tall figure, his lips tight. 'This is worse than nursemaiding a bear cub,' he fumed.

Roger leaned over to poke him in the ribs. 'Does not that make you Mother Bear, my friend?' Marc gave him such a look even Soraya jerked in alarm.

'I vowed to protect him,' he growled. 'God rot his merrymaking soul, what was I thinking?'

Roger laid a gloved hand on his forearm. 'You thought of your duty, Marc. Your honour. And rightly so. We are knights. Our lives are foreordained, our days pledged in service to our liege lord.'

'I will not be a knight for much longer,' Marc replied. 'Not

Richard's man, anyway. Chances are I will spend the rest of my days keeping the Plantagenets from gobbling up the land of the Scots.'

Roger's blond eyebrows shot up. 'You would fight against Richard of England?'

Marc noticed Soraya watching him closely, her face carefully blank, her eyes darkened. 'Saladin would laugh should he hear of this,' she said. 'Fighting against Philip of France and Leopold is one thing, warring against one's own countrymen—'

'The Normans are not my countrymen,' he snapped. 'I will always fight for my home. For my own land.'

'But first,' Roger insisted with a deepening frown, 'you must keep faith with King Richard, for so you have sworn.'

'Aye, I will not betray Richard.'

'I would not take Richard lightly, my friend, even if he does make merry at every tavern we visit. We are deep in the lands of his enemies. Each day we draw closer to Austria. And Leopold.'

Marc swore under his breath. 'God willing, we will slip unnoticed across Austria, circle to the west toward Salzburg and thence journey to Zurich. Richard has kin there, on his mother's side.'

'Pray God someone steals that stallion he rides before a German knight challenges him, monk's robe or not, and Richard replies in Norman French.'

Soraya glanced up, then quickly dropped her eyes to the slushy road over which they stepped their mounts. Richard, far enough ahead that he could not be seen, could still be heard.

'Hurry up, de Valery! I am famished.'

'Oh, no,' Soraya murmured. 'Not another tavern.'

Roger trotted after the king. 'Saints help us.'

Marc gazed thoughtfully after his friend. 'The king is being foolhardy, is he not?'

'Of course, my lord.' She shook the pony's reins. 'But I would not say such words to anyone else.'

'Do not jest. Could he be recognised?'

'Do not ask, Marc. To any but a halfwit, Richard flaunts himself every hour. We will know soon enough.'

At the first hostel they came upon, Richard stopped and sniffed the air. 'Rabbit! I smell rabbit roasting on a spit.'

The king slid off his mount and marched toward the inn yard, his tattered black robe billowing out behind him.

Roger dismounted, grasped the bridles of both animals, and shot Marc an inquiring look.

'Oh, very well,' Marc muttered. 'I am hungry, too. Besides, we need grain for the horses.'

Inside the warm, noisy room, Marc ushered Soraya to a table well away from the swarm of travellers already gathering around the tall, friendly monk with a ready song.

He groaned and signaled the innkeeper. A pitcher of warmed wine appeared before them, followed by a wooden tray of roasted meat and three loaves of black bread.

'How will we pay for this?' Roger asked between mouthfuls of bread.'

'I know not, my friend. It seems we have run out of money. Let us eat first and worry anon.'

Roger chuckled and pointed a rabbit haunch toward Richard, holding court across the smoky room. 'Already he is invited to sup with the only two sober men inside these walls. Maybe he will win the wager,' he said dryly.

Marc watched a man position himself near the doorway, neither joining in the revelry nor leaving the premises. Soraya saw him, as well, and she glanced at Marc with a warning in her eyes. From the kitchen, at the back part of the large room, drifted the scent of burning meat.

'Excuse me, lord.' Soraya rose. 'Saqii and I must answer a call of nature.'

Marc shot her a look. 'Be careful,' he said in an undertone. 'Do not leave the inn yard.'

She gathered up the dog in her arms and moved toward the door. Roger busied himself with the food and wine, but Marc watched her make hand signs to the tall man blocking the doorway, saw him smile and step aside to let her pass.

She was gone for a long time. Too long. Marc stuffed down a sudden sense of unease and kept his eyes on the door. Men tramped out, and more tramped in until he thought the thick, sweat-scented air would choke him.

Enough. He rose to go after Soraya, but at that instant she dashed through the door and flew across the room to the king's side. Rising on tiptoe, she spoke in his ear. Richard's face went white as milk.

Soraya grasped Richard's wrist and frantically pulled him into the kitchen at the back. Quickly she grabbed up a dirty apron, looped it around Richard's body and tied the strings at his waist. Then she jammed a knife into his hand and guided his arm toward a cooked rabbit waiting to be carved.

The door banged open. Four bulky knights in iron helms and chain mail strode about the room peering into faces. The king turned his back to them and bent low over the carving board, pretending to slice meat off the charred rabbit.

Roger made a move toward him, but Marc grasped his arm. 'Say nothing,' he murmured. 'But be ready to fight.'

Roger sank back onto the bench and noiselessly unsheathed his short sword. Marc did the same.

Suddenly one of the mailed knights gave a hoarse cry and

pointed his dagger at the monk slicing meat in the kitchen at the back of the inn. The three others roared an answering shout and tumbled into the kitchen area.

Marc was on his feet and moving toward the king with Roger at his back when he saw Soraya smash an iron pan against the forehead of the first invading knight. Another caught her around the waist and flung her aside like a bag of barley meal.

Richard crouched, carving knife in hand, but a sword tip lodged against his Adam's apple and he let the weapon clatter to the floor. Slowly and with great dignity the king rose to his full height. His eyes blazed like blue flame, but he did not flinch under the prick of the blade at his throat.

'Richard of England!' the knight shouted.

Marc and Roger struck the man from behind, knocking him to the floor. As he fell, his sword nicked into Richard's neck.

'Stop!' Marc shouted. 'Do not kill him!' He charged to the king's exposed side and spun to face four drawn swords.

The king's voice penetrated the roaring in Marc's head. 'Do not fight,' he said in a low tone. 'For England's sake, do not fight them, for if you do, they will kill me first.'

Marc stared at his attackers, saw Roger fling himself forward and impale his blade in the first man's back.

'Stop!' the king roared.

Too late. One of the knights swung his axe at Roger, bashing through the mail legging and slicing into his thigh. Roger went down with a cry.

The same knight advanced toward the king. 'Richard of England! You are my prisoner.'

Marc drew back his sword arm to strike, but Richard reached a hand to his shoulder. 'Do not,' the king said from behind Marc. 'Instead take a message to my mother, Queen Eleanor. Tell her to raise a ransom.'

One of the knights stepped toward him, beckoning for Marc's sword.

'Surrender it, man,' the king murmured at his back. 'Unless you want to see me spitted like yon rabbit.'

Marc handed over his sword. Two men tore off Richard's grease-stained apron and bound his wrists in front of him. The third knight lay groaning on his belly, Roger's blade protruding from his back.

Roger struggled upright, managed to stand long enough to wrest his sword free, then collapsed to one knee. 'I cannot ride, Marc. I will find a physician and follow later.'

'No!' Richard's voice sharpened. 'Stay here and heal yourself, de Clare, then return to Jerusalem. Marc will travel faster alone.'

The last glimpse he had of the king was the subtle dip of his red-gold head as he passed Marc and was marched out into the night.

Chapter Twenty-Two

Soraya pressed the gold bezant into the innkeeper's meaty palm. 'For Sir Roger's care.'

Wide-eyed, the rotund man looked from the gold he clutched to the knight who lay bleeding on his floor. 'He shall have the very best.'

Marc knelt at Roger's side. 'I am sorry to leave you, my friend. I will arrange care for your horse until you can ride once more.'

Roger's lids closed. 'Go with God,' he muttered. 'And take the boy with you.'

Soraya saw Marc swallow hard. 'Aye, if Sor— If he wishes it.'

She knew then that she would travel with him to England, and that if she did, nothing would ever be the same again. Her life would change and she could never go back.

She would go on. She could not bear to leave Marc to face the dangers of such a journey alone.

'Come.' Marc took her by the elbow and propelled her to the inn door.

'Wait,' she said. 'Should we not pay for our supper?'

'Pay?' His mouth twisted. 'With what? Richard spent the last of our coins in Venice.'

'Then pay with this.' She laid four silver marks into Marc's hand.

He caught her wrist. 'Where did you get this?'

'I did not steal it.' She lifted her chin, and Marc recognised the odd mix of arrogance and honesty that had fascinated him from the moment he'd laid eyes on her.

Marc waited. 'Well, then? It is one thing to filch fruit and cheese from a market stall, quite another to steal from a man's pocket.'

Her chin went up a notch. 'I stole nothing. I sold something.'

'What?' he demanded. 'What did you sell?'

She gulped in a shuddery breath. 'I sold King Richard's horse.'

Marc gaped at her. 'You sold the king's horse,' he echoed, his tone dry. He pulled her through the doorway into the inn yard. 'You sold…?'

'You don't believe me! A pox on Frankish men for the blinders you wear. In Damascus my words would be believed. And valued. But here, in this barbarian land where women other than whores are not seen or heard, I am ignored.'

'You are not ignored.' Marc drew in a long breath. 'Would that I could ignore you!'

'And?' she prompted.

He scowled at her. 'And yes, I believe now that you sold Richard's horse. If he knew of this, he would flay you alive.'

'Perhaps. In the inn yard, a man asked about the beast, saying he would shortly need an extra mount. So I demanded three silver marks for the beast and another for the saddle.'

'Even Richard would not believe this. What did you expect him to ride, then?'

Soraya did not flinch. 'I purchased a replacement for Richard, a plain-looking mare suitable for a monk. Remember, you wanted to be rid of that stallion? You said such a fine animal drew too much attention to the king.'

'Aye, I did.'

'Therefore, I did what was needed. Only…" She looked away from him. 'There is more.'

Marc groaned. 'I have had enough surprises for one night,' he said in a weary voice. 'The king is taken. Roger lies wounded. What "more" could there be?'

Soraya stepped closer. 'The man who bought the horse was one of those knights who captured Richard. Chances are,' she said with a hint of mischief in her smile, 'wherever they take him, the king is again riding his own beloved stallion and is no wiser.'

Marc stared at her.

'So you see, while a large injustice has been committed, a small justice was accomplished, as well.'

Unable to speak, Marc mounted his horse in stony silence, then began to chuckle and then to laugh. He laughed until his belly hurt, all the way to the edge of the town and beyond into the rolling countryside.

The sun slid behind the mountain peaks in the distance and at once the air grew colder. Soraya wore the fur cloak and held Saqii's shivering body on her lap. Soon she was shivering, as well. She worked to hide her discomfort from Marc's eyes, but when she bent her knees and drew her sandaled feet up under the warm fur, he could not help but notice.

'We will rest in that abandoned hay barn ahead.'

Soraya was so chilled she could scarcely nod.

Marc sobered when he dismounted and took his first step inside the structure. The interior was dark as Hades and smelled of musty straw.

Soraya breathed raggedly beside him. 'It is nearly as cold inside as it is outside.' Her voice sounded raw and uneven.

He was careful not to look at her; he couldn't stand to see her weep. 'It cannot be helped,' he said gently. 'We are beggars, not choosers.'

He lifted off Jupiter's heavy saddle and rubbed the animal down with a handful of dry straw. The slow, repeated motions freed his mind to consider Richard's final command. Ride to Queen Eleanor. Aye, he would. If they even managed to get as far as England with winter upon them.

Soraya sank down onto the splintery floor, wrapped herself up in the fur cloak and tucked her wool-stockinged feet under Saqii's shaggy coat. 'What will we do now?' she asked in a weary voice.

'We will rest here for the night. Tomorrow…tomorrow I know not. The fastest route would be over the mountains and into Burgundy, but such travel will be difficult in winter. Besides, it leads us straight to Philip of France.'

'And therefore…?'

'If we ride farther to the east, there are other hazards, among them Leopold and his German barons. It will be difficult no matter what.'

He finished grooming his mount, discarded the straw and loosened the cinch. Then he hoisted the saddle back into place. He did the same for Soraya's small pony, working slowly and deliberately over the smooth brown hide to give himself time to think.

Days of travel would be dangerous, yes. But the nights would be worse. How could he lie next to Soraya and not touch her?

'I could—' he hesitated '—take you back to Roger at the inn. When his wound heals he could escort you back to Jerusalem.'

'Ah,' she breathed. 'Should you not ask what I wish?'

He swivelled away from the pony to face her. 'You do not know the danger. I have travelled these lands before. I know the countryside. Why should I ask you?' It came out more harshly than he intended.

She looked everywhere but at him. Minutes passed and the atmosphere between them grew so charged he could almost hear the air sing.

'It would be foolish not to give careful thought to what is facing us. And whatever else you may be, Marc, you are not a fool.'

He ran his hand over his stubbled chin. 'Would that I were. Would that I could turn my back on the king and the oath that presses me on.'

'But you cannot.'

'Aye, before God, I cannot.' He gave the pony a final pat, then went to Soraya and knelt at her side. 'I cannot turn away from you, either. There is but one course of action left.'

Under the smudges of dirt, her face went pale. 'Please, Marc. Do not send me away.'

'I must. Do you not feel what is happening between us?'

She looked up into his eyes. 'I do, yes.'

'That is why I must take you back to Roger. To Jerusalem.'

'I do not wish to return to Jerusalem,' she said, her voice unsteady. 'I want to go on. With you.'

Marc rose, grasped her shoulders and pulled her up to face him. His hands shook. 'Soraya. I do not know how to say what I must.'

Tears shone in her eyes. She pressed her fingers against his lips. 'Then do not say it.'

'I have to speak. God knows I cannot continue like this, being close to you day and night.'

'I, too, will speak. I would not leave you to do this thing

alone. You will lose precious time if you take me back to Roger. The captured English king can ill afford such a delay.'

He sent her a look so piercing her belly curled in on itself.

'You cannot remain.'

'Marc,' she said softly. 'In the spring, when you have done what you pledged King Richard, when you no longer need me, I can take ship from England.'

He gave her a little shake. 'God's teeth, what are you saying? There will never be a time when I do not need you.'

'Think, Marc. You are betrothed. You must marry when you return to Scotland. No man needs two wives, and I will never be a concubine. I must—'

'No.' He tipped his head back and shut his eyes briefly. 'I can bear wanting you and not acting on my desire. But I do not know if I could stand your leaving me.'

Her mouth twisted. 'We must not think of such things now. We must make plans to reach England. I know that you must marry elsewhere, Marc. I want to come with you as a friend. A companion, for right now that is what you need.'

Marc gazed into eyes so full of tears they glistened like two emeralds. 'I could curse God for making you a woman. You have more courage and honour than most knights save Roger de Clare and Richard Plantagenet.'

She looked away. 'Why have you resaddled your destrier?' she asked suddenly. 'And my pony, as well?'

'Because I think we are being followed. We need to be ready to leave at any moment.'

Her eyes widened. 'But…'

'Leopold's knights will not allow word of Richard's capture to reach England. I carry that word.'

She said nothing. After a moment she gathered together a pile of straw and curled up under her warm fur cloak. Marc dropped beside her, positioned his body against her spoon-fashion, and felt Saqii settle at their feet.

He lay in uneasy silence. He could smell the scent of her skin, could stir the fine hair at the back of her neck with his breath. He wrapped his arm about her waist and she snuggled her spine against his belly. His manhood swelled and began to ache, but he did not move. These few hours he would spend close to her would be agonizing, but he would remember them all his life.

'I would tell you something,' he whispered.

She nodded and lay still, waiting.

'Little by little those awful memories of Acre are fading. And my pain over my brother's untimely death eases. It is you, Soraya. You are the healing music in my heart.'

As Soraya drifted off to sleep, she thought that she would remember these words forever.

At dawn the still morning air carried the sound of hoofbeats and jingling bridles. 'Horsemen,' Soraya whispered.

'Aye. Get ready to ride.'

The noises stopped outside the barn where they hid. Marc stood quietly, tightened the cinches on both animals and mounted his horse in silence. He motioned Soraya to do the same.

Following his example, she lay as flat as she could across the pony's neck and waited, holding her breath.

The rickety barn door creaked outward. Through the gaping space Soraya saw four, maybe five roughly garbed men burst through the opening, swords drawn.

'Ride!' Marc shouted. He charged straight into the clutch of swordsmen, Soraya half a length behind him. Two men fell from their rearing mounts; the rest scattered like crows.

They outran the pursuing horsemen, rode without stopping for another hour and at last halted their spent mounts near a field of cabbage. The outer leaves were brown and shriveled with frost, but Marc dismounted, softened the soil around the plant with his eating knife and yanked up a fat head mottled with patches of grey mold.

He broke off two inner leaves, one for Soraya. It was so cold it made their teeth ache, but it was better than starving. They devoured almost half of it, stashed the rest of the head in the supply bag hanging from Marc's saddle.

As swiftly as they could they remounted and headed cross-country over the frozen fields, through olive groves and forests thick with pine and giant cypress. Marc knew Soraya was exhausted; he himself was closer to it than he would admit. Every human being on this earth had his breaking point; he wondered how close Soraya was to hers. She was brave, perhaps even foolish, to follow him halfway across the world without complaint.

They pressed on, skirting the snow-covered foothills and avoiding the clearly marked old Roman roads until they reached the town of Salzburg. Saints be praised, the sun was shining.

'A sign from God,' Marc said as they skirted the city walls.

'Part of a natural cycle,' Soraya insisted. 'All things in nature are balanced. After snow comes sun, after death comes new life.' She held up a bulb of some kind with tiny yellow-green shoots poking forth.

Marc laughed. 'You may worship a seed if you like—I pray to God for sunshine.'

She tossed her head under the fur hood. 'Nothing but sun makes a desert,' she said with an impish grin. 'God gives us some of each, heat and cool winds, in His own good time.'

'Aye,' he acknowledged. 'But I hope to climb through yon mountain pass without freezing the toes off our feet.' He pointed ahead toward two towering white peaks. 'Therefore, I pray for sun.'

Soraya stared at the forbidding landscape ahead. She was not afraid, exactly. She was too cold and hungry to feel much of anything beyond the sharp pangs in her empty belly.

She hated this land! Nothing but ice and moaning wind and too few empty barns or animal byres attached to abandoned huts for adequate shelter. The few folk they encountered stared at them dumbly, looked away without answering when spoken to, without asking if they were hungry. In Damascus, in Baghdad, even in Jerusalem under siege, the first words spoken to a stranger were always, 'Have you eaten today?' In spite of their beautiful churches and ornate palaces, the Franks were truly barbarians.

She feared she would hate Scotland, as well. She would be a stranger. A foreigner. There would be no place for her in Marc's world.

They approached the base of the snowy peak where the sun glinted off the blinding white ground. The silvery globe hung low in the sky; soon it would sink toward the tips of the highest mountains. They had no time to lose. Already eagles circled the peaks, returning to their eyries as the cold increased.

The narrow ascending path was rocky and slippery with ice. The horses plodded up the treacherous trail for hour after hellish hour until at last Marc called a halt. He motioned Soraya forward and pointed.

She stepped her pony to his side and peered down. 'Oh!' she gasped. 'It is so beautiful! Another world, all white, lives in that valley on the other side of this mountain. Look, there are tiny houses, and a church! And barns! Marc, there are lots of snug little shelters just waiting for us.'

'Suisse-land,' he announced. Switzerland.

'We are safe, then?'

'For the moment.'

All she could think about was food to fill her empty belly and how warm her toes would feel next to a hearth, and then the howl of a wolf prickled the hair on her neck.

A cloud slipped over the lowering sun, and the cold grey light grew dim. If they were caught up here, wolves would attack. And if they did not, she and Marc would surely freeze to death.

Again, the wolf howled. Closer.

Then an ominous, low rumble rolled around the mountain-side, growing louder as she scanned the steep field of snow before her. Her scalp prickled.

'Away!' Marc shouted suddenly. He plunged forward, over the crest and out of sight. She jerked her pony's reins but before she could scramble after him, she heard a sharp crack and the mountainside below her gave way.

'Marc!' she called.

A cloud of white skimmed down the steep slope before her, picked up speed and hurtled onward in a widening wall of snow. The ground under the pony's hooves shook.

'Marc!' she screamed again. 'Marc!' She screamed his name until she could no longer hear her own voice against the rumbling snow. The wall of white had gobbled him up.

The pony took a hesitant step forward. Another thin crack and the snow crumbled away under her. She yanked the reins hard to the left, but the pony sank up to its fetlocks and tried desperately to thrash its way out of the path of the tumbling ice.

Far below her, a speck of something dark shot out to one side, like an olive pit.

It wasn't an olive pit. It was a horse. And a man, tumbling over and over until both came to rest an arm's length apart on a little hillock of snow.

The stallion struggled and pawed its way up onto its feet. The man lay motionless.

'Marc!' Her cry echoed back to her. '…arc…arc…'

By the time she reached him, she was sobbing uncontrollably, the tears freezing on her cheeks. Without taking her eyes off Marc's body she slid off the pony's back and floundered through the thick white powder

He lay face up, arms spread, one leg folded under him. His skin, even his closed eyelids, were grey. She pounced on him. 'Marc! Marc, wake up!'

With hands that were numb she grabbed one shoulder and shook him as hard as she could. 'Marc! Damn you to perdition, open your eyes!' She brushed the snow off his torso, looking for wounds. He lay so still she could not believe he lived.

She scraped ice away from his forehead and mustache and abruptly he jerked.

'I am dead, am I not?' he said in an uncertain voice.

'No!' she screamed. She started to cry again.

He opened his eyes. 'Then,' he said, struggling for breath, 'you are not an angel?'

'No,' she shouted. 'I am not an angel. An angel doesn't wear a turban and a fur cloak. Marc, wake up!'

'Ah.' She heard the disappointment in his tone and suddenly she was infuriated.

'Don't you dare want an angel more than you want me!'

With a groan, he reached one arm up, cupped it behind her neck and pulled her head down until her lips touched his mouth. He kissed her with such heat and thoroughness she grew dizzy.

'Soraya,' he murmured. 'Don't give me orders.'

Her mouth was a finger's distance from his. His warm, unsteady breath smelled so sweet she wanted to sob with pleasure. 'Are you injured? Do you feel any pain?'

'Praise God I am only cold. And hungry.' He closed the small space between them with another kiss, then another, hot and demanding. His hand cradled the back of her head, pressing her mouth firmly, almost greedily onto his. Fire kindled below her belly.

When she opened her lids he was gazing at her with a puzzled expression. 'Soraya,' he whispered, closed his eyes and whispered it again. 'Soraya.'

It took them until well past dark to stumble on down the mountainside and find a deserted stone and timber byre. The crude building was almost buried beneath the snow.

Light-headed with exhaustion, they fell onto the rough wood floor and, without speaking, rolled into each other's arms. Marc pulled the fur cloak over their shivering bodies, and they slept until cockcrow.

Chapter Twenty-Three

They traveled for weeks, through Innsbruck and Zurich, then on to Besançon, Auxerre, sleeping in cow byres, forests, even caves. They hid from other riders, especially those clothed in chain mail, and turban-swathed merchants, perhaps Venetians, perhaps Arab. And monks. They knew only too well that a holy man's robes could be a disguise. They ate when and what they could.

They skirted south of Paris and two days later crossed into the Angevin duchy at Alençon, drenched with rain and spattered with mud. It seemed endless. And when they finally reached Normandy and Bayeux, it was even worse. Day after day, rain sluiced from Soraya's sodden headwrap down the back of her filthy tunic and on to drench the mud-encrusted grey wool stockings Marc had found for her.

She hated this miserable, sloppy land even more than Austria, where mountains crumbled away under her feet. Here, she had no feet; they disappeared below her ankles in puddles of brackish water or oozing slime beds.

The port town of Barfleur, with its rose tile roofs and collection of wind-beaten boats in the crescent-shaped harbor, seemed colder even than the mountains.

They had to find a ship. After travelling for weeks now they could go no farther north unless they swam across the channel. But finding a ship turned out to be more difficult than slogging through the wintry landscape.

'*Non.*' Another ruddy captain spat in Marc's face. 'Not in this weather. When it dries out, then we will see. Mayhap then I will take you across to England. To Portsmouth, you say?'

'To any place on English soil. I cannot wait long, man. I carry a message for the queen.'

'You? *Mon Dieu!* You don't look like any messenger to me. You and your lad, too. You both look like drowned water rats. Tell me another joke, *mon ami.*'

Without a word Soraya caught up Marc's supply bag and rummaged in its depths. She passed a small object wrapped in white silk into Marc's hand.

'You will believe this, I think.' He carefully unfolded the silk to reveal the king's privy seal. 'Richard the king, see there? I am sent by your duke and king of the English, Richard they call Coeur de Leon. *Compris?*'

'*Oc,*' stammered the sea captain in Provençal. 'Yes, yes. You are a crusader knight, eh? One who marched to Jerusalem with Richard? Tell me, sir, has the Holy City been taken?'

Marc ignored the question. 'I serve Richard, and I need a service from you, for your royal duke.'

'Anything,' the captain sputtered. 'Anything for Duke Richard. And for Queen Eleanor, as well. I come from Aquitaine, *compris?*'

The captain gazed across the sleepy harbour to the sea beyond, where towering green-black waves swelled in the screaming wind. 'Anything, that is, except cross the great channel in such a storm. My ship would founder. I would never see my wife and babe again. And you and your message would be lost.'

'When?' Marc demanded.

'When the wind from the north drops. I would risk my life for Richard Plantagenet, but not my ship. Not even for Richard would I be such a fool.'

Marc folded the bronze seal into its wrapping and handed it back to Soraya. 'We will wait, then. Is there an inn nearby?'

The captain pointed down a narrow street to a red-roofed structure with two floors and a generous inn yard.

Oh, to sleep on a bed. Soraya's bones ached from nights spent on wet, cold barn floors or the bare ground. Last night they had crawled into the rotted-out stump of a chestnut tree. She shut her eyes, imagined warming her numb legs by a fire and eating something that didn't taste of mold.

A boy no older than seven or eight unloaded Marc's stained supply bag and led the tired horses away to feed and shelter. Marc shouldered the hemp bag and he and Soraya stepped into the cozy, crowded inn and unobtrusively slid onto a bench at a dimly lit corner table. A blaze crackled in the kitchen fireplace and the smell of woodsmoke and something tantalizing made her mouth water. Sausage? Roasting chicken?

The serving maid sent them an inquiring look. Marc held up two fingers, and in moments she emerged from the kitchen with two wooden cups of ale, some bread and hard, white cheese, and a plate of juicy sausages to share.

'Truly,' Soraya moaned after her first bite, 'I have never tasted anything so delicious.'

They were so starved they did not speak again until the empty plate shone in the firelight and their second cups of ale were empty.

Marc swallowed the last morsel of cheese and grinned at her. 'Hunger is humbling, is it not? And now—' he signaled the serving maid again '—for a bed.'

'*Oui*, we have lodgings, *monsieur*,' she reported. 'If you will not mind sharing with five other gentlemen. One of them is sitting just over there.' She gestured toward a man seated alone at the behind Marc.

Soraya tipped her head to see past Marc and let out a gasp. 'Brother Andreas!' she whispered. 'It is Brother Andreas! He is wearing a monk's cowl, but I know that face.'

The monk sat in profile, his attention riveted on a haunch of venison he was laboriously carving with an eating knife. Her heart turned to stone. 'What should we do?' she murmured.

'Sleep,' he said quietly. 'We are half-dead from cold and fatigue. We will sleep until the sun comes out and the ship sails.' He beckoned the serving maid closer and slipped a coin into her grimy hand. 'We would be private, my squire and myself. I am expecting a visitor, a lady.'

'*Alors*, but of course.' The girl broke into a knowing smile. 'Walk up the outside stairs and turn to your right. The last chamber.'

Keeping his back toward Brother Andreas, Marc motioned for Soraya to pull the fur cloak over her head and hide her features. 'You go first.'

He gave her a little push, and she slipped through the doorway like a shadow. Marc waited three heartbeats, then gathered the last of the bread and held it up to his face as if still nibbling on it. Just as he stepped outside he shot a glance back at Brother Andreas.

The monk had not moved an inch, but still sat doggedly sawing on the venison with his knife.

Thank God for dull blades. He positioned Soraya behind

him and crept up the back stairway. Feeling his way down the dark hallway, he bumped into a latched door. It opened easily and he stepped across the threshold

The room was black as the inside of a chimney. Cautiously Marc moved about, sweeping his hands before him. Ah, a candle. And flint.

Light flared, revealing a basin half-full of scummy water and a damp washing cloth lying beside it. 'Someone has just left,' he muttered. 'Or perhaps they charge by the hour.'

Soraya said nothing.

One bed, rope-strung on a sturdy ash frame, stood against the wall. The opposite corner of the room held a ragged collection of rolled-up pallets. Marc snapped the bolt on the timbered door, then sought Soraya's hand.

'We are safe.'

'Aye,' she breathed, looking down at their interlaced fingers. 'But if that is truly Brother Andreas below, we are also trapped.'

'There is a window.' Marc motioned to one side with his head. 'Over there. If the worst happens we can escape that way.'

She shuddered. The window was on the second level, at least fifteen feet above the ground.

Raucous laughter boomed through the floor, then came the rhythmic clatter of wine cups pounding in unison on wood tables. 'The Normans are noisier even than the Austrians,' she quipped.

'And they smell sweeter,' Marc said with a grin.

She wrinkled her nose. 'Not by much.' She removed her cloak and draped it over a low chest next to the bed. 'Tomorrow,' she said, starting to unwind her turban. 'Tomorrow let us find a market. My tunic is more tattered than a ship's worn-out sail.'

Her dark curls tumbled free and he caught his breath. He

ached to touch her hair, to smooth his fingers across her skin, her bare arms.

'Tomorrow,' Marc replied, watching her hands fold the length of now-grimy silk, 'we will find a barber to cut your hair.'

'And a new tunic.' She raised her arms, pointing to the split side seam and the ripped hem.

'Yes,' he said quickly. 'A tunic.' One that better covered the swell of her breasts and closed up tight at her neck so he could not catch glimpses of the creamy flesh of her bosom and her shoulders. Such a garment would have to cover her from head to toe, like a nun.

Another outburst of merriment drifted from below. Soraya kicked off her sandals and drew the damp wool stockings off her feet. 'Let us sleep, if we can.'

She selected two pallets, unrolled one on the bed and spread the other on the floor. Marc unbuckled his sword belt, grinning at the muffled jolts heard from the inn beneath them. A lusty song rose and he winced. 'Normans,' he said in a dry voice, 'dance like elephants and sing like—'

'Camels,' Soraya finished.

He smiled, drew off his surcoat and reached for the lacings on his mail shirt.

'Do you sing, Marc?'

The question made him laugh aloud. 'Sing? Aye, after a fashion.' While he rolled up his mail, he began a tune. ''Lo, my love, come thou with me, far from the mountains, far from the sea…'

''Tis a Scots air,' he explained. 'My father, who was French, would sing it to my Scots mother when he thought no one was listening.'

Soraya could not speak over the apple-sized lump lodged in her throat. Her eyes stung and suddenly she gave a hoarse sob and covered her face with her hands. Marc stepped close and curved his arm about her shoulders.

'I sing worse than a camel, do I?' he said gently.

She nodded her head, then shook it and turned into his arms, burying her face against his shoulder. 'Not worse,' she sobbed. 'Better. Everything you do is better.'

She wound her arms about his waist. 'Marc,' she said in a muffled voice. 'What will become of me when you reach your home in Scotland?'

He grasped her trembling shoulders and leaned his cheek against her hair. 'I do not know. I know only that it is my duty to return. Among other things, I must see to my lady mother.'

Soraya lifted her head and they stared at one another. 'Remember that night on the ship from Jaffa? When I tried to kill you and you held me and…?' Her voice caught.

'Aye, I remember. Even then I felt something between us. I cannot lose you, Soraya.'

'We must…must think of tomorrow.'

'No. Not of tomorrow. We are here, together, at this moment. That is all that matters.'

His low voice faded into heavy shouts thundering from below. 'Drink! Drink! Love and be merry, for life is short.'

'We are doubly trapped,' she said, her voice trembling. 'I belong nowhere.'

Marc pulled her closer. 'Aye, mayhap. God forgive me, but I would rather die here, with you, than go on without you.' He bent to kiss her, but a pounding shook the door.

'Open in the name of the king!'

He held her a moment longer, then pressed his forehead to hers and closed his eyes. 'If this should mean my death, Soraya, flee to Queen Eleanor. You will be safe there.'

'Marc!' She clung to him. Deliberately he set her aside,

buckled on his sword belt and withdrew the blade. Facing the door, he shouted, 'Which king?'

'Philip of France!' The voice spoke in mangled Norman French.

Soraya's face drained of colour. 'Stay behind me,' Marc ordered.

'What business does the king have with a knight and his squire returning from the Holy Land?'

'You will learn soon enough. Open the door!'

'Get ready,' he said over his shoulder. Soraya crouched beside the low chest where her cloak lay and frantically rewound her turban.

Marc moved forward a single step, touched the tip of his sword to the bolt and slid it back. Feet apart, he raised his sword and waited.

A short, swarthy man in the blue and gold colors of France burst through the opening. Another man, taller but similarly clad, tramped in on his heels. At the sight of Marc's unsheathed blade, the first man halted, but the taller man behind him stumbled into him, pushing him forward onto Marc's sword. The point of the weapon nicked the chain mail the short man wore under his gaudy uniform and he sprang back. He dropped the sword he carried and it clattered across the floor.

'I would not kill an unarmed man,' Marc said. He kicked the man's sword toward him, watched him grab it up, then whipped his own blade to nudge the hollow of the Frenchman's exposed neck. 'State your business,' he snapped.

'I...' The man's black eyes hurriedly scanned the room, touched on Soraya huddled near the chest and moved on. 'Where is Richard of England?' he shouted.

'I know not,' Marc replied. 'And if I did know, I would not tell you.'

'You would protect that false enemy of France?'

'I would, and I do. Now get out before I spit you like a leg of mutton.'

The short man started to relax his stance. Marc allowed him to back away from the blade at his throat, but in that instant the taller man behind him lunged for Marc, sword drawn. Marc sidestepped and the man hurtled on past him.

For a split second Marc took his eyes off the dark man still in front of him, and in that instant his attacker threw himself forward.

Marc heard a muffled shout at his back, but before he could turn to look, his blade caught the short Frenchman at the neck. Blood welled. The man's knees buckled.

He snatched his sword back and turned to meet the second man. He swore aloud.

The sight that met his eyes made his blood congeal.

Chapter Twenty-Four

Behind him, the tall Frenchman's head was completely enshrouded in Soraya's fur cloak. Marc watched the man flail blindly with his short sword while Soraya skipped away from the slashing blade. Suddenly she whipped the cloak off the man's head and shoulders and tossed it over the tip of his weapon.

While he struggled to free his sword, she darted forward and plunged her small jeweled dagger at the base of the man's thick neck. He gurgled a scream and toppled backward.

Boots thumped down the hallway outside the chamber. After a quick look at Soraya, Marc raced to the window and sliced the translucent oiled paper out of the opening.

'Climb onto the sill,' he ordered. He then turned toward the door but waited until he heard the scrape of her body against the frame until he pivoted to face the intruders.

Four brutish-looking men in blue-and-gold surcoats stumbled over themselves as they poured into the tiny room. Marc blocked one man's blade and feinted to avoid a blow from his left.

'Soraya, jump!' he shouted.

'I cannot!' she screamed.

He feinted again. 'Don't look down. Close your eyes and roll forward.'

'I c-cannot!'

'For the love of God, why not?' He couldn't turn to look; more Frenchmen were swarming through the open door.

'Because Brother Andreas is waiting in the inn yard below!'

Brother Andreas? A dozen assailants in front of him and Brother Andreas below? What a choice.

Marc fought his way toward the window where Soraya perched. Keeping his back to her, he slashed at the advancing mob of men. Step by deliberate step he edged to where he could sense her shaking form behind him.

'Forget Brother Andreas,' he shouted over his shoulder. 'He is the least of our problems at the moment.'

'I will do as you say,' she said in an unsteady voice. 'But—'

'Just do it,' he interrupted. 'Jump. Now!'

He heard her suck in a deep breath, then heard a slight rustle, then nothing. No sound rose from below the window, not a cry, not a thump, just maddening silence.

Two men drove their bodies toward him. He swung sideways, caught the forearm of one, who crumpled in pain. The wounded man rolled into the path of the fighters behind him, slowing their advance.

God's teeth, he must do it now, make his leap to freedom. He twisted, tossed his sword out the window, and dove headfirst after it.

Soraya pushed her way out of the spiky purple bush that had cushioned her fall and ducked to escape the sword that came hurtling from above.

Brother Andreas grabbed up the weapon, and Soraya's heart stopped.

'Quick!' the monk bellowed. 'This way.'

She stared at him for a split second. His round face was scrunched up like a dried walnut shell. This way? What way?

The monk made a quick, impatient gesture toward the corner of the inn. *'Vite! Vite!'*

Just as she started toward him, Marc sailed through the air in front of her, his head tucked down into his knees. He smashed noisily into the same spreading purple bush she had. In an instant he was on his feet, facing brother Andreas, who was now armed with Marc's sword.

The monk moved forward, taking small, purposeful steps, and Marc prepared himself to dodge the first cut. But Brother Andreas halted a mere blade's length from Marc's body and for a long moment neither man moved.

Soraya sprang onto the monk's back and pressed both palms over his eyes. He shook her off like a bear shedding water, and when she hit the ground the wind whooshed out of her. Unable to move, she watched in horror as Brother Andreas moved forward one more step. He stood close enough now to slice Marc's chest with the sword.

She shut her eyes. She could not watch him die.

But she heard nothing, and after a moment she opened her lids to peek. Surely she was dreaming!

Brother Andreas was handing the sword to Marc, hilt first. The instant Marc grasped it, the monk spun away, beckoning them to follow.

They raced after him, around the corner of the inn to the yard where, to her amazement, Jupiter and her pony stood saddled and ready. Angry men swarmed down the outside stairway, a cacophony of clanking swords and thudding boots, and Soraya scrambled to mount.

Marc jammed his sword into the scabbard at his side and

pulled himself into the saddle. He was halfway out the slat inn-yard gate, miraculously standing open. She glanced over her shoulder, saw Brother Andreas, his smile so sweet he looked unearthly, position himself between the onslaught of shouting attackers and the gate.

The monk went down under their trampling feet and lay still.

They waited two whole days, hidden in a freezing cold slate-roofed windmill a dozen yards from the quay. On the morning of the third day—a Sunday, Marc surmised, because the church bell began to clang—the sun rose and burned off the fog that shrouded the harbour. The red-faced captain of the *Robin Joyeux* hoisted his sail and was just unwinding the mooring rope when Soraya and Marc appeared. Quickly they stepped the horses they had secreted in a villager's stable near the windmill onto the gangplank.

A gold coin found its way into the captain's calloused palm. He goggled at it, then smiled broadly. '*Bien*. We sail.'

Already Soraya felt queasy. She dismounted halfway up the gangplank and eyed the harbour behind here. A street vendor ambled along the quay, his wooden tray of offerings balanced in front of his belly on dingy red straps.

She stuffed the pony's lead into Marc's hand and sped down the gangplank after the man. She had spent all but one gold bezant and some silver deniers, still hidden inside the waistband of her trousers.

Her only purchase was a pouch of dried ginger root. The shabbily dressed vendor sent her a curious look. 'That is all? You wish nothing more?'

'That is all. *Shukren*.'

'May you walk with God,' he murmured.

'And may your tribe increase,' she responded automatically.

Once she was back on the ship, Marc's narrowed eyes pinned her. 'What have you stolen now?'

'I did not steal anything.' She handed him a piece of the ginger. 'For *mal de mer.*'

Marc could not hold back a chuckle. 'You did not 'borrow' it? You are losing your skill?'

'Look for yourself. The vendor is there, on the quay. He carries all kinds of—' She broke off, her eyes widening. 'That man, the vendor! He spoke to me in Arabic!'

'Ah,' Marc said with a laugh. 'I see that you are still skilled at drawing attention away from your transgressions.'

Soraya caught the sleeve of his surcoat and jerked hard. 'And you are still skilled at being impossible! Do you not understand the import of my words? He spoke to me in Arabic! How would he know to use Arabic?'

Marc's grin faded. 'Aye, I see now. He could be a spy.' He studied the vendor, who was disappearing down a narrow lane. 'Then again, perhaps he is just an Arab purveyor of ginger root.'

She doubled up her fist and smacked him in the chest with all the strength she had. For the next hour she alternately nursed the reddened imprint of chain mail links on her hand and vomited over the deck railing.

All day the ship plowed through the still-choppy sea. At dusk, Marc bundled Soraya below deck to escape the cutting wind, then sat beside her while she nibbled on the ginger root and threw up into a wooden slop bucket.

The crossing took thirteen hours, and when the craft bobbed at last into the wide, welcoming harbor at Portsmouth, Soraya could scarcely stand.

'*Pauvre petit,*' the captain murmured as they waited to disembark. 'Is the boy all right now?'

Marc nodded but continued to support Soraya's shoulders.

The captain frowned. 'The crossing, I am sorry for the…' He searched for a word, making wavy motions with his hand. 'For the up and down.'

Marc clapped the man on the back. 'A small matter, now that we stand on English soil.'

Never did he think he would be grateful for English soil. Even if it was not his Scots homeland, their safe arrival meant he was certain to fulfill Richard's royal charge.

And England, for the moment, meant safety. God knew he hadn't drawn an unworried breath since they first made landfall in Italy.

Since before Acre. He watched Soraya pacing on deck, her arms folded tight over her stomach, her head tilted up. He knew she was still queasy from the rolling of the ship, but, as usual, she was putting up a brave front.

The Lord had blessed his journey with Soraya's presence. She took the sting out of their privation. And more. She had lightened his black grief over Henry's death at Ascalon. Marc shook his head in half disbelief. Even crouched in hiding, cold and hungry, wearing filthy, lice-ridden garments, just being with her warmed his soul.

And heated his blood to molten desire. Soraya was unique among women; he knew now that he could no longer deny that he loved her.

When the horses were unloaded and led down the wood ramp, she met him at the bottom of the gangplank. 'Just look!' She pointed toward the land that sloped up from the sea. 'How beautiful and green everything is! Everywhere you turn, green trees, green hills, even green flowers.'

'That is not a flower,' he said, laughing. 'That is a signpost, painted green.'

At the first crossroads, Marc dismounted to read Soraya's green 'flower.' Winchester. The arrow pointed north.

'A half-day ride,' Marc said with a grin. 'We should arrive at Queen Eleanor's court by suppertime.'

Queen Eleanor's court. For the first time in a week, Soraya's heart crawled into her throat. The queen of the English would likely think she was a common servant. Or worse.

Chapter Twenty-Five

They rode cautiously, Marc in the lead on Jupiter, a ghostly grey shadow which Soraya followed with her gaze focused on the paving stones under her pony's hooves. A thin sliver of a moon hung in the darkening sky.

Such straight, wide roads the Normans used. As did the Frankish lands, even Austria. Remnants of the old Roman empire, she supposed. She had seen such roads in Syria, as well. Every land the Romans had conquered, they had criss-crossed with routes designed for fast movement of foot soldiers and supply carts.

She preferred the narrow, twisting streets of great cities, Damascus and Constantinople. Byzantine cities. Would she never see the massive churches and exquisite mosaic-tiled mosques again? Part of her was sick with longing for her sun-drenched homeland.

Now she allowed the question that had nibbled at her ever since sailing away from Jaffa to Cyprus and now to England: Where did she belong?

And who was she? Was she still Khalil's adopted niece, now that her beloved uncle no longer lived? Was she still a spy for Saladin, even though she was far from Jerusalem, far from the undercurrents and power struggles of siege and chicanery and warfare?

Who, then? She could not help glancing down at the threadbare tunic she wore, the torn and ragged trousers of once-fine linen. She looked like the poorest orphan. No longer graceful. Not clean. Not even female. She was lost, even to herself.

And Marc's betrothed awaited him in Scotland.

The road swerved west, following the river. In the deepening twilight the water was silvery blue with green shadows moving beneath the surface. One shiny, sleek trout arched into the air and landed with a soft splash.

Dark trees with rounded shapes grew along the banks, so thick they blocked the gold flush of the sun dipping behind the topmost branches. Not olive trees, but... She peered closer at the thickets of undergrowth. Could someone be following them?

'Marc?'

He pulled up his mount and waited. "Tis not far, Soraya. A few leagues and we will be warm and safe in Eleanor's court."

Her stomach grumbled. 'And fed, I hope.'

'Of that I am certain. The queen is known to be generous to Richard's loyal servants.'

The queen. She had never laid eyes on a queen, not a real one, a queen in her own right. Byzantine royalty often married commoners, once even a prostitute, though the woman was said to be quite beautiful. Saladin's women were never seen. Even the name of his favourite was unknown outside palace walls.

A growing dread weighted her belly, as if her insides were turning to stone. What would the great Eleanor of Aquitaine see when she laid her royal gaze upon one such as herself, a ragged, filthy intruder in a foreign land?

A shudder racked up her spine as if a lance were grating over each bone.

'Do not lag, Soraya. Stay close behind me.'

She obeyed without protest. She *wanted* to stay close to him. He was the only thing she knew and understood in this strange land.

More than that. God help her, she would always want to be close to him.

The towering castle at Winchester was constructed of dressed grey stone. Light glittered from myriad windows on upper levels, as if the inhabitants enjoyed a surfeit of fire hearths and gloried in the burning of candles. Her heart skipped at the thought of warmth.

A wooden barricade surrounded by a deep ditch of oily-looking water barred their access. They clopped across the narrow moat bridge and Marc demanded entrance at the west gate, then ushered Soraya through the reluctantly raised portcullis at the outer bailey, past a grumbling guard who cast them dark looks of suspicion. Stiff with fatigue and fright, she did her best to ignore him.

In the inner courtyard, a muttering groom led away their mounts, and another lad, a sleepy-eyed page dressed in a wrinkled green tunic, led the way into the great hall.

Soraya stopped short. The ceiling soared over her head. Fires crackled and snapped at two massive hearths, one at each end of the huge room. Tapestries and thick, multipatterned carpets covered all the walls but one, and on that hung a huge, round wooden table, fixed just below a triple-paned glass window.

A guard intercepted them, blocking their way with his lance.

'I must see the queen,' Marc announced.

The burly man glanced up and down at Marc's grimy surcoat. 'The queen has retired. Who are you to demand audience?'

'I am Marc de Valery.'

Instantly the lance was lowered. 'Ah, yes. The Scot.' The man sniffed and surveyed Marc's worn leather sword belt and the rusty mail sleeves that showed under his ragged surcoat. 'I thought as much.'

Soraya shrank inside her tunic, painfully aware of her travel-stained garments, her dirty, wind-chapped cheeks, her grubby hands and broken fingernails. If only she could arrange her head wrap to hide her face!

'There is a rank smell about you, Sir Marc. Before you see Her Majesty, perhaps you would like to—'

'I bring an urgent message for the queen. A matter of life and death.'

'To be sure, to be sure. Still—'

'Come on, man, take me to Eleanor! I have news of the king.'

The man turned white and spun on one leather boot. 'Wait here.'

They waited. Soraya's palms began to sweat. She glanced around the deserted hall, then wiped them on the front of her tunic.

A rustling sound drifted near, and then a commanding voice broke the quiet. 'King? Which king? That whelp Philip of France, or that slippery scamp of a son, John, who fancies himself king?'

A tall, regal figure swept forward to confront Marc. Dressed in a scarlet velvet gown with fingertip-length gold-lined sleeves and a braided girdle, Great Eleanor descended on them like an imperious whirlwind. Her face, framed in a gracefully draped wimple of soft gold linen, betrayed nothing.

Marc dropped to one knee. 'Your son, Majesty. Richard Plantagenet.'

Eleanor's intense blue eyes widened for an instant, but her pale, elegantly boned face showed no emotion. 'My son,' she said, her tone matter of fact, 'is on crusade. In Jerusalem.'

At her gesture, Marc rose. 'He is not, madam. He is taken prisoner near Vienna.'

Eleanor did not respond. Instead, she turned to Soraya. 'I advise you, de Valery, to teach your squire better manners. You are to kneel before the queen, boy.'

Soraya fell to her knees and bowed her head, but she glimpsed the queen's face for a single unguarded moment; sheer anguish burned in her piercing eyes. The queen had used the reprimand as a diversion, to hide her emotion. The woman was clever. Controlled. She had eyes like a hawk, Soraya thought. Eleanor missed nothing.

Of course. The woman was the queen of England. Power and majesty radiated from her very fingertips. Soraya was drawn to her as a moth is drawn to light. And, for some reason she could not fathom, Soraya liked the queen.

'There is more, Your Grace,' Marc said in a quiet voice.

'What more?' Eleanor demanded. 'Did you see my son taken in Austria?'

'Aye, Madam. Five German knights accosted us at an inn.'

'I tried to disguise him as a cook turning meat on a spit,' Soraya blurted. 'But—'

'A cook!' The queen turned on her. Soraya shrank away and covered her face with her hands. What had she done?

But Eleanor began to laugh. Her face turned rosy, and she laughed until she had to hold her side with one bejewelled hand.

'A cook,' she said, wiping her eyes. 'Turning a spit…I do admire your quick thinking.' At once she sobered. 'My son would not be silent at such a time. What message then does he send me?'

Marc nodded. 'He bids you raise his ransom.'

Eleanor surveyed him with eyes like two hard blue stones. 'And so I shall,' she said, her voice glacial. 'God rot the Duke of Austria. Leopold will pay for this.'

She motioned impatiently to Soraya, still on her knees. 'Oh, get up! Get up! There is much to—'

Soraya stood as she was bid, but the queen stopped mid-sentence. 'Well, well.' She flicked a glance at Marc, then returned her penetrating eyes to study Soraya. Her queenly gaze probed Soraya's face, then the torn tunic, moved down to her trouser hem, back up to her turban.

'My goodness,' she snapped. 'I can scarce believe it.' Her masklike visage cracked into a smile that grew wider and wider as her eyes sparkled with amusement. 'What better to take my mind off my burdens than…a clever puzzle to unravel,' she murmured, tilting her head. She nodded decisively. 'I am fond of puzzles.'

Soraya's nerves tightened under Eleanor's perusal. She wished she had never entered the great hall in the first place, wished she had gone to the stable, with the horses.

The queen raised her voice. 'William Marshal!'

A man-at-arms stationed at the far door called out the name, and echoes reverberated and finally faded into a pregnant silence.

They waited. In a few minutes, a burly man with sharp dark eyes and a watchful look about him entered and strode straight to the queen, bowed and reached his hand to hers. Eleanor began to speak before he had brought the royal fingertips to his lips.

The queen's voice dropped to a conspiratorial murmur, and Soraya caught only an occasional word. '…Leopold… ransom….'

'And,' Eleanor added as the earl stepped away, 'see that this knight and his…squire have food and lodging.'

Marshal said nothing, just nodded, pivoted on one heel and strode out the door he had entered. The queen stood for a long moment looking after him, a satisfied smile on her lips. 'Tomorrow,' she began, 'we will see to baths and fresh garments for you both.'

At the mention of a bath, Marc's weary, lined face relaxed. 'Thank you, Your Grace. 'Tis kind of you.'

'Nonsense! The Feast of Twelfth Night is tomorrow eve. I should not appreciate two such—' she looked them over, her sharp eyes twinkling '—dilapidated diners at my table.'

A laugh bubbled out of Soraya's throat.

Eleanor pinned her with a steely gaze. 'What is your name, child?'

'Soray, Your Majesty.'

The queen pursed her lips. 'Very well, Soray. I will send for you in the morning, after you break your fast.' Without a backward glance, Eleanor swept out in a swirl of scarlet velvet. Marc and Soraya stared at each other.

A page came to escort them to a cozy chamber high in a castle turret, where they ate their fill of cold meat and warm, spiced wine and with grateful sighs fell, fully clothed, onto the large blue-curtained bed.

'What would the queen want with me?' she whispered.

'I know not, Soraya,' he replied in a drowsy, contented voice. He drew her close, laid his arm across her waist as he had each night since Richard's capture in Austria. 'Go to sleep.'

'Perhaps she intends to instruct me in court manners? So I will not embarrass her at the great feast?'

'Aye, possibly. You must remember not to "borrow" a wine goblet or a salt cellar,' he said with a chuckle.

'Or a roast chicken or a fruit tart, which would be more to my liking.'

'Exactly so,' he mumbled in a weary voice.

She would make him proud, Soraya thought.

Still she could not erase from her mind the amused expression on the queen's face, or the pleased but crafty look in those penetrating blue eyes.

Chapter Twenty-Six

'Come, come!' Queen Eleanor tutted, propping her elegant, veined hands on her hips. 'Do not take me for a fool, child. You rode all the way from Jerusalem, why do you hesitate at a bath, which takes no bravery at all?'

Soraya studied the queen, so beautiful in the flowing gown of sky-blue damask it was hard to notice anything else in the sumptuous apartment. 'But it does take bravery, Your Majesty. You will understand when I disrobe.'

'Then do so,' Eleanor said with undisguised relish. 'Surprise me, if you can.'

Soraya looked everywhere but at the queen. The entire chamber blazed with light from tall windows of intricately paned glass, and banners of scarlet and gold hung from the walls. Plantagenet colors. The lions reminded Soraya of Richard, crowned with red-gold hair and capable of unreasoning fury. She could certainly see where he inherited that trait. She expected an outburst of Eleanor's anger at any moment.

She unwrapped her turban and stripped off her gathered trousers. Last she shrugged out of the dirty tunic and began to unbind her breasts.

'Goodness,' one of the serving maids gasped.

'Quiet, Margit,' the queen barked.

Soraya clasped her arms over her naked chest. Grey-haired Margit gave a little squeak and clapped a hand over her mouth.

Eleanor smiled, her eyes sparkling with enjoyment, snapped her fingers and pointed to the copper bath tub.

Soraya stared at the warm, inviting water with sudden misgivings. Was not Eleanor surprised at her sex? Except for flashes of amusement in the dark blue eyes, the queen's face wore its usual imperturbable expression, and Soraya wondered what lay behind it. Did nothing surprise Great Eleanor?

She lifted one leg and stepped into the tub. The warm water lapped deliciously against her calf. She plunged her other leg into the tub and splashed down into a sitting position.

Instantly a bucket of water emptied onto her head.

'Margit! Bette! Do not drown the child, simply wash away the grime!'

The two maidservants huffed and fluttered over Soraya with scrub cloth and perfumed soap, cleansing away weeks, or rather months, of…well…boyhood. Soraya pressed her forehead against her knees to hide her smile. She didn't care that Eleanor was not surprised; what mattered more at this moment was the exquisite feel of silk-smooth soap perfumed with roses on her bare skin.

Perhaps the English were not as barbarian as the Franks. At least their queen appreciated the finer offerings of a civilised culture. Indeed, Soraya could see how the queen could exploit such assets to her advantage—rich red wine offered to travellers and merchants would open their pouches of silver coins for Richard's ransom. The delicate, sheer face powder Eleanor wore, together with those sculpted cheekbones, would beguile the most penny-pinching bishop or abbot, regardless of their vows of chastity.

How Uncle Khalil would have admired this woman!

Scrubbed until her flesh glowed, her hair rinsed in water perfumed with orange blossoms, Soraya emerged from the bathtub to meet Eleanor's calculating look.

'Bette, the wardrobe chest. The large one.'

It took both round, dimpled Bette and the older Margit to drag the carved wood chest from an adjoining room and position it next to the polished silver mirror on its bronze stand. Bette flipped the lid clasp and lifted up the top.

'Now,' the queen murmured, 'let me think.'

'Your Majesty,' Soraya ventured. "Are you not distressed at discovering de Valery's "squire" is…me?'

The queen studied her with narrowing eyes. 'De Valery's squire.' Suddenly she laughed. 'I am not blind, child. And I do like a clever girl. Did you think I could not tell male from female at a single glance?'

The queen did not wait for an answer. 'Who are you, then, since you are obviously *not* a squire?'

'My name is Soraya al-Din. I grew up in Damascus, but my mother and father were Circassian. I was educated in a sultan's harem, though I was allowed to worship in the Greek church.'

'Do you ride, Soraya of Damascus?'

'Aye, madam, I do.'

'Astride?' Eleanor demanded. 'In skirts?'

'I do.'

'Good,' the queen snapped. 'I cannot abide those simpering ladies who cannot control their mounts with their knees.'

Margit lifted a pale rose wool pelice from the chest and held it up to Soraya's shivering body.

'Too insipid,' Eleanor said. 'The girl is cold, Bette. Put a shift on her.'

The younger maid dropped a soft linen garment over Soraya's head and settled it over her hips to brush her bare toes. Margit brought another gown from the pile of clothing in the chest, this time a yellow silk with wide, overlong sleeves lined in cream sarsenet.

'Too floppy,' Eleanor pronounced. 'The girl is slim. And such breasts! And all this time you kept them wrapped up, like a squashed sweetmeat?'

'I had to. I had to pretend.'

Eleanor's voice softened. 'So you did, under the circumstances. Come, Soraya of Damascus, I say we shall be friends.' She cast a look at old Margit's spine, hunched with age. 'I crave youth around me. And intelligence.'

Bette stepped forward with an armload of garments, crimson, gold, and such deep blues!

Eleanor pointed. 'The emerald silk. Perfect.'

The servant held the dress up to Soraya and rotated her toward the queen. Eleanor smiled. 'You are quite lovely, my girl. Perhaps I should adopt you. I have too many sons, all greedy and quarrelsome.'

'Not King Richard,' Soraya murmured. Eleanor did not hear.

'Now that your knight, de Valery, has delivered the king's message, do you travel to Scotland with him?'

The question caught Soraya off guard. Did she? She would not be accepted as a female stranger or a disguised squire. She would never belong in Marc's world. They had no future together.

'I think not, madam.'

Eleanor's thin, arched eyebrows shot up. 'Why not?'

Soraya stepped into the silk gown Bette held for her, slid

it up over her shoulders and turned so the serving maid's quick fingers could lace it up the back.

'Because, madam, Sir Marc is already betrothed. Her name is Jehanne of Chambois, and he is to marry her upon his return.'

'Do you think to give him up, child? Are all Circassians such fools? My dear, when I first fell in love with my Henry, I was married—married!—to Louis of France. It mattered not.'

She sighed and looked away. 'Later, of course, when our cubs grew unruly, Henry locked me away. For sixteen long years I was alone.'

Soraya caught her breath but did not speak. What could she say to a woman who had borne all that God and the devil could inflict? 'Why would King Henry do such a heinous thing?'

Eleanor apparently guessed the question. 'Love is very close to hate, you see. Poor Henry. He could never distinguish one from the other.'

Soraya lifted her arms for Margit to adjust the low neckline of the beautiful green gown. Not since her years in the harem had she felt such fine fabric against her skin. And that was…six summers past. After so many years wearing loose trousers and tunics, she wondered at her pleasure in wearing the elegant green silk gown.

'My situation is different, Your Majesty. Sir Marc does not take his duty lightly. He will do what he must.'

Eleanor's head jerked up. 'Are you suggesting my Henry did not? A king's first duty is to his kingdom. Henry did what he had to in order to preserve it.'

'And a Scottish laird's duty is to his lands and his people. The death of Sir Marc's brother at Ascalon left the Rossmorven estate in Marc's hands.'

'Admirable indeed,' Eleanor said.

Soraya swallowed hard and looked the queen in the eye. 'I am trying to...I must accept what must be.'

'Must you, now?' Eleanor said, her voice gentle, almost teasing. '*Alors*, Soraya of Damascus, we shall see.'

Eleanor's commanding voice rang above the noise of the great hall, where linen-swathed trestle tables seated a hundred or more guests—knights and their ladies, bishops, earls and dukes.

'I would ask something from all of you here assembled.' Poised halfway down the stone staircase, wearing a flame red wool gown with the Plantagenet lions embroidered in gold thread about the hem, she was an impressive vision. A queen to her fingertips. A modest gold crown rested atop her carefully draped head veil.

Looking neither left nor right, the queen advanced down the steps. 'Tonight we celebrate Twelfth Night, as you know. In keeping with the tradition of giving gifts on this eve, I require from each of you two things: first, a prayer to God for my son, King Richard, who languishes in a German prison....'

A collective gasp traveled over the assembled company, then dead silence. 'Your king needs your prayers. But more than that, your king needs your silver, for he cannot return to England until his ransom is paid. One hundred thousand marks.'

Another gasp, this time of outrage. But whether because of the monstrous amount or because imprisonment of a king was unheard of, Marc did not know. Clever woman, Eleanor. She had entered the hall last, after all the guests were seated, moving like a regal crimson swan. Wherever her eye fell, her presence was immediately acknowledged with a respectfully bowed head.

Marc, seated at the high table next to William Marshal, at

the queen's right, with Soraya next to him on the other side, watched the queen progress slowly among her subjects, followed by a tall knight carrying what looked to be a wooden wash tub. Coins clinked into the vessel as Eleanor passed; coins and bracelets, silver necklaces, even silver-handled eating knives. 'For Richard,' men murmured as the collection tub made the rounds.

No one could refuse Great Eleanor, and well she knew it. Marc dropped in his last silver denier and prayed Soraya would refrain from donating the small jewelled dagger she always wore at her waist.

Come to that, where *was* Soraya? The place beside him intended for her was still empty. He reached for his wine cup and scanned the hall. He choked on his first swallow.

Trailing in Eleanor's wake floated the most breathtakingly beautiful woman he had ever seen. As she drew near, Marc stood up, as did every other man at the table. God in heaven, she was transformed!

The folds of her green silk gown swept the floor as she moved, a gown that reminded him, with a sharp blow to his midsection, that she was a squire no longer, but a woman. An exquisite woman, with flawless skin the color of rich cream, a narrow waist girdled with gold links, and breasts that swelled at the gown's low neckline. Breasts that made his mouth go dry.

Queen Eleanor's route brought her to the high-backed chair of honour, but instead of taking her seat, she raised her hand for quiet. 'I present to you a newcomer to this court, Soraya of Damascus.' The queen nodded once at Soraya, sent her a dazzling smile, and settled into her cushioned chair.

Soraya took her place beside Marc. He couldn't speak a word for the fullness in his throat. He could scarcely believe what his eyes told him. His Soraya had bloomed into an extraordinary flower.

No, not *his* Soraya. He grabbed up his wine goblet and gulped down three quick swallows. *His* Soraya was slim and straight as a reed, her face dirty, her green eyes dull with fatigue, with an annoying stubborn streak and a laugh that warmed his soul.

What had happened to *that* Soraya?

He leaned close to her ear, breathed in her scent of cinnamon and oranges. Her thick, dark hair, curled softly about her face, shone like black satin.

'So that is why the queen summoned you,' he whispered. 'To turn you into a *peixit*.'

'A what?'

'A *peixit*. A Scottish faerie, or a pixie, if you will.' A queen, he wanted to say.

'I think Queen Eleanor is a master at manipulation,' Soraya said under her breath. 'She used me as a diversion, to take the sting out of the one hundred thousand marks for ransom for King Richard.'

Marc stared at her. 'Did you like being a diversion?'

She gave him a smile that stopped his heart. 'I like being female once more, yes.'

He breathed in her spicy-sweet scent. 'I miss Soray, just a little.'

She shot him that smile again; he felt its warmth all the way to his toes. 'You are joking, of course.'

'I am not joking.'

She sent him an amused look. 'And,' she added, 'you are lying. Again.'

'I am not lying. We were close, Soray and I. We suffered the same privations, froze in the same snow, ate the same food. Slept in the same…' His voice halted.

'We cannot do so now,' she murmured. 'I am no longer your squire. In truth, I do not know who I am.'

'I have lost you, then?'

'Say instead that you must set me aside, Marc.'

He caught her hand under the table. 'I cannot.'

A band of minstrels and dancers spilled into the hall, singing and hooting like a chorus of geese. 'Hail to the Lord of Misrule, And to his good consort, too. We come uninvited, To please those beknighted, And all lords and ladies…for Yule.'

The guests groaned at the bad verse, but began banging their wine cups on the table in welcome. The troupe marched about the hall in high spirits, playing shawms and lutes, fiddles and nakers. After Eleanor's sombre plea for silver to save King Richard, the minstrels' revelry was received with cheers.

The queen signaled her approval with an imperiously raised hand, and the raucous merriment was unleashed.

Except for Marc and Soraya, who sat unmoving as two stone statues, gazing into each other's eyes. Soraya bent her head toward him. 'What are we to do?' she murmured under the roar of the players.

A stricken look came over Marc's face. 'I cannot give you up,' he said softly. 'I know not what to do, but I cannot lose you.'

'Marc,' she whispered. 'What if…' She jerked upright as one of the musicians shoved his lute in front of her.

'By order of Queen Eleanor, Soraya of Damascus is commanded to play.'

Marc shoved the man aside. 'Be off, man. The lady has no skill on this instrument.' He started to hand it back, but with a sniff, Soraya lifted it out of his fingers.

'Think you I am not educated in the arts?' she asked him. She slid from her place and perched on the raised dais, cradling the lute in her left hand. She struck a chord and the noise dropped to nothing.

She sang in Arabic, a haunting melody with a refrain quickly picked up by the guests. Between verses, she improvised countermelodies and subtle embellishments, holding Marc's gaze for an instant before she started the next verse.

In his grey eyes she saw surprise. Fascination. Adoration. And finally resignation. She knew it could never be, and she put her aching heart into the song, a maiden's farewell to her lover.

When she reached the end of the song, shouts and clapping rose from the packed hall, but she could not look up. Not until she blinked back the tears stinging under her lids.

Chapter Twenty-Seven

Soraya handed the lute back to the goggle-eyed minstrel. 'Well done, my lady,' the young man intoned. She glanced up at him, but her attention was caught by a figure standing in the shadows at the far wall, a plump man with a face as round and shiny as a gold coin. He looked back at Soraya, nodded once, and tucked his fiddle under his chin.

She caught her breath. Brother Andreas! He was alive! One of his eyes was bruised purple-black, but she would recognise him anywhere. She thought he had died helping them escape in Barfleur.

What was he doing here at Queen Eleanor's court?

He began a tune with a spirited rhythm and a soaring melody, played against a single drone note. A dance, she surmised. Without a break in his music, the fiddler began circling the hall, increasing the tempo until guests gathered in the center to form a double circle. The women moved in one direction, facing out; men circled in the opposite direction, facing the women.

''Tis a carole,' Marc said in her ear. 'You move opposite your partner until you meet again and...'

'And?'

Most couples kissed at that point, but he did not want to tell her that. In truth he did not want to dance with her, fearing he would never be able to let her go at the end.

'Do you see Brother Andreas?' she murmured.

'Aye. Brother Andreas is a spy for Eleanor.'

Her eyes widened into two clear green pools. 'A spy! How do you know?'

Marc laughed softly. 'I confronted William Marshal, and he admitted it, after a time. Marshal is the Earl of Pembroke and a renowned warrior. He forgave my rude questions and spared my honour, but he could just as easily have struck me dead.'

Perhaps the earl *should* have killed him. His body was in torment. He ached to fold Soraya into his arms, kiss her, make love to her. Without her, his soul was parched. He turned to face her, studied her face. Was she feeling it, as well?

She seemed lit up from within, her eyes glowing, her hands never still, moving from the neck of her gown to her hair, her girdle. He had never seen her so on edge. He could not begin to guess what she was thinking.

'All this—' she flung her arm over the crowded hall '—is too much for me to grasp. Perhaps I have fallen asleep and this is just a strange and beautiful dream?'

Marc touched her hand. 'Before you wake, come dance the carole with me.'

Their eyes met. 'With pleasure.'

She did not drop her gaze until they joined the circle, matching palms as the other dancers did, and began to move opposite each other. During the slow, dignified steps, the dancers stopped and touched hands with the new partner facing them, then moved on until the original partners met again and paused in greeting.

Marc found his hands shaking as he moved in the intricate pattern, waiting for the circle to revolve completely so Soraya would once again stand opposite him. How he ached to press his mouth to hers.

When they met again, Soraya leaned toward him. 'I—I scarcely know how to say what I wish to say.' Her cheeks flushed deep rose.

Her words sent a flame into his groin. 'And what is that?' They stepped away from each other, then back in the same pattern.

'I like being close to you,' she murmured. 'I like dancing with you. T-touching you.'

Marc could not breathe. 'For that you must wait,' he said. The carole ended and he walked her toward the shadows at the back of the hall. He ached to kiss her. But when they reached the hearth fire, they had to halt for five young pages who staggered past them carrying trays loaded with roasted venison and chicken, bowls of flavored puddings and loaves of fine-grained bread.

'Are you hungry?' Marc asked.

'I am not,' Soraya confessed.

''Tis strange, is it not? After all these weeks of near starvation, the glut of dishes in this hall does not interest me.'

'We will be hungry before morning. I should fill my pockets—oh! I forgot, I have no pockets! Only this silk purse on my girdle.'

Marc glanced at the golden links encircling her slender waist. 'Later perhaps we might "borrow" the wash tub now collecting coins.'

'Too obvious,' she replied in an undertone. 'The art in "borrowing" is to take little and hide it well.'

'Aye,' he said, grinning. 'I will think on that.'

The musicians started a new dance, the rhythm slow, the shawms giving way to lute and fiddle. Marc led her forward and without saying a word turned her to face him. He curved his hands at her waist, as the other dancers were doing.

'Lift your arms and touch my shoulders,' he murmured.

Her fingers burned his flesh through surcoat and tunic. The blood began to pound in his head. He wanted to do more than touch her. More than kiss her. He wanted to lie with her.

He looked into her face and was stunned to find her eyes held an unspoken yearning. In that instant he knew she wanted it, as well.

My God, they were man and woman, and they were in love with each other!

He kept his hands at her waist. She kept hers on his shoulders, and only their hands kept them apart from each other. The enforced separation honed their awareness, made him sharply conscious of the heat between their bodies, the longing he now knew Soraya was feeling as desperately as he was.

What aching temptation this simple bransle created! The distance between them, no more than two hand spans, sizzled with an odd, dark excitement he had never felt before.

'Soraya,' he breathed. 'Tomorrow I must ride for Scotland.'

'I know,' she said quietly. 'I can see it in your eyes.'

'I know the queen invites you to sleep in the dormer with her other ladies. That is a great honour.'

'I do not care about such an honour.'

'Eleanor wants you to remain here, with her, does she not?'

Soraya nodded. 'She does. She says I make her laugh.'

'Do not sleep with the women,' he said. 'Tonight I want you to be with me.'

'You are bold, Marc.' Her voice was so soft he thought he dreamed it.

'Aye, I am that. But this may be all we will ever have of each other. Let us take it. Let us know joy with each other.'

'Yes,' she whispered. 'And may tomorrow take a thousand years in coming.'

The revelry of Twelfth Night grew louder, the games and bawdy pantomimes more rowdy as the minutes passed, culminating in presentation of the King's Cake and a drunken selection of the Lord of Misrule. Marc paid no attention, not even when Brother Andreas shouted with childlike delight at being chosen king, and the short, rosy maidservant Bette his queen.

Marc focused his gaze on his dazzling Soraya, moving like a breath of heaven at his side. As if by prior signal, they stepped away from the dance at the same instant, and without speaking moved to the dim area at the back of the great hall. No one paid them any notice.

Attention was focused on the high table, where Brother Andreas now sat in Eleanor's place, and dinner guests fought over trays of miniature fruited cakes soaked in brandy. Laughter rose until it drowned out the musicians and the jugglers. Marc held out his hand to Soraya and uttered a single word.

'Come.'

They mounted the three flights of stairs, climbing up and up until the sounds of merrymaking gradually faded into silence. The only light came from a single wall sconce, which Marc lifted away from its holder and held aloft. There were no servants, no guards, no squires; all were below.

The total quiet felt magical, as if every earthly activity had come to a halt but for the soft, irregular breathing of a man and a woman, and the beating of two hearts.

Marc placed the candle in the sconce at the third-floor landing and lifted Soraya into his arms. His chamber was the last one on this passageway. He kneed open the heavy oak door and stepped inside to total darkness.

'There is a hearth, but no fire is laid. I did not think to need one.'

'We do not. Your arms are warm.'

He steadied her feet on the plank floor, then moved to the door and shoved the wooden bar closed. Kneeling at the small hearth, he scrabbled in the wood box beside it.

'What are you doing?' Soraya said.

'Building a fire. We are wine-warmed now, but that won't last the night.'

When the flames licked against the stone fireplace, Marc rose and came to her. His mouth on hers made her light-headed with joy, and as his lips grew more demanding she felt as if she were a bird, floating over the floor beneath her feet. His tongue touched her earlobe, dipped into the shell and a wash of desire flooded her. His tongue was… His mouth was…

It was all mad ecstasy. If it went on much longer she would scream she wanted him so much. How she wanted her bare skin against his.

He lifted his head. 'Take off your gown.' His fingers fumbled with the lacing at the back, and then she felt a breath of cool air on her heated flesh. She shivered when he pulled the voluminous sleeves away from her arms and shoulders, then shuddered with pleasure as his hand dipped below the neckline of her shift.

'Yes,' she whispered. 'Yes, touch me.' She raised her arms above her head, writhed in an ecstasy of anticipation. 'Touch me all over.'

Her shift whooshed off over her head, and then his hands were on her breasts, her throat, her belly and below. She arched to meet the finger he slipped into her, remembering she was untouched, thinking what a glorious feeling he could create with something so simple, his finger inside her. He moved deeper and she began to moan. At first the sound startled her, but when she realized it was her own voice she heard she smiled and rocked with his motion. What he was doing felt magical!

'Soraya.' His voice was low and thick. His breath against her nipple made her float out of herself.

'Take off your tunic,' she demanded. 'And your chausses, and your…'

'No.' He breathed hard for a moment. 'I cannot touch you and undress at the same time.'

Without answering, Soraya slid off his surcoat and drew his tunic over his head. Just as his hand found her again, she loosened his chausses and dropped to her knees to slide them off. When his male member appeared she leaned forward and touched it.

He sucked in air. When she moved her hand he breathed in more roughly. She liked it, that she could affect him so. Before she knew what was happening he rose to his feet, grasped her shoulders and sidestepped out of his undergarment. Then he pressed her backward onto the soft, lavender-scented counterpane. She stretched deliciously, feeling smooth silk against her naked skin, and then Marc spread her thighs apart and dipped his head to taste her.

She cried out, and did so again when he began to explore her with his tongue. It was soft and then rough and raspy, and then hard. Determined. She could do nothing but give herself up to it, let him suck and lick and bite and, oh! The feel of his mouth, of him.

He rose over her, pressed hard at her entrance, pushing into her as he cried her name. A sharp sting of pain bit at her deep inside, and his mouth covered her cry.

He began to move inside her, in, out, then in again. Slowly.

Then even more slowly. Something was happening to her, building in her. She clenched her hands, unclenched them, buried her fingers in his dark hair. Her mouth burned. She opened her lips, ran her tongue over them and listened to his breathing begin to match hers. It was so exquisite.

'Marc,' she whispered.

An explosion of wrenching delight lifted her up, out of herself, and she pulsed and clutched and screamed as wave upon wave of ecstasy bore her away.

'Soraya,' Marc groaned. Then he shouted her name once more. 'Soraya!'

When she could hear again, she realised he was saying something over and over. 'I love you. I love you.'

Of course. She knew that they loved each other. No man could make her feel such wondrous things without love.

'I know,' she murmured. 'In my heart I will always be yours.'

He raised his head from the bed where they lay entwined. 'I know not what waits in Scotland. I know only that I love you. I belong to you. Always to you.' Tears shone in his eyes. With one hand he pressed her head against his neck. 'I will love you all my life.'

He smelled of sandalwood and soap. She would always remember him just like this, soap and sandalwood and the sweat that sheened his body when he was inside her.

Chapter Twenty-Eight

Long after Soraya drifted into sleep in his arms, Marc lay awake staring up at the low wood ceiling. There would never be a night with Soraya that lasted long enough. He knew this with a certainty he had not felt since following Richard on crusade three years past. Then he had believed in God's cause, spoken by Urban II in the churchyard at Clermont. He believed in Richard Plantagenet's honour as a warrior knight, and in his own honour, as well.

He had also believed he would one day see his brother again, would journey back to Scotland in Henry's company, proud of their part in rescuing the Holy Land from the Saracens. He had believed other things, as well.

Now he lay sleepless, painfully aware of all he had not learned: How to live with the screams of dying men in his ears, hostages betrayed and slaughtered. How to assume lordship of Rossmorven now that Henry was dead and the land fell to him. How to honour his betrothal to Jehanne.

How could he leave his heart and soul here in England and ride away from Soraya in the morning?

She made a small sound beside him and curled closer. Her

hair smelled of cinnamon, and a faint perfume wafted from her bare skin, scented with roses and something spicy.

Soraya was his heart, his soul. His life. He would never stand being apart from her.

But he must. He had vowed to return to Scotland, and now he must do his duty. He lay in torment until the sky seen through the single narrow window turned grey and then peach, and at last he slept.

When a shaft of bright sunlight fell across his face, he woke suddenly and turned toward Soraya. The sheet was cool, the pillow, as well. She was not here! Not sitting at the fire, not eating the cold roast chicken and cheese he had smuggled from the kitchen.

He lay awake, waiting. An hour passed and she did not return. Had she gone to Eleanor?

Had she fled to Portsmouth and taken ship for Jerusalem? He could not believe she would do so, not without saying goodbye. Not after last night. As unpredictable as she could be, she could not have left him with no word, not after what they had found in each other's arms.

But where was she?

He rose and dressed in chain mail and tunic, made his way down to the outer bailey. Eleanor was there, bidding farewell to two bishops and a retinue of men at arms. Marc caught a squire on his way to the stables and requested that his mount be brought to him. While he waited, he puzzled over Soraya.

And then a cold truth tore into his heart. If she had wanted to say farewell, she would be here.

Stunned with disbelief he managed to kneel before Queen Eleanor and speak over an aching throat. 'I thank you for your kindness, Your Grace.'

'You brought me a gift, de Valery—news from my son. It is only fitting to honour such a messenger. Ride with God.'

'Your Grace, please tell Soraya…' He could not continue.

He rose, numb with grief, to clasp the hand William Marshal extended to him. Hooves thumped behind him, and Marc turned.

The young squire led Jupiter forward. Perched on top of the animal's broad back sat a grinning Soraya. She looked so pleased with herself he didn't know whether to laugh or strangle her.

She gazed at him from the high-backed saddle, her green eyes sparkling. The small brown pony was roped to the stallion, a small wooden chest tied on its back. Her fur cloak covered what looked to him like a calf-length sky blue tunic with blackwork embroidery at the neck and from its folds poked a bright-eyed, shaggy Saqii.

She wore no turban. Instead, a scarf of yellow silk framed her face, held in place by a snug hood of ermine tied under her chin.

Speechless, Marc stared at her while the queen and the Earl of Pembroke walked away toward the keep without looking back. They had known!

He mounted behind Soraya without a word and guided Jupiter toward the town gate, so befuddled with joy his body shook. The moment they were through the portcullis and over the drawbridge, Marc reined up sharply outside the castle wall.

'Do you know what agony you caused me, waiting for you? Wondering why you did not come?' He cursed the unevenness in his voice.

'There was no other way. The queen insisted.'

'God in heaven, Soraya… God in heaven, never, *never* disappear like that again.' He found himself shouting, but the knot in his chest began to loosen. 'Swear it! That you will not leave me. Swear it!'

'I will not leave you, Marc. Unless you send me away, I will be with you until the stars fall. I do not know *how,* since you journey to Scotland to be married, but…"

She gave her head a decisive shake. 'I cannot think of that now. What I will think of is breaking our fast! Look what the cook gave me.' From inside her cloak she drew half a roast chicken wrapped in clean linen and a wedge of white cheese. Unable to speak, Marc waved the food away.

Soraya nibbled in silence as they rode, the wind biting at their cheeks, the hills still frost-runed. She did not want to think about how she could stay with Marc despite his betrothal. But she must think about it.

She mulled over the problem all the long, mud-splattered way to Rossmorven, which took three bitterly cold days and nights. Unforgettable nights. When at last they rode onto Marc's land, through the checkerboard of farm fields and pastures of grazing cattle and up the rocky hill to Rossmorven keep, she still had no solution.

The countryside was stippled with dark green brush— heather, Marc called it—that cloaked the hills and green vales like a rough carpet. They stepped their horses carefully along the narrow lanes that ran between the fields and grazing areas for small herds of black cows. A dense forest of fir trees bordered the fields on one side; on the other were copses of hazelnuts and juniper.

It looked to be a sparsely populated land, unlike Italy or Austria, with their overcrowded towns and awful smells. But she didn't know if she could be happy here; it was so cold, so spare.

Marc gazed hungrily at everything, drinking in the landscape and smiling and smiling. The closer they drew to the castle the more cheerful Marc became. Soraya grew more and more nervous. The black stone keep loomed stark and forbidding against the grey sky, as if warning. *'Stop. Go no farther. You are not welcome here.'*

Marc began a song in a guttural, unintelligible language. 'Gaelic,' he explained. 'About a sailor coming home from the sea.' He sang a dozen verses before he broke off to greet the people who poured out of their thatched wattle cottages and lined the roadway. Many reached out their hands to touch his horse. 'Is that you, Marc? Glad yer home, laddie,' a tanned, wrinkled man shouted in bad Norman French. 'And all in one piece, too!' He directed a curious, unsmiling look at Soraya, and her heart shrank.

Marc replied in Gaelic, and a cheer went up.

'By St. Andrew,' another yelled, 'our Marc has returned. All will be well, now.' But once more, the smile on the ruddy upturned face lapsed into a frown at the sight of Soraya.

He loves this place, Soraya thought. And the people love him. *But they do not love me.*

They made slow progress toward the castle, besieged as Marc was with well-wishers—farmers, tradesmen, women in tidy kerchiefs with reddened hands, and here and there a child peeking from behind a skirt and shyly waving.

'Ah, 'tis good to be home,' Marc said at every affectionate outburst of welcome. He stopped often, conversing in Gaelic with knots of men gathered along the edge of a barley field, their woolen caps respectfully doffed. To a man, they eyed Soraya with distrust.

Except for the night they spent together at Eleanor's court in Winchester, she had never seen Marc so happy. *Two things only does a man need,* Uncle Khalil had said. *Something to occupy his hands and mind, and someone to love.*

Now Marc had both—his inherited estate and herself.

Her heart kicked against her ribs. He also had a woman to whom he was betrothed.

No wall surrounded the black stone structure before them, just a tall fence of wooden stakes. Situated on a hill of rock, bordered on two sides by a meandering arm of the sea, the place was impregnable. The huge rectangular building had steep-sided walls, near twenty feet high, Soraya calculated, and she counted three levels in the keep that loomed at the back. She also counted four square towers and a wall walk connecting them. But no guards patrolled the battlement, and no men at arms stood at the stairway entrance to the keep.

A servant boy scampered forward and took their horses, promising to deliver the small chest of clothing Eleanor had pressed on her. 'Use what God gave you, but remember my advice,' the queen had insisted in her speech of farewell.

How could she forget? She could still hear Eleanor's voice, ringing with authority, words of queenly wisdom inserted among the wardrobe admonitions. 'Brown is not your best color. Be sure your kirtles are soft, as no man wants to run his fingers over a porcupine. Wash your hair with perfumed soap.'

'Very well,' she murmured under her breath. 'My hair is washed and scented with attar of roses. Now what?'

It was clear that she and Marc would not be able to occupy the same chamber. She did not want to cause pain to his betrothed; it was blatant enough that she was travelling with Marc; she need not twist the knife.

A man-at-arms, the only one she had seen thus far, appeared just inside the entrance to the great hall. The old man looked so frail she guessed he would be unable to draw the sword from his belt, much less strike a blow with it.

'Fergus.' Marc nodded at the elderly man.

'Is't you, then?' the man croaked. 'Master Marc?'

'Aye, it is me.'

'By St. Ninian! Let's have a look at you, laddie.' He peered up at Marc, inspected him head to toe with tear-sheened blue eyes. He spared not a single glance at Soraya.

'You're all growed up, you are.' She struggled to comprehend the mix of mangled Norman French and Gaelic the old man spoke.

'Fergus, where are the guards?'

'Oh, they be down at the training field. King William has need of good knights.'

Marc met Fergus's gaze. 'Tell Robert the steward I want to see him.'

''Taint Robert no more, lad. ''Tis a new man. A Frenchman,' he said with a scowl.

The two men spoke in lowered tones, and Soraya surveyed the large hall. A long trestle table sat against the whitewashed wall at one end; another, shorter table and a high-backed chair sat square in the centre of the room. A fireplace burned at each end of the hall, but neither was close enough to warm anyone except the two hunting hounds snoozing at the hearth.

'And Fergus?'

'My lord?'

'Send Brigid to me. My guest will need tending. I will be in the lady Margaret's solar.'

Fergus halted on his way to the stone stairway. 'I fear Lady Margaret be not ready to receive—'

Marc grinned. 'My mother is never ready to "receive," but I warrant she will be ready to see her son after these long years!'

'Marc!' The old man wheeled toward him, hand upraised. 'Do not.'

Marc paused midway up the steps that led to the family living quarters. 'Do not what?'

Fergus made a helpless gesture with his shaking hands. 'Do not…frighten her. I mean, lad, do not surprise her. Lady Margaret doesn't like surprises.'

Marc laughed. 'No woman likes to be surprised in her private chamber. But she is my lady mother, man! And I can wait no longer.'

He beckoned Soraya to accompany him, grasped her hand and held it tight. 'I have not seen my mother in eighteen years, not since my fostering with my uncle Louis in France.'

Soraya could scarcely keep up with him. Up another set of stairs, then down a long hallway to a wide door at the far end. Marc rapped on it.

No response came from within, so he knocked again. 'Mother?'

Still no answer. He frowned, then pressed down the iron latch and swung the door open. 'Mother?'

A small figure sat facing away from the door, her tiny slippered feet propped on a hassock near the blazing fire.

'Mother?' Marc said softly. Then he was across the floor and kneeling before the small, white-haired woman. She patted his dark hair absently, then turned inquiring blue eyes on Soraya.

'Jehanne? Who is it? I cannot see.'

Marc slowly lifted his head from his mother's lap and gazed into her heart-shaped face. 'Do you not know me?'

'Of course I know you,' she snapped. 'Do you think I am an old woman?'

Marc drew her delicate form into his arms, kissed both her wrinkled cheeks and held her for a long moment.

'It is Etienne, is it not?' she said against his shoulder. 'I knew it would be you.'

Soraya watched the smile ebb from his face, and her heart twisted.

'It is Marc,' he said in a quiet voice. 'Your son.'

The feet scrabbled on the hassock. 'I have no son called Marc. All I have is my dearest Etienne.'

'Dear God in heaven,' he breathed. He turned a white, anguished face toward Soraya. 'Etienne was my father. He has been dead for years.'

A knot lodged in Soraya's throat. 'Give her time,' she murmured. 'Your man Fergus warned you she does not like surprises. Perhaps she will remember later.'

Marc folded his mother in his arms again. 'I have come from across the sea, come home to Rossmorven. To you. Try to remember, Mother. I am Marc. Your son.'

'Yes, my dearest,' the old woman whispered. 'I have been waiting. It seems so long, dearest husband. So long...'

Marc lowered his head, his eyes closed. The woman's delicate blue-veined hand smoothed his hair over and over.

'Etienne,' she murmured. 'My Etienne.'

Chapter Twenty-Nine

‹My name is Brigid, my lady,’ the young woman said. ‘The laird said I was to see to your needs.’

Soraya turned at the voice. The young woman, no older than herself, looked at her with a closed, unfriendly countenance and expressionless blue eyes.

‘My thanks, Brigid.’ She had left Marc with his mother, tiptoeing out the door when Fergus beckoned to her and showed her to a chamber not far from Lady Margaret’s solar. In fact, she had been gazing out the narrow window at the farmlands to the south. A cloud had just rolled away from the sun, and a lovely, gold, late-afternoon light softened the austere landscape.

‘The laird also said to see what you might need before I brewed up the tisane for Lady Margaret.’

‘Have you lived here at Rossmorven long?’

‘Aye, my lady. Since I was born, fourteen winters past. The old laird was alive then, and since my mam were handfasted only but not wed in the kirk, the laird took her in and gave her duties so’s she could pay for her keep. Mam works in the buttery now. She makes the finest cheese, and in her spare time she sews for Lady Margaret.’

'How long has Lady Margaret been…?'

'Confused like? Ever since the laird died. But it has grown worse of late.'

'Oh? Why is that?'

The girl gave her a long, hard look, then stepped out the chamber entrance and looked right and then left before she quietly pulled the plank door shut. 'If ye must know, it has to do with my mistress, the lady Jehanne. She…by St. Mary, I shouldna' say much, save that she speaks more sharply since her young years are fast passing. Lady Margaret, now, she's off in some other world. No matter what, she speaks soft and does no harm.'

Soraya moved to the small wooden chest Eleanor had gifted her with and propped open the lid. 'When did the old laird die, do you remember?'

'Aye, let me think. The lady Jehanne were twelve winters when Mam bore me. She came from France for her betrothal to the laird's son. Let me see…Marc were ten and she were eight. After the ceremony, Marc and his brother left for their fostering, but Jehanne stayed here at Rossmorven. I was but a wee girl when the old laird died. He were always kind to Mam and me when he were alive.'

'And then?'

Automatically Brigid bent and lifted out the wool surcoat and cranberry red gown that lay folded in the chest, smoothed the wrinkles and laid the garments across the narrow bed. Someone had trained the girl well. Lady Margaret, perhaps.

'Well, and then both master Henry and master Marc sailed away to France to be squires. Master Marc has not laid his eyes on Lady Jehanne for all these years, until now.'

'Eighteen years,' Soraya murmured. And now Jehanne would be twenty-six summers. Why had she waited so long?

And then another thought struck. God in heaven, they would scarcely know each other. God forgive her for tempting him away from Jehanne.

She lifted several folded kirtles out of the chest and peeked to see what remained. A nightrobe only, and on the bottom...

A lute! She cried out in delight. Eleanor must have packed it as a gift. Soraya could just hear her commanding voice. 'The land of the Scots is a wild, untamed place. Give the girl something to *do*.'

'Oh, my lady!' Brigid's voice was hushed with awe. 'Can you play?'

In answer, Soraya lifted the instrument and plucked a simple melody. Entranced, the maidservant fell to her knees. 'We've had no song nor dance since Lady Jehanne... For such a long time. It makes my heart sing to hear a tune once more!'

Soraya knew at that moment she had made a friend. She played another verse. When she finished, Brigid reached a tentative hand toward the hem of Soraya's gown.

'Forgive me, my lady, but I canna' help asking. What be you to our Marc?'

Soraya bit back a smile. 'You mean, who am I and what am I doing here?'

Brigid nodded. 'Aye, you have the right of it.'

Soraya laid the lute aside. 'In truth, Brigid, I do not know how to answer you. To Marc I am friend, and more. And though I know he has been betrothed to Jehanne for many years, I care for him. I would do nothing to hurt him, and everything in my power to see him happy.'

Brigid's pale blue eyes filled with tears. ''Twill not be easy.'

'I know. And sometimes I am frightened.'

'Oh, my lady, be not afeared of this place. 'Tis housed

visitors before. I would fear only…' She broke off and began to twist her apron.

Soraya understood. 'I am weary, Brigid. We have ridden hard from Winchester, and three days in the saddle has tired my bones.'

Brigid scrambled to her feet. 'Shall I order a tub, then?'

Soraya opened her mouth to reply, then realised she could not explain why she needed no bath. Last night she and Marc had luxuriated in a shared tub at an inn near Jedburgh.

'Nay, not a tub. I will rest some before supper.' And before meeting Jehanne.

'Supper is served in the lower hall at sundown, my lady.' The maid disappeared for a few minutes, then stepped back inside with a fur coverlet over her arm. 'Ye might well need this, my lady. Winter nights be cold in this land.'

Soraya choked back a laugh. Cold? In this snug, warm chamber with a fire blazing on the hearth? After the frozen, blustery nights she and Marc had spent huddled in hollow tree stumps or pacing about the small confines of that stone windmill in Barfleur to keep from freezing, she would never, ever complain of being cold. Chilly, perhaps, but never cold.

All at once she thought of Damascus, of her quarters at Uncle Khalil's gracious, sprawling house. She had left such luxury behind. Perhaps, she mused as she spread the fur over the narrow bed and pulled it across her shoulders, perhaps she had left it behind forever.

She closed her eyes, but a shard of doubt crept into her thoughts. Marc loved this land, and its people. What if she did not?

Would it be enough to love just the man? To be his friend and watch another woman bear his babes?

* * *

The evening meal in the hall was a harsh awakening for Soraya. At first, there was no sign of Jehanne. The only other diners were seven men at arms just returned from the training ground and smelling of sweat and mud, and an ancient priest, Father Cuthbert, whose long fingers were permanently ink-stained, perhaps from copying manuscripts.

Marc sat in the center of the linen-covered table, Soraya on his left. The first and only course consisted of dry, grainy bread, cheese so hard she could not pierce it with her eating knife, and slices of fish. *Raw* fish. And some kind of honey-coloured drink that burned her throat and made her eyes water.

No wonder the Scots were so terse in their speech. Their tongues must be pickled!

And then, just as she picked up her eating knife to lift a morsel of fish to her mouth, a tall, elegant-looking woman in a well-cut gown ostentatiously click-clacked down the steps, her hard-heeled red leather slippers peeking out from beneath her hem.

The latest fashion, Soraya guessed. No doubt from France. Not designed for walking in muddy lanes. Jehanne's feet, she noted, were large. The grey wool gown outlined a generous form, lushly curved.

Jehanne paused before the sparsely loaded table, then signaled to the kitchen. Two servant boys staggered in carrying a towering dessert cake on a tray. They plopped the creation at the empty place at the table, and Jehanne swept slowly and very deliberately to the place reserved next to Marc. Her dark eyes were hard as slate.

Marc rose and bent forward to kiss her cheek. 'Jehanne,' he murmured.

Jehanne snapped her head in Soraya's direction. 'I see you bring a guest to my—' she hesitated '—to *our* table.'

'I do. May I pre—'

'And what is she?' Jehanne interrupted in a strident voice. 'Virgin? Wife? Or widow?'

Marc's head came up, but before he could speak, Soraya answered. 'I am none of those, lady,' she said quietly. 'My name is Soraya al-Din. I come from Damascus, and I am a woman, as you can see. But my status beyond that is my own private affair.'

'So,' Jehanna replied, her voice silky. 'You are a toy Marc found in the Holy Land.' She slid into her place beside him.

'Jehanne—' Marc began.

'I am not a toy,' Soraya returned, her voice controlled. 'Though it is true that Marc found me in the Holy Land. In Jerusalem.'

The priest suddenly came to life. 'Praise be! Perhaps you can tell us of King Richard's success over the infidel Saladin?'

'No success, Father Cuthbert,' Marc said. 'Saladin has made truce with Richard. There is peace in Jerusalem, but the city still rests in Saracen hands.'

'Peace!' Jehanne exploded at the word. 'Why not Saladin's head on a pike?'

'There was no need,' Marc countered. 'Saladin is an honorable man. I cannot always say the same for the English king Richard.'

Jehanne lowered the knife she was using to slice up the cake. 'What has happened to you, Marc, that your vision has grown so clouded?'

'My vision is not clouded. I was there. I know whereof I speak.'

'Oh, do you?' she snapped. Her voice was like a cracking whip. 'You know nothing. Nothing!'

Marc stared at her for a long minute. 'What has happened

to you, Jehanne,' he said quietly, 'that your vision has grown so bitter?'

She slammed down the cutting knife. 'What has happened?' Her voice was choked, on the edge of fury. 'I will tell you what has happened while you were off being an honourable knight with the king of the English. I have spent eighteen years—eighteen years!—waiting for you.'

'Jehanne,' the priest began. 'Daughter…'

'I am not finished!' she blazed. 'I heard news of every noble lady at my father's estate in Chambois marrying and dandling babes at their breasts. I watched myself grow old waiting for my time!'

The priest rescued the cake knife, pulled the platter toward himself and began slicing pieces. 'God sees all, daughter. He will reward you as He sees fit.'

He handed a slab of the fruit-heavy dessert to Jehanne on the flat side of the knife. Her white face grew mottled with angry red splotches. 'He cannot reward me enough for my lost youth,' she shouted. She struck the knife away with her fist and the slab of cake went flying onto the floor. Saqii pounced on it before the deerhounds opened their sleepy eyes.

Jehanne shot upright. 'What animal is that?'

Marc rose, as well. 'It is a pup. A pet. We…I found it in Italy.'

'Well, Sir Dog-Lover, get rid of it!'

Soraya swivelled away from the table and scooped up Saqii. Holding the trembling dog to her chest, she ran for the staircase.

'Soraya!' Marc's voice. She paused halfway. Behind her she heard a crash of pottery and a high female screech.

'Marc, what are you doing? Let go of me!'

Soraya pivoted to see Marc's hand pin Jehanne's arm to her side. Furious, she jerked away, overturning a pitcher of ale, and raked her nails across his face.

'This is my home, Jehanne,' he said in a low, steely voice. 'I am master here, not you.'

'We are betrothed, Marc. It is as much mine as yours. I have earned it.' She slapped him hard across the face.

He caught her hand. 'You will stop this, Jehanne. Stop it, now.'

'We will be wed soon,' she screamed at him.

An ominous silence fell. Soraya caught the hem of her gown in one hand and fled on up the stairs.

Three days later, as she cautiously descended the stairs, Soraya heard the buzz of voices in the great hall. She perched on the top stone step and watched Marc make his way through the mass of people—people she recognized from farms and the village, gathering before their laird for Justice Day. One by one, the men, and a few women, entered the keep in their muddy boots and trudged to where Marc sat at the table in the center of the room, holding the traditional laird's court.

Soraya leaned forward to listen.

'If it please ye, lord, Henny the fish wife cheated me on Thursday last when she—'

'I did no such thing!' a plump, red-haired woman screeched. ''Twas you said you'd rather have a fat pike than a skinny salmon.'

There were whispers about Jehanne, as well, which Soraya tried not to overhear. 'Spends money on herself, she does… Aye. She should be helpin' the people and providin' for the old laird's widow, Lady Margaret.'

It went on for an hour, and then two, with accusations and complaints and angry recriminations. Marc listened, asked questions and made decisions that were fair, even wise, Soraya thought.

The court continued all that day. At one point Soraya

slipped the rest of the way down the steps, retrieved a pitcher of cool spring water and two dippers from the kitchen and set it next to Marc with a few whispered words. 'In the desert, all share the oasis.'

He grinned, scooped up a dipperful, then invited the petitioners to share the water with him.

'Sam the miller be hoarding grain.'

'That's a false lie…'

'Nay, 'tis a true one,' the accuser said to a rumble of laughter. Even Marc chuckled. Then he fined Sam the miller two pence and a pan of oats, to be paid to Angus Shortbeard before the spring planting.

Marc finished the day with a handshake from Angus and a slap on the back from Sam the miller. What he really needed, he thought as the last of the villagers filed out of the hall, was an hour with Soraya. Just the touch of her hand.

Soraya had kept out of the way for the most part, since Jehanne spared no effort to curb her tongue and the vicious barbs she directed at Soraya were hurtful. But, Marc noticed, Jehanne didn't make an appearance on Justice Day. Fergus said she disliked the rank smell of the peasants and hearing the grumbles of discontent that were directed at her.

The instant the hall was empty, Marc tramped wearily up the stairs to Soraya's third-floor chamber. He knew it was her only refuge from Jehanne's constant whining voice and the unending strife she stirred up everywhere she went.

'God forgive me,' he said with a groan. 'Sometimes I wish I had never come back to Rossmorven.'

Soraya drew him inside and closed the door. 'Come. A man deserves some peace in his own house.'

'It is more than the petitioners,' he said. 'More than

Jehanne.' He sank onto the stool by the fire and ran his hands through his hair. 'Much more.'

She stood before him, took his hands and placed them about her waist. 'Tell me.'

He shook his head. 'I would not be disloyal to her.'

'Tell me,' she insisted. 'You must talk to someone.'

He pressed his forehead against her belly and wrapped his arms tight around her. 'There is Father Cuthbert, but I cannot…'

'Then talk to me.' She bent to lay her cheek against his hair. 'I can do little, I know. But I would lighten your burden if I could.'

Marc exhaled a long breath. 'The steward, Jacques, has been falsifying my account books. Jehanne brought him from Chambois, to repay a family debt, and she will hear nothing against him.'

Soraya nodded.

'Today I sent the fellow back to France. Jehanne resents my action. In truth, she is beyond fury.'

'Jehanne will resent all your actions when they do not follow her wishes.'

'Aye,' he said heavily.

'Forgive me, Marc, but in your long absence and your mother's confusion, Jehanne has served as chatelaine of Ross-morven for these many years. It must seem inconsiderate of us to return together. I can understand how she must feel.'

'I had no choice. I do not wish to live without you.'

'But it is Jehanne who is chatelaine.'

He closed his eyes. 'Aye, I know. My men avoid her. The servants fear her temper. Even in the village, among the cottars, there is discontent. They welcome me, but Fergus tells me they turn away at the sight of Jehanne.'

Again Soraya said nothing.

'There are other matters besides crops and feed for the cows,' Marc added. 'Women's matters that need attention—births and fevers and extra food for the old and the poor. I cannot do it alone.'

'She ignores such things, is that it?'

'Jehanne does not go among the people, as my mother did before she…. Oh, God.'

She smoothed one hand over his thick, dark hair. 'And your mother grows ever more distant.'

'My lady mother still does not know me. Her eyes see back to another time.'

'Lady Margaret is advanced in age, Marc. Be grateful that is all she suffers. There are worse things than confusion that befall the old ones.'

'Aye. She is not aware of what is happening to her mind, but at least she is not in pain.'

'It is you who suffer, because you love her and you are gradually losing her. Even Jehanne, who must be fond of Lady Margaret, must be hurting.'

'Not Jehanne. The servants tell me things….'

'And? Is there more that troubles you?'

'Aye.' He lifted his head and held her gaze. 'The grinding wheel at the mill is split. Someone is poaching deer from my forest, not one of the villagers, someone else. And there is Father Cuthbert and his accusing looks.'

He took both her hands in his. 'But at least I no longer hear the screams at night. I no longer dream of Acre.'

'And?' she queried again, her voice gentle.

'And,' he repeated. 'And I am not here with you at night. I see you at the noon meal and at supper, but it is not enough.'

'You are attending to your duties, Marc. I know you must do so.'

'What of you, Soraya? How do you occupy yourself in this spiderweb?'

She laughed softly. 'I play the lute Queen Eleanor sent, in your mother's garden when it is fair. Or in her solar. Lady Margaret likes music. I go down to the kitchen sometimes. Elgitha is teaching me to make pastry.'

'Pastry! What in God's name for?'

'To eat, of course. Buns and pies and tarts and… Yesterday I tried to bake mince tarts and a savory salmon pie, but I burned them both. Elgitha fears I will never learn.'

Marc smiled for the first time in two days. 'And what else do you do?'

'I gather herbs in the meadows. Fergus found a place in the cellar where I can hang them to dry. And I gather wildflowers, as well. Have you not noticed the bowl of woods iris in your mother's solar? And the red lilies—at least I think they are lilies—in your own chamber?'

Marc made no answer, just gazed at Soraya with a bemused expression. All at once he thought of Richard. Wherever the king was imprisoned, Marc hoped he would find something to sustain him, as Soraya had sustained him.

'Also I help Father Cuthbert with his inks and his copying. He is not good at Greek. And,' she said with a small grin, 'I try to avoid Jehanne.'

'Are you not discouraged, my Soraya? Angry that we are not together?' He stood and took her into his arms. 'Tell me.'

'I am angry sometimes, yes. But we are together now. We might sleep in the same chamber if we did not fear the disapproval of Father Cuthbert.'

'I will come tonight. I will not survive another day if I cannot hold you close.'

Chapter Thirty

And so it went for a fortnight. Jehanne fumed and fretted about the castle like a black spectre. Marc visited Lady Margaret each morning in her solar, but the days passed and still his mother did not know him.

Worst of all, Marc missed his nights with Soraya and often felt too heartsick to share his burdens with her. Often he thought of King Richard, held somewhere in Austria. The man would have no companion for solace. How Marc would be envied by the English monarch.

The servants and most of the villagers began to treat Soraya with uneasy respect, except for Jehanne. The castle was large enough that the two women rarely saw each other except for the main meal in the great hall, and Soraya took care to sit as far from Jehanne as she could to avoid her sharp tongue. Sometimes, when Fergus or one of the servants warned her that Lady Jehanne was in an especially foul temper, Soraya skipped the meal entirely. Later, Brigid would slip into her chamber, her apron pockets stuffed with bread and cheese.

Soraya knew she would not starve at Rossmorven, but some days she felt she might die of loneliness.

The tightrope she was walking began to fray one clear, brisk afternoon when she was spending an hour on her hands and knees weeding Lady Margaret's herb garden. Jehanne bustled into the enclosed square searching for Brigid and found Soraya instead.

'What are you doing here?' Jehanne snapped.

'Weeding,' Soraya replied calmly. Her heart was anything but calm; it skittered inside her chest like a frightened sparrow. 'Lady Margaret is fond of the apple mint for her tea, so I thought to give it more room to spread.'

'You need not,' Jehanne announced.

Soraya did not look up, but went on tending the mint bed. 'I do not mind. I enjoy it.'

'I meant that you need not do it at all.'

'It was Lady Margaret who asked—'

Jehanne twitched her blue wool skirt with impatience. 'Let me speak frankly, lady. You are not welcome here at Rossmorven. You do not belong here.'

'That,' Soraya said, her voice even, 'has been apparent from the beginning.'

'Marc is betrothed to me. Me! I have waited these eighteen years for him to return and keep his pledge. To honour me with what is rightfully mine.'

Soraya glanced into the woman's face. 'Why did you wait all that while?' she said carefully. 'Eighteen years is a long absence from someone you love.'

Jehanne's mouth twisted. 'Love! A marriage is not for love, lady. I waited these years for the land, of course. Marriage is to bind great families together.'

'If you do not love Marc, why marry him, then?'

'You might as well ask why birds mate in the spring. It is the way things are done. I bring a modest dowry, and Rossmorven has always been a rich estate. You—' Jehanne pointed a shaking finger at Soraya '—bring him nothing. Nothing!'

Soraya swallowed a gasp. Then she rose and confronted her rival face-to-face, weeding trowel in hand. 'That is untrue. I bring my love for him. And I bring myself.'

'You think too highly of your person, lady. The lord of Rossmorven cannot feed his cottars, his servants, his men at arms on such a puny diet as love. Survival—' Jehanne hissed the word '—that is what is important.'

'There is survival, and then there is survival,' Soraya said softly. 'There is more to life than breaking one's fast each day.'

Jehanne snorted. 'Then you are indeed a fool. Perhaps you have never gone hungry?'

'Nay, lady, I have often gone hungry. For weeks on end, the least of our concerns on the journey across the continent to England was filling our stomachs. A woman like you, Jehanne, knows nothing of life outside your own small, sheltered world.'

Jehanne blinked and her face whitened.

'But,' Soraya continued, 'you do have a point. For a lord, with responsibilities for his land and his people, the choice between love and survival is perhaps not possible.'

Jehanne looked straight into Soraya's eyes. 'Marc needs an heir.'

Soraya nodded. 'Granted.'

Jehanne's eyes hardened. 'I have worked hard for my place here. I do not intend to give it up.'

'Not all battles are so simple, Lady Jehanne. The wish to unite two souls, two bodies in marriage should be freely given.'

'I care not for "shoulds".' Jehanne's voice tightened. 'I can force Marc to keep his pledge. He owes this to me.'

'I do not believe one human being owes another such intangibles as things of the spirit.'

Jehanne's chin came up. 'Then it is you, lady, who knows nothing of life.'

Soraya let the comment pass. 'You do not care about his feelings? His happiness?'

'I do not. I care only that he honours his bargain. I care about my future as the lady of a great house. Of Rossmorven.'

Soraya nodded, then caught and held the narrowed gaze of the woman who faced her. 'You say I know nothing of life. Perhaps I know nothing about life in this Scottish land, but I know this much: *I do* care for Marc. And that leaves me no choice but to offer the only thing I can.'

'What could you possibly do for him, unless it is to leave Rossmorven?'

'I will not leave Rossmorven, or Marc, unless he sends me away.' She turned away from Jehanne and again bent over the bed of mint. But that night she did not sleep.

The following day a gale blew in from the east and a driving rain began at dawn. Soraya resigned herself to a day inside the keep. Once again, Marc was shouldering the obligations of Justice Day. He ordered a roaring fire built in the great hall fireplace and pitchers of warm spiced wine for the petitioners who straggled in, drenched from the storm, to state grievances or seek retribution.

As always, Soraya watched with interest from her hidden perch on the stairs.

John the digger had been beaten over the head with a peat shovel when he tried to collect his wages twice in one day, claiming he had not been paid at all.

The day before, Molly the goat girl had fended off the blows of the butcher's wife, who was furious because her best linen petticoat had been snatched from her clothesrope and gobbled up by a hungry nanny.

Then a hugely pregnant Mistress Ann, the stonecutter's wife, argued so passionately on behalf of her light-fingered nephew that her water broke. 'Owwww!' the woman wailed.

Soraya was down the steps and halfway across the hall when she heard a rough voice call, 'Where is the mistress, then? She should lend aid.'

'No matter,' another voice answered. 'T'other lady will help.'

Soraya slipped an arm about the peasant woman's bulging waist and started up the stairs. 'Brigid,' she called to the wide-eyed maidservant at the kitchen entrance. 'Prepare a chamber and bring clean linen.'

'Aye, my lady.'

'And send for Elsbetta, the midwife.'

'Oh my lady,' the stonecutter's wife cried. 'I thank—Owww!'

The woman's cries could be heard all afternoon, and as the proceedings in the great hall continued, the stonecutter, whose name was Willem, purposefully drank himself into a stupor and fell asleep by the fireplace.

Marc's head began to throb at the rumbling noise of shouting voices, the stink of wet woolen tunics and hose covering unwashed bodies. Despite the unrelenting rain, the villagers crowded into the hall and drank freely from the pitchers set on the table. He would have a riot on his hands if he didn't stop the flow of wine.

At the end of what seemed an interminable day, yet another voice boomed. 'I, too, have a complaint.'

Too weary to even look up, Marc reached for the goose-quill pen and turned over a new page in the record book.

'Name?' He studied the thumb-worn edge of the parchment.

'The Earl of Carrick.'

Marc groaned inwardly. Another case of his cattle straying

onto some neighboring lord's land—half the hills of Scotland were spotted someone's wandering cows.

'What is your complaint?' Marc asked, again without looking up.

'My complaint? I have ridden all this day in this soup you Scots call a "light mist" to speak to the lord of Rossmorven on a matter of imp—'

Marc glanced up. 'Roger! Roger de Clare!'

Roger leaped nimbly over the table serving as Marc's desk and the two men clasped each other like long-lost brothers. Roger clapped his arm over Marc's shoulders. 'You look tired, my friend. Can you dismiss these hordes of your countrymen and spare me an hour?'

Marc would like nothing better. He waved the gathered villagers away and led Roger through the throng and up the stone steps to his private solar on the second floor.

'The Earl of Carrick?' he queried.

'Aye,' Roger said, a note of boyish pride in his tone. 'Richard's doing. He's back in England, safe and in good spirits, but one hundred thousand silver marks poorer.' He followed Marc into the large room and took the chair offered.

'The king ordered you back to Jerusalem, did he not?'

'He did. But by the time the wound in my thigh healed, Queen Eleanor was on her way to Germany with the ransom. I joined her instead, thinking to guard the queen and her treasure.'

'"Thinking to"? Did you not guard her?' Marc handed his friend a cup of wine.

Roger sent him a wry look. 'One does not "guard" Queen Eleanor. No man in his right mind would dare ruffle a hair on her royal head, and as for the ransom, it was delivered in secret a week earlier, by William Marshal and a troop of hand-picked knights.'

'Then what brings you this far north, Roger? Carrick lands, as I recall, lie to the south.'

Roger nodded. 'I am here because of an oath I made to your servant boy, Soray. I promised I would take him back to Jerusalem.'

Marc didn't know whether to laugh or weep. Soray—Soraya—back to Jerusalem? Never.

'Roger, I have much to tell you. But—' he stood up slowly '—I have duties waiting in the hall below. We will talk tonight, after the evening meal. In the meantime, rest yourself. I will send someone to see to your needs.'

'Send Soray?' Roger suggested.

Marc laughed for the first time in what seemed like days. 'That I will not, my friend. You will understand why at supper.'

That evening Marc fended off Roger's questions about Soray and waited impatiently for Soraya to appear. When she glided down the steps in pale gold wool with a sheer net veil covering her hair, Roger looked at her uncomprehendingly and leaned toward Marc. 'Now there is a beauty, fit for a—' He broke off and half rose from his seat.

Soraya gave a cry and flew across the floor to throw her arms around the speechless knight. He didn't recover his voice until Soraya had kissed his cheek and squeezed his hand and laughed up into his puzzled face.

'God in heaven,' Roger blurted. 'How…?'

At that moment, Jehanne marched into the hall. Marc rose and gestured toward her. 'May I present the Lady Jehanne of Chambois? Jehanne, this is Roger de Clare, Earl of Carrick.'

Jehanne jerked and her eating knife clattered onto the floor. Her eyes glittered oddly.

Roger bowed to both women, then allowed Soraya to lead him to a seat next to her, far down the table from Jehanne.

'The Lady Jehanne seems…out of sorts,' he murmured.

'Fear not,' Soraya replied. 'Jehanne does not like me. She will not come within striking distance.'

'I cannot think how I missed such beauty,' Roger said, staring at Soraya. 'I cannot think…'

Soraya laughed. 'Do not think, Sir Roger. And do not stare at the Lady Jehanne as you do me. Jehanne is Marc's betrothed.'

Roger's head came up. 'Ah. I see. No, I do not see. What—'

'Later,' she whispered. She cut up a slice of chicken on her plate and closed her teeth over a morsel of breast meat. Later she would tell Roger about Jehanne, about everything. Suddenly she found the great hall over-warm, the air smoky and hard to breathe.

After the meal, everyone but Roger and Marc retired and the newly made earl sank onto the wooden bench beside his host and propped his elbows on the empty table. 'You cannot do this, Marc. I have never known a braver knight, or a man whose word of honour meant more. You cannot go back on your oath.'

'The bargain was made not by me but between my father and her father. Is breaking that pledge any worse than massacring the thousands of innocent men betrayed at Acre?'

His friend slowly shook his head. 'One sin does not excuse a second.'

'That I know, my friend,' Marc said in a dry voice. 'Would to God I could see an honourable way out.'

'There is no way out. You owe the lady Jehanne your name in marriage. You owe Rossmorven an heir.'

ˌMarc flinched and closed his fist around his wine cup. 'I know all too well what my obligations are. Is there a man in God's kingdom who does not feel his shoulders buckle under the burden? Who upholds his "honour" but feels his spirit wither, his soul grow parched?'

Roger splashed more wine into his own vessel. 'Honour in this world is defined by a king's command. And a lover's pledge. At bottom, there is only church law and man's law.'

For a long moment Marc said nothing. To Roger, one's role in life was uncomplicated. How he envied the man.

'And when church law and man's law are not the same?' Marc queried. 'What does one do then?'

Roger lowered his wine cup. 'You mean as happened at Acre?'

'As at Acre, yes.'

'Acre scarred you, Marc. It twisted your vision.'

'Aye.' Marc poured himself more wine. 'I did what was wrong in the name of honour. I found it hard to live with.'

'Every man there did the same.'

'So they did,' Marc agreed. 'That does not make it right.'

Roger laid one arm over his shoulder. 'Marc, Marc. Think, man! Life is short. One does the best he can.'

The best he can. 'And here at Rossmorven, the choice is the same,' Marc acknowledged. He lifted his head. 'I see what must be done. What I do not know is whether I can do it.' He drained his cup. 'But I must at least try.'

'Fergus!' he called loudly

The elderly man-at-arms stepped forward. 'Yes, my lord?'

'Have young Martin saddle my horse.'

Chapter Thirty-One

Soraya spied Marc coming toward her across the meadow and she straightened, her cutting basket over her arm. The look on his strained face made her swallow hard, and she looked down, studying the flowers she carried. The tumble of wild iris and henbane and tiny roses reminded her of her situation at Rossmorven—a mix of sweet and bitter.

'Walk with me,' he said when he reached her.

'What is wrong?' She could not stop the question. His features looked drawn and tired, and his eyes betrayed a dimming hope.

'We must talk. I cannot go on like this.'

Without a word she stepped to his side, laid the scissors in the basket and took his hand. 'Come. I have found a path down to the firth.'

He gave her a weary smile. 'Aye, I know of it. Henry and I used to fish from the rocks.'

As one, they turned east and made their way across the meadow toward the fringe of dark green trees bordering the cliff edge. Below them the blue-green sea swirled, lapping at the rocks with greedy fingers of white foam.

Marc gazed down at the water. ''Tis a time as unsettled as the tide, is it not?'

Soraya turned toward him. 'It is not the times that are unsettled, but the discontent we have stirred up. Say instead that it is an unsettled *matter*.'

'Aye. Still I would not change it.'

'Marc, is it wrong to want this? Is our own happiness too much to ask for?'

'In truth I do not know. But, Soraya, neither do I care. The burdens that come with Rossmorven will crush me if I take no joy in them. Without you, I would take no joy in anything.'

He stopped and took her hand. 'Do you like this land, with its hills and the sea roaring all night?'

Soraya smiled inside. 'I did not think so at first. But I do. I listen to the sound of the sea from my chamber window, when all else is quiet.'

'As do I,' he said quietly. 'All through the night. I cannot sleep for wanting you.'

Soraya squeezed his hand. 'It cannot go on. It must end, one way or another.'

'Aye. That is what I came to tell you.'

Her heart stuttered, stopped, then double-skipped on. 'I can say nothing save that I love you, and that you know already.'

'Say it anyway. I need to hear your voice saying it.'

She halted and half turned toward him. 'I love you, Marc. I pray for your happiness.'

He closed his eyes, and she spoke again. 'You know that I will love you all of my days.'

'No matter what befalls us?' His voice trembled slightly.

'No matter what. I will carry you in my heart. Always.'

He looked into her face, folded his hands about her shoulders. 'I have decided what I must do. I want to marry you, Soraya.'

She could only nod for the tightness in her throat.

'Then will you? Be my wife?'

Still she could not speak. Far below them cold, green waves boomed against the dark rocks, tossing white spray to the heavens. She stretched to kiss his cheek, then brushed her mouth against his. 'Yes. Yes, I would be your wife.'

He caught the back of her head and pulled her to him. 'I love you, my Soraya,' he said against her lips. 'I love you more than you could ever know.'

He kissed her deeply. She reached her arms about his neck and the flower basket tumbled to the ground and rolled a few feet away. In the middle of his kiss, she could tell he had begun to smile, for his lips widened, then parted.

She would never have enough of him. If she lived to fourscore summers, when he touched her she would always feel the impulse to pull off her gown and underkirtle and lie with him.

He groaned and lifted his head. 'I am leaving within the hour. Riding south to Winchester.'

She opened her eyes wide. 'Why?'

'To seek a way through this snare we are caught in.' He kissed her again, then released her and strode off across the meadow.

Before Marc went to the stables, he sought out Jehanne in her chamber, where she sat with her back to the tall, narrow window, working a square of embroidered silk.

'Jehanne, I...'

She did not look up. 'Marc, is anything amiss?'

'I wish to dissolve our betrothal.'

She sat quite still for a moment, then shifted the silk on her lap and surveyed him with hard black eyes. 'Do you now?'

'I will arrange another marriage for you, a better one.'

Jehanne snorted. 'Better? Better than what? I have had no marriage at all for these eighteen years.'

'I mean, a better match for you than myself. A richer prospect. A title, if you wish it.'

Her eyes flared momentarily, then dropped to her embroidery, but she said nothing.

'Jehanne.' He reached both hands toward her in entreaty. 'For the love of God, release me.'

She looked up at him, her sharp-eyed gaze resting on the neck of his forest green linen tunic. When she spoke her voice was harsh. 'I have everything I want here at Rossmorven. Everything except your name. Grant me that and I will stay out of your way.'

'I do not intend to live separate from my wife.'

'But you cannot make *her* your wife,' she said, her voice icy. 'You can make *her* only your whore. And if I judge the lady correctly, that is not enough.'

'You are correct. It is not enough. But I have had my fill of doing the wrong thing for the right reason.'

Jehanne rose and faced him. 'So, you would break our betrothal. You bastard.'

'Sometimes I wish to God I truly were.'

She said nothing, just pushed him, slowly and deliberately, out through her chamber door.

Six tense days and agonising nights passed while Marc was away. To Soraya, the castle seemed filled with his presence, but she noted that Fergus and Brigid and the other servants were on edge. She heard the grumbling of the cottars when she walked past their fields to the meadow to gather lilies and puffballs.

Something was afoot.

Roger sidestepped her questions, and Brigid reported that

Jehanne was in such a strange state of lassitude, combined with outbursts of temper, that Soraya kept to her chamber.

Midafternoon on the sixth day, Marc clattered into the bailey, covered with mud, his face white and drawn. He dismounted, stumbled into the keep and hauled himself up the stairs to Soraya's chamber.

She heard him coming, recognised the soft chink of chain mail and his halting footsteps, and she flung open the door. At the sight of his gaunt features she caught her breath.

He reached for her, and his eyes… God in heaven, his eyes! Red-rimmed with exhaustion, they were sunken in dark shadows.

'Marc.' She breathed the word, then pulled him inside, shut the door and bolted it.

'Marc, are you well?'

'Soraya,' he panted. 'Had to see you…filthy from travel, but I had—'

'Come,' she said. She drew him forward, began to loosen the mail shirt.

'Wine,' he croaked.

She reached to the table behind her and thrust a cup into his hand. 'It is your Scot's brew.'

One swallow and he choked. Another swallow and his ragged breathing began to even out. She pulled the mail shirt off over his head, untied the leggings, stripped him down to his braies. Then she led him to the bed, lay down beside him and drew him into her arms.

'Love you…' he muttered in a scratchy voice. Before she could respond, he was asleep.

He slept the rest of that day and all that night, waking only once to accept a swallow of ale and a few morsels of the cheese tart Soraya had retrieved from the kitchen. She had made the tart herself, but the crust was tough and chewy, and by the time she poked a bit into his mouth it was so soggy from her tears she winced when he swallowed it. But he smiled up at her anyway.

At dawn the following morning, Fergus tapped on the chamber door. Soraya opened it at once.

'There be a messenger, my lady. The man says 'tis from the English queen.'

Eleanor! 'Prepare the solar, Fergus. Marc will be there within the hour.'

'Send for Jehanne,' Marc murmured from the bed.

Soraya nodded. 'Fergus, ask the Lady Jehanne to join us.'

The old retainer touched his forehead. 'Aye, that I will.'

When the door closed behind him, Marc sat up and caught Soraya's hand. 'Remember this: whatever happens from here on, it is you I want. Only you.'

Marc conducted Soraya to one of the five chairs in his solar, then waved the messenger knight into the seat across from her. At the last moment, Jehanne entered, elegant and remote in a sand-colored kirtle and dark fur surcoat, walking stiffly beside Roger with her clawlike hand on his arm. Marc seated her, then took the chair between the two women and pinned his gaze on the messenger.

'I understand you bring a message from Queen Eleanor of England? And that the queen directs it be delivered in the presence of the three of us?' He glanced at Jehanne, then Soraya, and nodded. 'Proceed.'

The young knight rose and spread open a tight roll of vellum. 'From Eleanor, Queen of England and Duchess of Aquitaine, to the lady Jehanne of Chambois, greetings. My son, Richard known as Lion Heart, wishes to reward a loyal and deserving knight with marriage to a high-born lady, such as yourself. Two esteemed knights will compete for this honour, Duke Thierry of Rennes and Count Clarence of Brittany. Both are to receive lands and manors in England, but only one will win your hand in marriage.'

Jehanne sat motionless, her mouth open.

'Therefore, we authorize a royal tournament in your honour to determine the better man, to be held at Winchester the first Saturday in April in the year of our Lord 1194.'

Jehanne half rose, cheeks flushed, her dark eyes glowing, hands clasped over her chest. 'A tournament,' she breathed.

'My lord, there is a postscript addressed to you.'

'Read it,' Marc said shortly.

The knight swallowed, then lowered his voice and quietly read the postscript from Eleanor to Marc. 'The heart has its own truth, if you have the courage to follow it.'

The messenger rerolled the vellum and laid it on the table before Jehanne. Marc nodded to dismiss the young man, then turned. 'Jehanne, I would speak with you. In private.'

Jehanne nodded absently, her eyes on the retreating knight.

Within the hour, Jehanne swept back into his solar and plunked her wide hips onto a backless chair.

Marc rose. 'Wine?'

'No. Well, yes, thank you.'

His eyebrows went up. Jehanne seldom drank wine unless it came from France, and this did not. Was she nervous?

His gut clenched. Even as children, he could never anticipate what Jehanne's reactions would be. *Would she or would she not?*

'I scarcely know how to begin,' she murmured. She swallowed a healthy mouthful from her cup and raised her dark eyes to Marc's. 'You must wed me. Keep to your pledge.'

Marc's heart sank. How was it that she still wanted him and not a duke or a count?

'At least that is what Father Cuthbert says,' she continued. She downed another gulp of wine.

'I see. Father Cuthbert advises that we must wed.'

'He does.' Two bright splotches of color washed over Jehanne's pale cheeks. 'But I—I am sorry, Marc. I know it is what we should do, but I cannot. I…do not love you.'

His heart stopped. 'That would seem a small matter, for neither do I love you. Love, as you have so often pointed out, has naught to do with it.'

'Well, then…' She gazed down into her half-empty cup, and Marc waited, his pulse hammering in his ears.

She sent him a swift, sly glance. 'I could give you a child, Marc. An heir to Rossmorven.'

'Aye, you could.' He was finding it hard to breathe.

'It is your duty to provide an heir. Are you not tempted by such an arrangement?'

'I am not tempted, no.'

'Not even for a son?'

'No, Jehanne. Not even for a son.'

She released a great sigh, but whether of relief or resignation he could not tell. *Would she or would she not?*

'I wish…' she began.

Marc held his breath and shot a look at her. Her eyes were chilly, calculating. When she spoke her voice was calm. 'I wish you to release me from our betrothal.'

He stared at her, afraid he had not heard correctly.

'Will you?' she asked again. 'Agree to renounce our betrothal? I am…let us say, struck by a sudden curiosity to see the wider world. To visit the English queen.'

Marc was on his feet in an instant. Lifting away her wine cup he took both her hands in his. 'Aye. I will release you.'

She smiled. Marc pressed his lips to her cool forehead. 'I will be grateful for your generosity to my dying day.'

'Ha! In a year's time you will forget me,' Jehanne snapped.

'Nay, I will not.'

'Then,' she said, her voice sharp, '*I* will forget *you.*'

She brushed her lips across his cheek and swept out of the room.

Chapter Thirty-Two

In the morning, Fergus took word to the villagers that the laird wished to speak to them. Then he sought out Soraya, who was pruning the rose in Lady Margaret's walled garden.

'Best lay out some more ale, my lady, before they arrive.'

Soraya stopped with her trimming shears poised before a wild pink roses. 'Before who will arrive? What is happening?'

'Nothin' yet.' The old man's eyes slid away from hers. 'But 'twill, soon as the people come to the great hall. Now, I got me duties, so if you'll excuse me…'

He was gone before Soraya could recover her tongue, but by noon, it was indeed apparent that something unusual was about to occur. She found the great hall crowded with every man, woman and child at Rossmorven, whispering among themselves. Two squires set up the trestle table Marc used as a desk on Justice Day, dragged his high-backed walnut chair into position at the center and then pulled four additional seats to flank Marc's. Soraya eyed the arrangement with a sudden rush of unease.

Jehanne entered and was seated on Marc's right. She held a scented kerchief to her nose, apparently against the earthy stench of the peasants. Roger conducted Soraya to the chair at Marc's left.

Marc nodded to those assembled, waited for quiet and at last began to speak. 'I call you here because there is something I wish to say to you. There is a matter I would settle.'

A rumble rolled around the hall, growing louder as it circulated from farmer to shopkeeper to stonemason. It faded abruptly when Marc raised one hand.

'I care deeply about Rossmorven and its people. And as your lord I recognise my obligation to you.'

'None here doubts that, yer lordship!' someone shouted. A chorus of 'ayes' followed. Again Marc raised his hand.

'As you know, the Lady Jehanne and I were betrothed when we were children. Many long years the lady has kept faith with me, but she now feels she can no longer honour that pledge. She is hereby renouncing our betrothal.'

At his side, Jehanne nodded stiffly in assent.

The blood drained from Soraya's brain as a rustle of whispers circled the hall. Marc again waited until it was quiet.

'I will live my life in service to you, as lord of Rossmorven, but on one condition. I wish to marry the lady Soraya, seated here at my left.'

A burst of talk began, then quickly died as Marc once again raised his hand. 'I would have your assent by tomorrow at dawn. Should you decide you will not accept Soraya al-Din as my wife and the mistress of my holdings, I have asked William, King of Scots, to name a new lord for these lands.'

'Never!' someone shouted. ''Taint right.'

'Hear me out,' Marc said quietly. 'I acknowledge that the lady is not of noble lineage. And she is not of Scots descent. But I would have her, and only her, for my wife.'

'Who's this "Sarah Aldin"?' someone mumbled.

'The lady in the green gown, you dolt. The one who boiled up that posset for your Alix when she couldn't breathe.'

'Aye, her. She is not a Scot, then?'

'Nay.'

''Twon't matter,' said the first man. 'She is a good lady.'

''Twill matter. Father Cuthbert will never allow it.'

Marc paused at the open door of Soraya's chamber as the maidservant sped down the passageway toward him. 'Yes, Brigid, what is it?'

The girl dropped a quick curtsey. 'Sir Roger wishes to speak with you. Both of you, he means.'

'And where is he?'

'In your solar, lord.' She dimpled. 'Helping himself to your wine.'

'Come.' Marc grasped Soraya's hand and together they went down the stone steps to his private solar. For some reason she could not name her heart constricted in dread.

Roger put his cup down on the mantel and grasped Marc's hand in greeting. Soraya studied the earl's eyes for a clue.

'You wished to see us?' Marc inquired.

'Aye, I do. I…it is a delicate matter.'

Soraya sent Roger a warm smile. 'Let me guess. You need Marc's help to retain your new lands? You wish to stay with us until summer to avoid the muddy road back to Winchester? Ah, I know. You have conceived a taste for our apple brandy and would learn the making of it?'

Roger took both her hands in his. 'All of the above, Soraya. And whatever else you can think up on the spur of this moment, for both Marc and I need a bit of wit right now.'

'And what lies at the top of your list of wishes, then?'

'Ah. Well. I…' He swallowed audibly, but kept Soraya's hands in his. 'I wish you to know that if…if…'

Marc spoke up, his voice quiet. 'If the people will not accept Soraya. If I don't retain Rossmorven. Aye? Speak, man!'

'If it comes to that, you will both be welcome at Carrick Castle.'

Marc gripped his hand on Roger's shoulder. 'I am more grateful than I can say, my friend. 'Tis an unsettled time.'

Roger cleared his throat. 'It is unsettled because you are challenging the old ways. A hundred years of tradition.'

'Aye,' Marc said. 'Perhaps an outmoded tradition, one that needs to change.'

'Your people…' Roger began.

'My people have no love for Jehanne.'

'But,' Soraya interrupted, 'they would retain you as their lord, were it not for me.'

'Perhaps. It does not matter. We are bound together by far more than tradition. I will not live apart from you.'

'But a marriage… Lord God in heaven, it goes against everything we have known.'

Marc leaned toward Soraya. 'We must trust the people of Rossmorven. And, if we are to forge a new path, we must trust ourselves. It is *not* wrong to love each other.'

A pregnant silence fell, broken at last by Roger. 'Your supply of wine is low, my friend.'

'The hospitality of Rossmorven is endless,' Marc replied with a grin. 'Brigid,' he called out the door. 'Bring more wine, will you?'

Brigid arrived a few moments later with a brimming pitcher and two additional wine cups.

'Where is Lady Jehanne?' Roger asked idly. 'Nothing worthwhile comes for free,' he reminded.

'She is…packing, sir,' Brigid replied. 'Filling up her trunks with a right good spirit.'

Soraya gasped, then stared at Marc. 'Packing?' they said in unison.

'Packing?' Roger echoed. A smile warmed his eyes.

A laugh caught in Soraya's throat. 'It would seem that Queen Eleanor understands women as keenly as she does her sons.'

'Queen Eleanor is herself a woman,' Roger said.

'And the queen knows her quarry,' Soraya added with a smile. 'Though it would take more than a tournament in my honour to lure *me* to England's court. In this case, the snared fox has herself set the bait.'

'*Quoi?*' Both men goggled at her.

'You are men,' Soraya said with a smile. 'You are not expected to understand how a fox thinks. Or a woman, either.'

With that, she left the two friends alone.

Before dawn the following morning, Soraya stood at the window of her chamber peering down at the bailey below. Shrouded in darkness, the area was a mass of shadows; no light showed but for the glowing embers at the smithy's shed. She clasped her forearms across her waist and tried to quiet the roiling of her belly. What would this day bring?

Along with the first rays of the sun came an unpleasant surprise. Jehanne tapped at Soraya's chamber door and without waiting for invitation, stepped inside. She wore her usual severe grey kirtle and black overgown, and her expression matched her garments.

'Good morning, Jehanne.'

'*Oui*, it is morning, is it not?' she replied, her voice silky. 'The day those unwashed peasants of Rossmorven will decide your future. And,' she added with a sneer, 'Marc's future, as well.'

Soraya straightened. *Her* future, yes. But not Marc's. Whatever the cottars decided, she could not take him away from Rossmorven. The estate was his life. He loved it, from David, the old man of the corn who distilled that fiery liquor the Scots were so fond of, down to the tiniest newborn babe that now blessed the cottage of Willem the stonecutter and his long-barren wife.

'I would never take Marc away from Rossmorven.'

Jehanne eyed her slantwise. Despite her growing unease, Soraya caught and held the woman's gaze. 'What is it you wish, Jehanne?'

'I want to know what is expected at court. I want to know about Queen Eleanor of England. What is she like?'

Soraya hid her surprise at the question. Then she remembered that Jehanne, for all her high-flown airs, had never been to court. Jehanne had chosen to keep herself closeted at Rossmorven for almost twoscore years.

'What is Eleanor like?' she mused aloud. 'She is not "like" anyone but herself. She is unique. Why do you ask?'

'Will she bend on a matter?'

Soraya's hand made an involuntary motion. 'A matter? What matter?' Something in the question nudged her memory.

Jehanne did not answer.

'No,' Soraya said. 'Eleanor is frighteningly intelligent. Do not think to bargain with her. Or, worse yet, try to deceive her. She does not bend to anyone or anything.'

Jehanne's pale forehead wrinkled into a frown. 'I wonder if the queen would allow—'

Soraya studied the woman's suddenly apprehensive expression. 'Do not think to trick her, Jehanne. Or to wheedle a favor. Eleanor will see all in an instant and she will chew you up and spit you out before you can blink.'

The tall woman came to attention. 'How should one…that is, how should I conduct myself at Eleanor's court?'

Ah, so that was it. Jehanne wanted personal advice. How it must cost Jehanne to humble herself in this way.

'I believe I had an advantage in that I liked the queen of the English, and I think she sensed this. And, without meaning to, I made her laugh.'

Jehanne tossed her head. 'I may not like this queen, but I wager I can hold my own with her. She is French, after all, even if she is from L'Anguedoc. Scandalous region,' she muttered. 'Full of ill-mannered troubadours singing bawdy songs.'

'My lady,' Soraya cautioned softly. 'Forgive me, but you have not yet taken Eleanor's measure.'

Jehanne stared at her in silence, her face shuttered.

'What is it you want from the English queen, Jehanne?'

'That is my affair,' she shot back.

'Do not try to manipulate Eleanor, or I fear you may face her wrath.'

'*Mais non*, Soraya of Damascus. It is *I* who fear for *you*. Think on it. What will you do when Marc sets you aside?'

A chill swept through Soraya, but she raised her chin and met Jehanne's dark eyes. 'I will manage.'

'I suppose you could always come to Queen Eleanor's court,' the older woman said slyly. 'But let me speak frankly. I hate to think of the two of us in the same castle.'

Soraya drew herself up. 'I, too, will be frank, Jehanne. I have served as friend and companion to Marc through danger, through terrible loss, through weeks of near-starvation and waning strength, grinding cold, and shelters so rude you would shrink from entry. I have gained Marc's love and regard, and I do not mean to give it up. I will remain with Marc because he asks it, and because I have earned that right.'

Jehanne stared at her, and in her eyes Soraya saw a glimmer of grudging respect. Without another word, the woman swept out the chamber door and on down the passageway.

Soraya almost laughed aloud. God in heaven, how Eleanor would relish playing cat and mouse with the proud lady of Chambois. She felt halfway sorry for Jehanne.

A shout from the great hall below reverberated up the two floors to her chamber. The people of Rossmorven were gathering. Her mouth went dry as a thistle. These were the people in whose hands Marc had placed his future.

And hers.

Chapter Thirty-Three

Robin the tanner spread his thick arms to encompass the mass of peasants jammed into the great hall. 'The way we see it, our Marc will make a fine laird. We wouldn't take kindly to losin' him.'

Joy shot into Marc's heart. Instinctively he glanced at Soraya, seated at his side, her face impassive. He knew she was trying hard not to let her raw feelings show. He also knew she would never ask him to choose between his people and her. He must make that choice himself.

The tanner signalled that he had more to say, and Soraya's face turned the colour of whey. Aye, they wanted him. But what about Soraya?

A black thought intruded into his mind. If it came to that, he knew his Soraya. She would straighten her shoulders and go on. Perhaps back to Jerusalem with Roger. Ah, God, he could not bear to think about it.

Marc shouted for quiet, and Robin nodded his thanks. 'Now,' the tanner said expansively, 'about the mistress of Rossmorven. To a man, we—'

'We don't want that foreigner,' someone yelled.

Soraya went absolutely still.

'She ain't bad, just got a burr stuck in her drawers,' a woman shouted.

A burr stuck in her...? Marc smothered a snort of laughter. It wasn't Soraya they meant, but Jehanne.

'She's French,' a deep voice called.

'So's the laird, lackwit. His father was French.'

Marc rose. 'I do not intend to wed the Lady Jehanne,' he said in clipped Gaelic.

A buzz of discontented voices rolled around the hall. Robin shushed them, then pivoted to face him. 'A betrothal's made afore God. Father Cuthbert says a man cain't set it aside so easy.'

Marc's jaw tightened. 'Well, then?' he queried, still using Gaelic.

'Well, then,' the burly tanner repeated. 'Here's how 'tis. The people, we want you to stay, lord. And we know you were pledged to the Lady Jehanne.'

'That is true,' Marc said quietly.

'But we don't want the Lady Jehanne.'

'Agreed.' Relief flooded him. Thank Christ for the good sense of a hardheaded Scot. But there had to be more.

'It is Soraya al-Din I want to marry.'

At the sound of her name, Soraya began to tremble. Marc touched her shoulder, then resumed his seat beside her. Reaching his hand under the table, he gently squeezed her fingers.

'As to yer lady, Sarah Aldin,' the tanner continued, 'we don't know nuthin' about her save that she's comely and not stinger-tongued like t'other lady.'

'Aye,' Marc murmured. 'She is not stinger-tongued.'

'But Father Cuthbert, he says this here Sarah don't belong to you because...well, because you're promised already.'

'The once-promised lady no longer wishes to stay at Rossmorven.'

Robin's mouth opened, then closed, then opened again. 'Excuse me, lord. Don't think I heard you right. The lady Jehanne don't want—I'm losin' my wits. And my courage.'

'Courage!' someone bellowed. 'Robin needs some courage!'

Brigid disappeared into the kitchen and reappeared with a pitcher and a cup of something, which she pressed into the tanner's meaty hand. He tipped his head back, downed the contents in two gulps and began to sputter.

'Lor',' he wheezed. 'By Saint Ninian, that be courage and more!'

Under the table, Soraya released Marc's hand and clenched her fists. He curved his palm over her knotted fingers, watching Brigid refill the tanner's cup. At the same instant the maidservant bent her head to hear something Robin was whispering into her ear.

Brigid turned away and glided toward the table where he and Soraya sat. 'Here, my lady, ye might need this.' She presented another brimming cup.

Soraya swallowed a sip of the amber liquid. 'My thanks, Brigid,' she rasped when she could speak.

The maidservant bent toward her. ''Twon't be long now,' she whispered. 'Robin's drunk a wee bit more "courage."'

From her apron pocket Brigid produced a third cup for Marc. 'Brace yerself, my lord,' she murmured as she poured it full.

Marc downed a healthy gulp and skewered Robin the tanner with a hard look. 'Now, master tanner, you will speak of Soraya al-Din.'

Soraya's gaze focused on the stocky man who held her fate in his calloused hands. The tanner fidgeted with the rope belt at his waist, shuffled his feet. But, Marc noted, he would not meet Soraya's eyes.

His heart contracted as the obvious truth sank in. They did not want Jehanne as mistress of Rossmorven. But they did not want Soraya, either.

Her eyes sought his. In one swallow she drained half the fiery liquid and tried to smile. Her gaze was steady, but he found his own vision suddenly blurring.

Soraya's head felt as if it spun like a child's top. Marc's eyes continued to look deep into hers, but he was speaking to Robin the tanner.

Robin jerked like a puppet on a cord and opened his mouth to emit a tumble of gutteral words. Gaelic again. Then more words, her name once more, and something that amused the crowd, for a swell of laughter washed over the hall.

Marc spoke again, barked, really, and the tanner flinched. The people jammed together in the overcrowded hall quieted until Soraya could hear nothing but her own unsteady breathing.

'Say it!' Marc commanded. 'You will have her as your mistress.'

Robin gasped out some words. *'Tha sinn a' gabhail ri!'*

What did that mean? Soraya downed another gulp from her cup. Along with a growing dizziness, she became aware of an odd sense of detachment. All at once she cared not one pomegranate kernel for the will of the cottars.

She would ask Roger to take her back to Damascus.

'Gabhail ri!' the crowd roared. They shoved forward toward Marc in a solid mass, and four men pulled him out of the high-backed chair and hoisted him on top of their shoulders. *'Gabhail ri! Gabhail ri!'* they chanted as they marched around the hall.

Soraya shut her eyes. She tried to shut her ears, as well,

but over the bedlam she heard Robin the tanner's deep voice. 'Sarah Aldin! *Tha sinn a' gabhail ri!*'

Roger…where was Roger? She would saddle her pony and…

The men paraded Marc twice more around the hall. Just as he came abreast of her again, he reached down for her hand. His eyes shone with happiness.

Sarah Aldin?

That was her! In spite of everything—the betrothal, tradition, even Father Cuthbert—the people had chosen *her* to be mistress of Rossmorven? Marc's wife?'

She half rose from her chair, felt her mind slow and the sounds fade. A grey veil dropped over her vision.

The next thing she knew she was lying on the floor among the rushes and Marc was bending over her, laughing.

Laughing! She had swooned away like a goose-brained maid and Marc was laughing?

He leaned close. 'Aye,' he said, his voice coming from far away. 'Wake up, my Sarah Aldin. You will make a bonny bride.'

'I am awake,' she breathed. Then she closed her eyes and once more floated into blackness.

Chapter Thirty-Four

❧❧❧

From the window in Marc's solar, Soraya watched a mounted man, a knight, enter the bailey and slow his horse to a standstill. A carved wooden trunk was tied on the back of his mount. He shouted at a hovering servant. 'Carry this trunk into the hall. And fetch the lady Soraya of Damascus.'

Soraya flew down the stairs to greet the knight. 'Queen Eleanor of England,' he said without preamble, 'sends you a wedding gift.' He gestured to the foot of the stone steps where the large dark-grained wooden trunk sat unopened on the floor.

'Look inside, Soraya,' Marc said from beside her.

Soraya hesitated, then knelt beside the trunk. A burst of laughter rose from the trestle table behind her, where Roger and the knight, and now Marc, sat sharing talk of Eleanor and King Richard, along with brimming mugs of mead. She hid a smile. Men. At bottom, they were really just little boys who liked to play.

The trunk latch clicked and she raised the heavy lid. 'Your wedding gown, I think,' Marc called from across the room. 'And some other women's fripperies, no doubt.'

Soraya lifted out the most exquisite gown she had ever seen. Woven of gossamer silk of a pale sea-green embroidered at the neck and hem in a darker shade of green, it shimmered in her arms.

'Oh,' she murmured. A unison chorus of 'oh's' echoed from the knot of gathering servants.

There was also a sleeved cloak of forest green velvet, a sheer cream-coloured veil and a circlet of gold encrusted with emeralds to hold it in place.

And at the bottom, wrapped in white silk, lay her old turban and the jeweled dagger. *Oh.* Bless the queen for remembering. Her throat tightened into an ache.

'My darling girl, don't weep over it!' Marc called. 'Go and dress for our nuptials!'

Soraya stepped quickly to the table, leaned down and pressed a kiss on Marc's warm cheek, then turned to the messenger knight. 'I send my thanks to Queen Eleanor.'

'Stop weeping, now,' Marc grumbled softly.

But she saw that his own eyes were shiny with tears.

Touched more than she could say, Soraya signaled to a servant boy to carry the trunk up to her chamber where she would dress for the late-afternoon ceremony.

Just as she started up the stairs herself, a rich voice rose, singing a ballad in Gaelic. Something about a beautiful maid waiting at the well for her lover. As she climbed higher, the voice followed with a second verse, and then a third. By the time she reached the third floor passageway that led to her chamber, all the men were singing.

Late that afternoon, when the pale winter sun slanted through the tall windows of his mother's solar, Marc knelt at Lady Margaret's feet. Taking her hands in his, he looked up into her face and his heart tumbled over. Her blue eyes were gazing straight into his.

'My son,' she said in a small, clear voice. 'You have returned.'

His eyelids burned. 'Aye, my lady, I have.'

And by God's grace and a miracle, so had she. He could scarcely speak for the tears choking his throat.

'I am to be married within the hour, Mother. I came for your blessing.'

'It is Soraya, is it not?' Lady Margaret inquired.

'Aye, it is Soraya.'

'I wished it so. I have long waited for a bairn in this cold, drafty place. And I like the lass. She has made a great difference at Rossmorven. I believe it is her tisanes that have cleared my mind.'

Marc swallowed hard. 'The ceremony will be held in the chapel, after vespers. I want you to be there, Mother. Could you?'

'I do not believe I can walk from here to there without pain. But…' She tugged a ring from her middle finger. 'Give your bride this. Your father gave it to me when we were wed.'

His heart clenched. There were so many other things he wished to tell her, most important that Soraya at this moment was secluded in her chamber, bathing and donning the fine wedding garments Queen Eleanor had sent.

He lifted his mother's hand. 'I love Soraya, but I have a confession. I gambled Rossmorven for her.'

'Did ye now? You're a brave one, you are.'

'I did. And by the grace of God, I have won them both.'

Lady Margaret nodded, curling her fingers around her son's large, strong hand. 'Good,' she pronounced. 'And you won't forget about the bairn?'

Her smile, the first he had seen since his return to Scotland, lit up her small, pale face.

'I will not forget the bairn,' he promised. He bent his head and brought both her hands to his lips. Then he rose, leaned down, and kissed both cheeks and her forehead.

'Be happy,' she whispered.

'Soraya of Damascus,' the priest called in a commanding voice. 'Come forward.'

A frisson of excitement went through the small gathering, as if a single sigh had been exhaled in unison. Soraya stepped forward from the back of the small chapel on the arm of Roger de Clare and slowly made her way through those assembled toward the candle-lit altar where Marc stood waiting.

He had never seen a woman so beautiful. The green silk gown swirled in graceful folds as she moved. Roger matched his long steps to hers and looked every inch the proud father in his royal blue tunic over a long-sleeved undershirt of cream linen.

Marc's heart swelled under his richly embroidered crimson surcoat. Roger was a true friend.

And Soraya… She stole his breath. His Soraya glowed in the flickering candlelight, a shimmering vision in a gown that matched the color of her eyes, green and clear as the northern sea. Even through the sheer veil she wore he could see her gaze catch and hold his, a promise in the mysterious depths of her eyes.

She moved toward him with elegance, her face lifted to his, her shoulder-length hair shining like black satin under the jeweled circlet. Around her waist she wore the delicately wrought chain of garnets and gold wire he had presented to her but an hour ago.

Unless he was dreaming, this lovely, surprising, endlessly fascinating creature was to be his, forever.

At his side, Fergus laid a hand on his arm. 'Don't twitch, laddie. She will be yours soon enough.'

Nay, Marc thought. Not soon enough. He wanted to claim Soraya this very instant.

'Take her hand, laddie,' Fergus whispered. 'She will na' break.'

Her warm fingers entwined with his and for a long moment they simply looked at each other. A hush fell over the guests as the priest took his place in front of the silk-draped altar and cleared his throat to gain their attention. He beckoned them forward.

Soraya's gasp nearly undid Marc. 'Brother Andreas!'

Marc tore his gaze from Soraya and glanced at the prelate. Not Father Cuthbert but the plump monk, or spy, or whatever he was, grinned back at him.

Before Marc could quiet his galloping heart, Brother Andreas began to speak.

'Now, before these witnesses are come Marc Etienne de Valery of Rossmorven and Soraya al-Din of Damascus. Turn and face those here assembled.'

Soraya and Marc slowly pivoted toward their guests, and she gave another tiny gasp. At the edge of the gathering stood Marc's mother, Lady Margaret, her frail form supported by the ever-gallant William Marshal.

She glanced at Marc and saw that his eyes were wet. She squeezed his hand, looked away, and audibly sucked in her breath again.

Jehanne in a grey kirtle and blue wool overdress stood next to Roger de Clare, leaning on his arm and smiling up at him with the strangest expression on her face.

Brother Andreas spoke again. 'Turn now to me, who represents God Almighty on this earth, and swear your vows before this company.'

They turned again, and once more Soraya found her hand firmly clasped in Marc's. The priest motioned, and Marc and Soraya knelt side by side to pledge their lives to one another.

All through the long ceremony that followed, Soraya held Marc's hand so tight that when he released it to slip the incised gold band onto her finger, she found it had gone numb.

As one they turned to face each other, bending their necks until their foreheads were almost touching, and then Marc whispered something close to her ear.

'*Je t'aime*. I love thee.'

'I love thee, as well.' She spoke the words in Gaelic.

Epilogue

Lady Margaret of Rossmorven got her wish for a bairn. And for good measure, God granted twins to Marc and Soraya. Rosalynne Margaret and Richard William de Valery made the world aware of their existence early one crisp autumn morning in the year 1194.

At nine summers, Richard de Valery traveled south to foster with Roger de Clare, Earl of Carrick, and he returned to Rossmorven years later as a knight.

Of Rosalynne de Valery little is known except that she was betrothed to the son of the Scottish pretender to the throne. She did, however, keep a diary for the duration of her life.

Author's Note

Rossmorven is a fictional place. Soraya and Marc are entirely fictional characters. However, Richard the Lion Heart, Saladin, Eleanor of Aquitaine, and the knight William Marshal, Earl of Pembroke, did in fact exist in the late 12th century.

For purposes of the story, I have altered the route of Richard's journey from Jaffa in 1192. First, he did not stop at Cyprus; sale of the island to the Templars occurred later. Second, because of a storm, his ship actually landed on the east coast of Italy, rather than the west coast, as portrayed herein.

Richard was captured by German knights near Vienna; he was ransomed for 100,000 silver marks raised by his mother, Eleanor, and he returned to England in March 1194.

Saladin died of an illness in March 1194 in Damascus. Richard the Lion Heart died from a crossbolt arrow wound received in 1199 in Chalus, France.

Eleanor, Queen of England and Duchess of Aquitaine, died in 1204 at the age of 80 and is buried at the abbey of Fontevrault.

William Marshal, Earl of Pembroke, died in 1219 at his manor house in Caversham, England.

* * * * *

Turn the page for a sneak preview of
IF I'D NEVER KNOWN YOUR LOVE
by
Georgia Bockoven

From the brand-new series
Harlequin Everlasting Love
Every great love has a story to tell. ™

One year, five months and four days missing

There's no way for you to know this, Evan, but I haven't written to you for a few months. Actually, it's been almost a year. I had a hard time picking up a pen once more after we paid the second ransom and then received a letter saying it wasn't enough. I was so sure you were coming home that I took the kids along to Bogotá so they could fly home with you and me, something I swore I'd never do. I've fallen in love with Colombia and the people who've opened their hearts to me. But fear is a constant companion when I'm there. I won't ever expose our children to that kind of danger again.

I'm at a loss over what to do anymore, Evan. I've begged and pleaded and thrown temper tantrums with every official I can corner both here and at home. They've been incredibly tolerant and understanding, but in the end as ineffectual as the rest of us.

I try to imagine what your life is like now, what you do every day, what you're wearing, what you eat. I want to believe that the people who have you are misguided yet kind, that they treat you well. It's how I survive day to day. To think of you being mistreated hurts too much. If I picture you locked away somewhere and suffering, a weight descends on me that makes it almost impossible to get out of bed in the morning.

Your captors surely know you by now. They have to recognize what a good man you are. I imagine you working with their children, telling them that you have children, too, showing them the pictures you carry in your wallet. Can't the men who have you understand how much your children miss you? How can it not matter to them?

How can they keep you away from us all this time? Over and over, we've done what they asked. Are they oblivious to the depth of their cruelty? What kind of people are they that they don't care?

I used to keep a calendar beside our bed next to the peach rose you picked for me before you left. Every night I marked another day, counting how many you'd been gone. I don't do that any longer. I don't want to be reminded of all the days we'll never get back.

When I can't sleep at night, I tell you about my day. I imagine you hearing me and smiling over the details that make up my life now. I never tell you how defeated I feel at moments or how hard I work to hide it from everyone for fear they will see it as a reason to stop believing you are coming home to us.

And I couldn't tell you about the lump I found in my breast and how difficult it was going through all the tests without you here to lean on. The lump was benign—the process reaching that diagnosis utterly terrifying. I couldn't stop thinking about what would happen to Shelly and Jason if something happened to me.

We need you to come home.

I'm worn down with missing you.

I'm going to read this tomorrow and will probably tear it up or burn it in the fireplace. I don't want you to get the idea I ever doubted what I was doing to free you or thought the work a burden. I would gladly spend the rest of my life at it, even if, in the end, we only had one day together.

You are my life, Evan.

I will love you forever.

* * * * *

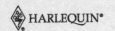

HARLEQUIN® *Romance*®

presents a brand-new trilogy by

PATRICIA THAYER

Rocky Mountain BRIDES

Three sisters come home to wed.

In April don't miss

Raising the Rancher's Family,

followed by

The Sheriff's Pregnant Wife,

on sale May 2007,

and

A Mother for the Tycoon's Child,

on sale June 2007.

REQUEST YOUR FREE BOOKS!

Harlequin® Historical
Historical Romantic Adventure!

2 FREE NOVELS PLUS 2 FREE GIFTS!

YES! Please send me 2 FREE Harlequin® Historical novels and my 2 FREE gifts. After receiving them, if I don't wish to receive any more books, I can return the shipping statement marked "cancel." If I don't cancel, I will receive 6 brand-new novels every month and be billed just $4.69 per book in the U.S., or $5.24 per book in Canada, plus 25¢ shipping and handling per book and applicable taxes, if any*. That's a savings of close to 15% off the cover price! I understand that accepting the 2 free books and gifts places me under no obligation to buy anything. I can always return a shipment and cancel at any time. Even if I never buy another book from Harlequin, the two free books and gifts are mine to keep forever.

246 HDN EEWW   349 HDN EEW9

Name	(PLEASE PRINT)
Address	Apt. #
City	State/Prov.	Zip/Postal Code

Signature (if under 18, a parent or guardian must sign)

Mail to the Harlequin Reader Service®:
IN U.S.A.: P.O. Box 1867, Buffalo, NY 14240-1867
IN CANADA: P.O. Box 609, Fort Erie, Ontario L2A 5X3

Not valid to current Harlequin Historical subscribers.

Want to try two free books from another line?
Call 1-800-873-8635 or visit www.morefreebooks.com.

* Terms and prices subject to change without notice. NY residents add applicable sales tax. Canadian residents will be charged applicable provincial taxes and GST. This offer is limited to one order per household. All orders subject to approval. Credit or debit balances in a customer's account(s) may be offset by any other outstanding balance owed by or to the customer. Please allow 4 to 6 weeks for delivery.

Your Privacy: Harlequin is committed to protecting your privacy. Our Privacy Policy is available online at www.eHarlequin.com or upon request from the Reader Service. From time to time we make our lists of customers available to reputable firms who may have a product or service of interest to you. If you would prefer we not share your name and address, please check here. ☐

HH07